GODENGINE

DOCTOR WHO – THE NEW ADVENTURES

Also available:

TIMEWYRM: GENESYS by John Peel
TIMEWYRM: EXODUS by Terrance Dicks
TIMEWYRM: APOCALYPSE by Nigel Robinson
TIMEWYRM: REVELATION by Paul Cornell
CAT'S CRADLE: TIME'S CRUCIBLE by Marc Platt
CAT'S CRADLE: WARHEAD by Andrew Cartmel
CAT'S CRADLE: WITCH MARK by Andrew Hunt
NIGHTSHADE by Mark Gatiss
LOVE AND WAR by Paul Cornell
TRANSIT by Ben Aaronovitch
THE HIGHEST SCIENCE by Gareth Roberts
THE PIT by Neil Penswick
DECEIT by Peter Darvill-Evans
LUCIFER RISING by Jim Mortimore and Andy Lane
WHITE DARKNESS by David A. McIntee
SHADOWMIND by Christopher Bulis
BIRTHRIGHT by Nigel Robinson
ICEBERG by David Banks
BLOOD HEAT by Jim Mortimore
THE DIMENSION RIDERS by Daniel Blythe
THE LEFT-HANDED HUMMINGBIRD by Kate Orman
CONUNDRUM by Steve Lyons
NO FUTURE by Paul Cornell
TRAGEDY DAY by Gareth Roberts
LEGACY by Gary Russell
THEATRE OF WAR by Justin Richards
ALL-CONSUMING FIRE by Andy Lane
BLOOD HARVEST by Terrance Dicks
STRANGE ENGLAND by Simon Messingham
FIRST FRONTIER by David A. McIntee
ST ANTHONY'S FIRE by Mark Gatiss
FALLS THE SHADOW by Daniel O'Mahony
PARASITE by Jim Mortimore
WARLOCK by Andrew Cartmel
SET PIECE by Kate Orman
INFINITE REQUIEM by Daniel Blythe
SANCTUARY by David A. McIntee
HUMAN NATURE by Paul Cornell
ORIGINAL SIN by Andy Lane
SKY PIRATES! by Dave Stone
ZAMPER by Gareth Roberts
TOY SOLDIERS by Paul Leonard
HEAD GAMES by Steve Lyons
THE ALSO PEOPLE by Ben Aaronovitch
SHAKEDOWN by Terrance Dicks
JUST WAR by Lance Parkin
WARCHILD by Andrew Cartmel
SLEEPY by Kate Orman
DEATH AND DIPLOMACY by Dave Stone
HAPPY ENDINGS by Paul Cornell

THE NEW
ADVENTURES

GODENGINE

Craig Hinton

First published in Great Britain in 1996 by
Doctor Who Books
an imprint of Virgin Publishing Ltd
332 Ladbroke Grove
London W10 5AH

Copyright © Craig Hinton 1996

The right of Craig Hinton to be identified as the Author of
this Work has been asserted by him in accordance with the
Copyright, Designs and Patents Act 1988.

'Doctor Who' series copyright © British Broadcasting
Corporation 1996

Cover illustration by Peter Elson
Original Grand Marshal design by Mike Tucker

ISBN 0 426 20473 5

Typeset by Galleon Typesetting, Ipswich
Printed and bound in Great Britain by
Mackays of Chatham PLC

*All characters in this publication are fictitious and any resemblance
to real persons, living or dead, is purely coincidental.*

This book is sold subject to the condition that it shall
not, by way of trade or otherwise, be lent, resold, hired
out or otherwise circulated without the publisher's prior
written consent in any form of binding or cover other
than that in which it is published and without a similar
condition including this condition being imposed on the
subsequent purchaser.

For Jim

Standing as I do in the view of God and eternity, I realize that patriotism is not enough. I must have no hatred or bitterness towards anyone.

Edith Cavell

Prologue

Broken Swords

2109 – Arsia Mons, Mars

Holding the sword horizontally in front of him, Old Sam switched on the suit's external speakers, hoping that the digital gain would make him audible in the thin air of the Martian tunnel. He swallowed, unsure of what to say, unsure of how to say it.

He said it. 'I am Samuel Robert Garvey Moore of the Second Battalion Third Brigade of the United Nations Armed Forces; I have killed more people than I can count.'

Pulling it downwards, Old Sam broke the ancient sword across his knee and dropped the two sections on the rubble-strewn ground. There, he had performed the ritual that the Doctor had instructed. Now for the final part.

'I come in peace,' he said.

For over an hour, Old Sam stood in the silent tunnels in the outskirts of the underground Martian city, waiting for a sign that his peace offering had been accepted – or even acknowledged. But the endless, whispering silence grew too oppressive for him to remain. Leaving the broken Japanese katana to gather dust on the ground, he stood up and left. He had done what the Doctor had asked of him; if the Martians chose to ignore the overture, that was their problem.

2110 – Jull-ett-eskul Seminary of Oras, Argyre Planitia, Mars

'It is a gesture,' explained Abbot Aklaar, pointing at the broken katana on the stone table in front of him. It had been brought to the seminary only hours ago by a pilgrim who had witnessed the events at Arsia Mons, but Aklaar had spent those hours meditating upon its significance. 'A symbolic gesture of peace. Obviously, some humans are better versed in our customs than we have imagined.'

'The humans offering peace after they have ripped the soul from our people – it is an insult.' Abbot Kyren turned his back on the broken sword, his beige robes of office swirling round him.

'You sound like a Grand Marshal of the Warrior caste rather than an Abbot in the Order of Oras,' said Aklaar, his voice vaguely chiding. 'With so many of our people dead or departed, we are the spiritual guardians of Mars. By instituting a formal peace with our neighbours on Earth, we can safeguard the future for our descendants.'

'Descendants? Descendants?' Kyren frowned, the smooth green skin of his forehead wrinkling over his yellow eyes. 'Only a handful of us are left on Mars now. Any descendants will be born on Nova Martia, never seeing the true Martian sun, never breathing true Martian air.'

Aklaar held up an admonishing finger. 'It is considerably more than a handful, Kyren; there are still hundreds of thousands of us here, and we owe it to them to come to an accord. We have lived in secrecy for too long, hiding in our cities and atoning for our crimes. The humans are not even certain that any of us still remain here. Yet after atonement must come forgiveness. That is what I propose.'

'Peace, Aklaar? Remember, there are still some factions on Mars that would baulk at such an idea.'

'The remaining Warriors?' Aklaar nodded. 'They are few, yet their opinions carry much weight, even now. We must contact them, persuade them of the wisdom of this new path.'

'And if the Warriors agree?' asked Kyren.

Aklaar placed his hand on the beautiful, broken weapon on the table. 'Then perhaps this will not be the last sword to be broken in the name of peace.'

2157 – Void Station Cassius, Edge of the Solar System

Julius Ericson leant back in his chair and sighed: another shift in the most boring job in the solar system. Void Station Cassius, in orbit around the planet of the same name, did nothing but stare into the black infinity that lay beyond the solar system, gazing outwards with unblinking cybernetic eyes.

'Coffee, Jules?' It was Lena Martin, his fellow inmate, carrying two mugs. Julius cheered himself up by remembering that their current assignment ended in two days' time; Lena and he would be replaced by two more unfortunates and finally be able to fly back to their respective homes on Earth and Mars. Personally, he couldn't wait to see his wife and kids again.

'Just what the doctor ordered.' He took a sip and placed the coffee on the desk. It was foul, but it was the best that they could hope for, this far away from civilization.

'Anything going on?' she asked, sitting in the chair next to him. It was a running joke – there was more chance of the sun going nova than anything actually happening out there.

'What do you think?' Julius laughed. But his laughter was cut off by a screeching alarm that filled the room. The proximity alarm. His eyes darted to the monitor, which had automatically switched to the view that was causing the furore.

Those same eyes widened in disbelief. 'Holy shit!' he whispered.

Wave after wave of jet-black saucers were dropping out of subspace in sector eight, huge black discs bristling with weaponry, materializing just beyond the Oort Cloud.

The Black Fleet.

Julius had heard of the fleet; they all had. They had all seen the news broadcasts from the once beautiful world of Sifranos, where a billion settlers had been exterminated and the world turned into a sterilized cinder. And then there had been the other fourteen colonies, also obliterated by the mysterious adversaries who came and went and left nothing but destruction in their wake.

But they were all far-distant colonies, worlds on the very edge of the Alliance. No one ever imagined that there was any threat to Earth – however powerful this unknown enemy was, they couldn't be stupid enough to attempt a head-on confrontation in the solar system itself.

Clearly, everyone was wrong. As the hundreds of saucers headed towards Earth at just under lightspeed – given the sheer number of ships, they would have had to have come out of subspace this far out to avoid problems with the sun's gravity well – Julius opened a channel to Interstellar Taskforce Command. The whole purpose of Void Station Cassius was being justified: it would take hours for the monitor satellites closer to Earth to even spot the invasion fleet, let alone mobilize any counter-defences. Julius reached out for the panel that would link the station directly to Taskforce Command on Earth.

His hand never reached it.

Under the impact of six photon impellers, the delicate assembly that was Void Station Cassius bloomed in an explosion of metals and plastics, threaded with boiling gobbets of organic matter, that lit up the frozen Oort Cloud which ringed the solar system. Leaving only an expanding cloud of debris behind, the Black Fleet proceeded towards the third planet in the solar system.

The Dalek Invasion of Earth had begun.

PART ONE

THE BRINGERS OF WAR

Chapter 1

Roslyn Forrester's subconscious mind fully accepted the fact that somebody was whistling classical music into her left ear. Why shouldn't they – it was a free universe. But although her subconscious made a valiant attempt to ignore it, the incessant military beat that pounded away inside her skull eventually forced her to react.

The whistling stopped.

Two things struck Roz when she opened her eyes: the sky was pink, and her right hand was clasped around the Doctor's neck. She immediately let go, allowing the surprised Time Lord to slump to the dusty red ground, where he rubbed his throat with an aggrieved expression on his lined and mobile face. 'At least the respiratory bypass system cut in,' he muttered. For a second, she was shocked by her reaction; you're behaving more like Kadiatu all the time, she mused.

Then she recognized the significance of the Doctor's tune. Rolling dunes of reddy-brown dust stretched away in all directions, with nothing – no buildings, no vegetation, nothing – to interrupt the desolation. Their current location was painfully obvious.

'Mars, the Bringer of War?' It had been a long time, but no one ever forgot a stint on the Red Planet. She definitely remembered hers, a particularly unpleasant period during her generally unpleasant time squiring Konstantine.

The Doctor cradled his fingers and then twisted them back until the joints cracked. 'Correct planet, correct Holst.' He jumped to his feet and smoothed down the silvery atmospheric density jacket that he was wearing over his usual cream linen one, and dusted off his trousers. And then he threw his arms open to encompass the landscape. 'Unless my areography is sadly mistaken, we are about ten thousand kilometres from Tharsis Plain. That's if I have identified *that* correctly.' He nodded towards the horizon, where a distant flattened cone broke the monotony of the sky, which darkened from salmon pink to deep crimson as it met the ground. Really distant, when you considered that the little cone was an extinct volcano twenty kilometres high and six hundred across.

'Olympus Mons,' stated Roz, mainly to establish her credentials. She sniffed the air: thin, but breathable, with that unmistakable burnt smell that characterized Mars, which put it somewhere between the mid twenty-second and the early twenty-fourth century, if she remembered the start-stop timetable of terraforming correctly. By 2310, Mars had gained an Earth-type atmosphere, including the pollution. 'How the hell did we end up here?' Mixed and jumbled images and sounds flashed through her mind – tortured materialization noises blurred into frantic bell-ringing, while brilliant orange globes danced around the console room and behind her eyes. But nothing would hang together, nothing would connect.

The Doctor plucked his panama hat from his head and spun it on a forefinger. 'The emergency emergency systems would have locked on to the nearest environment that offered safety.' He cast his gaze towards his feet, which were kicking the red dust with a life of their own. 'Unfortunately, Mars seems to have fulfilled the requirements. A pity; I would have preferred somewhere with a little more *atmosphere*.' Roz wasn't sure whether he meant that literally or not.

But there was something missing. Realizing what it was, she looked around, but the vista of red rocks and red dust was completely clear of anything even vaguely Cwej-shaped. 'Where's Chris? He left the TARDIS just after we did.' Then she said it. 'Didn't he?' Nasty feelings were doing nasty things in her stomach.

The Doctor produced his umbrella seemingly from thin air and started to doodle aimlessly in the sand. 'The TARDIS broke up because she was caught between a subspace infarction and a Vortex rupture,' he said quietly, drawing an oblong shape with a light on top. 'That particular combination of events curdled the Time Vortex throughout the solar system, and its psuedo-Euclidian geometry would have –'

That was too much. 'In terms that a simple cop can understand, Doctor; you lost me just before the word "infarction".' Then again, the way her head was behaving, words of one syllable would be of little help.

He frowned, smiled sadly, and started again. 'The forces which, er, interacted with the TARDIS screwed up the Time Vortex, to put it bluntly. As far as the TARDIS emergency emergency systems were concerned, Mars and Triton could have been next door to one another. Normal rules didn't apply.'

'Chris is on Triton?' Vile world. Didn't even merit a viscount, just a grossly distasteful baron with a liking for young boys, Roz remembered vaguely. She hoped for Chris's sake that he had landed somewhere else.

The Doctor shrugged. 'Just a guess. It could just as easily be Vulcan or Cassius. Or Earth, come to that. All we can be sure of is that he's safe, wherever he is.'

'Did you give him one of these survival kits?' She held up the white box.

The Doctor nodded. 'Although Chris's has been tailored to suit his personal needs,' he added mysteriously. 'Rest assured, Chris is safe – the TARDIS would have made sure of that. Safety is, of course, relative.'

Then it hit her: delayed shock as she finally understood what had happened. The TARDIS had been totally, utterly destroyed.

One minute, they were flying away from Benny and Jason's wedding in good – if hungover – spirits; the next, all hell broke loose. The first inkling that something was about to go terribly wrong was the low, insistent chiming of some distant bell from deep within the TARDIS, but they barely had time to register that before they were thrown to the floor; something had hit the TARDIS. Roz remembered clambering to her feet to see the Doctor running around the control console in desperation, his hands darting out over the controls with almost blinding speed. Electrical fires were igniting everywhere, filling the console room with acrid black smoke; as Roz found it more and more difficult to breathe, the Doctor started muttering about subspace infarctions and Vortex ruptures. Just before she passed out, the Doctor shouted out that he had activated the 'emergency emergency systems'... and then Roz had woken up on Mars.

And the Doctor had lost his TARDIS. 'Are you all right?' she whispered. The TARDIS was more than the Doctor's ship, she knew that. It was his home, his friend, his life... 'I mean –'

The Doctor replaced his hat. 'The subject is closed,' he stated with a finality that Roz knew not to argue with. 'I suggest that we find a slightly more hospitable environment before nightfall. Despite humanity's determined attempts to terraform this planet, it still gets rather chilly around these parts.' He pointed towards the crimson horizon, where a feeble brilliance marked the sun. It was rather too low on the horizon for Roz's liking.

'And it'll get chillier. I have been here before, you know.' Her posting to the Martian colony at Jackson City – a massive conurbation sprawled over Olympus Mons – had been a riot. Well, a lot of riots, actually. But the Doctor's icy tone cut short her recollections.

'No, Adjudicator Forrester, I did not know. But you're right: night will fall in about five hours, and then it will get very, very cold. Bitter.' And that coldness seemed to have started with the Doctor.

Fine, so they were on Mars. But there were many different flavours of Mars, depending on the era. 'Have you any idea *when* we are?' If they were beyond the late twenty-third century, the planet was fully colonized; there was a good chance that a reconnaissance flitter would spot them before too long.

'It's difficult to calculate the year solely from the amount of terraforming,' the Doctor explained. 'Mars was actually terraformed four times over a million-year period. By four different races, come to that.' He frowned, and looked up at the sky. For a couple of seconds he cocked his head as if listening to some galactic time beacon, and then sucked a finger and held it up. 'Er, 2157. May, I believe, give or take a month or two.'

'2157,' Roz repeated. And then she realized. '2157! But that means...' She trailed off and stared at the horizon, where a brilliant star was just rising. Earth. And in 2157, it was crushed under the tyranny of a cold and calculating alien intelligence.

'Exactly,' muttered the Doctor sepulchrally. 'Two hundred million miles away, the Daleks are in residence. And if that hasn't got anything to do with the TARDIS's demise, then I'm Rassilon's uncle.' A thin thread of hatred seamed his voice.

Roz narrowed her eyes at the unseen foe. History books referred to it as the Dalek Invasion of Earth, but it had been far, far worse than that. Earth was conquered early in 2157, but the other planets had fallen over the following five years. Mars fell later in 2157; it would be just their luck to escape the destruction of the TARDIS, only to find themselves on the front line of the Dalek invasion of Mars. The invasion had failed – a genetically engineered virus which feasted exclusively on Dalek wiring had seen to that – but a lot of good people, both humans and Martians, had died defending their planet. Her attention returned to Chris; the Goddess knew where he had landed, but if he was on Earth... The Doctor tapped her on the shoulder with his umbrella.

'I suggest we head towards Jacksonville. It might not be the metropolis that you know, but the colony is thriving just about now. Short of supplies, but thriving, none the less.'

Roz considered their distance from the far cone of the highest mountain in the solar system. 'But Jackson Cit– Jacksonville is over nine thousand kilometres away!' She looked at the small white box the Doctor had thrust into her hands just before she had plunged through the orange globe he had summoned in the console room. She doubted that the survival pack contained enough supplies to last them even a fraction of the time that it would take them to reach Jacksonville, perched halfway up Olympus Mons. Then again, food was the least of their worries: there was no free water on the surface – apart from at the poles – and the night-time temperature would soon plunge them into hypothermia, even with their survival jackets. What the Doctor was proposing was lunacy.

'Surely we should look for somewhere a little closer.' She racked her brain. 'Shelbyville is about a hundred kilometres due east, and Springfield is just next to Ascraeus Lacus –'

The Doctor shook his head. 'Fifty and seventy years too early respectively. The only other human colony currently on Mars is Arcadia Planitia, and that's even further than Jacksonville. So we should get moving.'

'You honestly believe that we're equipped to hike over ten thousand klicks?' she snorted.

He gave her a look of mournful sympathy. 'I know it's quite a trek, Roz, but we really have no choice, do we? But we don't have to travel overland; Mars is blessed with an extensive tunnel system about a kilometre under the surface. All we have to do is find the way in.'

'Natural tunnels?'

'Some of them,' he said quietly.

Of course, she realized. Mars was the former home of the Ice Warriors. Having spent rather too many hours at the bar with a particularly boisterous group at Benny and Jason's wedding, she was beginning to consider them one of the more decent races of ETs. 'Why don't we try to contact the Ice Warriors?'

'What Ice Warriors?'

'What do you mean?'

'This is 2157, Roz. The entire race vanished nearly a century ago, at the conclusion of the Thousand Day War.'

Roz sighed. 'Of all the times to end up on Mars, we have to do it without Benny.'

The history and culture of the Ice Warriors was archaeologist Professor Bernice Summerfield's speciality. Roz remembered what Benny had told her about the giant green lizards.

'They vanished. At the end of the War, the clean-up troops from Earth moved in, but they couldn't find a single Martian. The whole planet appeared to have been abandoned; the few

cities that Earth knew about were empty, deserted. Now we know that they'd decided to start a new life on Nova Martia, but at the time... well, it was quite a mystery. Some people claimed that the Martians were simply hiding, waiting to attack; others reckoned that the human military had used some secret bacteriological weapon to exterminate them. Created a bit of a stir.'

'They've gone, haven't they?'

The Doctor nodded. 'Gone but not forgotten. Not by me, anyway. But their tunnels and their cities are mainly intact; they're warm – at least comparatively – and there will be water. It will take some time, but we will reach Jacksonville.' He did a 360-degree turn before pointing out a direction. 'That's our best bet.' Then he paused.

'And remember –' He reeled a mysteriously found yo-yo in front of him, and Roz watched it creep up and down the string at a very odd rate. 'We're a hundred years before the gravitic web was laid; gravity is a third of Earth's.'

Roslyn Forrester, whose adjudication duties had taken her to planets where the gravity ranged from zero to what felt like infinity, began to prepare a jagged reply, before catching sight of the comet that was trailing through the sky. 'Look!' she yelled. 'Is that what I think it is?'

'If you think it's an atmospheric shuttle crash-landing, then yes, it is.' The Doctor set off at a run. 'Time to help,' he called over his shoulder. 'Swallow one of the little orange pills in the first-aid kit. Anti-radiation capsule; Mars is quite hot at the moment.' Then he was away.

Roz opened the box and marvelled at the collection of pills, vials and mysterious supplies within, before locating an orange capsule and placing it in her mouth. As it dissolved, she leapt to her feet, and immediately found herself half a metre above the ground. Indecorously landing amidst a plume of crimson dust, she watched the Doctor sprinting into the distance with a blatant disregard for the lower gravity. Then again, she decided, since when had the Doctor shown the slightest regard for the laws of physics? Taking careful steps, she bounced after him.

* * *

'Rachel; slave your station to mine and tell me what you think.'

Dr Felice Delacroix looked up from the board of readouts and frowned. Ten minutes ago, their latest attempt to punch a hole through subspace had gone rather spectacularly pear-shaped, blowing half the failsafes before dissipating into the void. Unfortunately, the readouts and twinkling alarms across her work-station suggested that the attempt hadn't dissipated quite as much as she and her co-workers had thought. Not for the first time, Felice wondered how much of what she had learnt at Cambridge belonged in the bin. 'It looks like we're getting feedback along the carrier wave.' A rather solid bit of feedback, come to that.

'Crap,' replied Rachel Anders, a dumpy, middle-aged woman with greying hair and a permanently sour expression. A grouch who just happened to be in charge of the research laboratory. A research laboratory which just happened to be the only thing left on Charon. And it was *Professor* Rachel Anders, of course. Never forget that. 'That can't happen.' She walked over to Felice's station and examined the monitors, elbowing her out of the way in the process. Immediately, her face screwed up in disbelief and she hissed one word. 'Shit.'

'Satisfied?' snapped Felice. Okay, so they were all under pressure on Charon, but Rachel's constant attitude problems didn't help matters. Anyone would think that Felice had deliberately broken the laws of physics just to piss her off. She tapped one of the displays. 'Something's definitely coming up the carrier wave.'

'But the Transit beam never focused at the secondary node,' Rachel muttered. 'There wasn't any way for matter to penetrate subspace and enter the stunnel stream.' In simple terms, the subspace transit tunnel they had attempted to create – a stunnel – had only had an entrance. Creating an exit was the purpose of their research. A desperate purpose.

'Something did,' Felice pointed out, mainly to be provocative. 'And it's going to resolve at this end in a little over two minutes.' She looked across the room to the huge oval of their stunnel terminus. Although it possessed none of the pizzazz of the old commercial termini such as Paris or King's Cross, it had one thing in its favour: it was the only terminus in the solar system that still functioned, a fact indicated by the infinite cylinder which stretched from the mouth of the oval into infinity ... or so it seemed. Actually, it was an optical illusion caused by the universe's interaction with the primary subspace meniscus. And reaching beyond that meniscus into the abstract dimension of subspace – with the blockade in place – might be their only hope of reaching beyond the solar system. Then again, since none of their attempts to achieve a stable, two-ended stunnel had worked up till now, its continued functioning was rather a moot point.

Transit technology had been all but abandoned years ago: human beings had never really trusted the idea of being scrambled into elementary particles and shoved through subspace, and the fiasco of the first commercial stunnel run to Arcturus hadn't helped its popularity. But some people – such as Rachel and Felice – still felt that the science could have useful applications, and the Earth government had grudgingly funded a small research complex about five years ago. That it had been placed on Charon – almost as far away from Earth as it was possible to be and still share the same solar system – had actually proved quite exciting at first; Felice had felt like a pioneer, pushing back the frontiers of science. It hadn't taken long for her to feel cut off and isolated, working away at problems that no one outside the base was particularly interested in.

However, events that had followed the invasion of Earth had given them a new purpose. The invaders had set up a subspace blockade across the solar system, making it impossible for any ships or supplies to drop out of subspace within the orbit of Cassius. And conventional travel was just as impossible; the Black Fleet simply blasted anything that moved.

Rachel, Felice and the others were possibly the only people in the solar system with the faintest chance of breaking that blockade – not that they had much to show for it at the moment apart from a succession of failed, one-ended stunnels.

But if *something* had managed to enter the one-ended

stunnel that Rachel and her team had accomplished, perhaps it wasn't quite as one-ended as they had thought. Then again – and perhaps more importantly – what the hell *was* hurtling through subspace towards Charon?

Rachel mouthed Felice's fears. 'Get a security team to the terminus room. Stat!' she growled into the work-station's comm grille. 'If it's one of *them* ...'

Felice stared along the seven-metre tall oval tunnel, her scientist side noting the swirling, phosphorescent wisps that were beginning to form as the automatic systems registered an incoming signal. Even if their visitor was one of the bastards who had claimed ownership of the solar system, there was no way of shutting down the stunnel from their end, not with the damage that the last attempt had caused. And if it *was* one of them, she hoped that a security team of frightened colonists would be able to stop it.

Because all the defences of Earth hadn't been able to.

The main doors of the stunnel chamber suddenly flew open and four black-suited figures in ill-fitting uniforms strode in. The uniforms had been culled from the corpses of the Charon Militia that had been found in the escape tunnels leading from the surface: as the continued bombardments had driven the few survivors of the colony underground, the Militia, holding the rear, had been annihilated by the final radiation burst that had managed to penetrate twenty metres of solid rock. Their successors were teenagers, terrified children holding their salvaged plasma rifles as if they were going to be the targets, rather than the enigma that was only a minute away from materializing in the meniscus.

Rachel began barking orders at them, terrifying them even further. 'You and you to the mouth of the stunnel, you two at the sides.' Felice suppressed a smile; forget scientific research – Dr Rachel Anders was definitely in the wrong profession. She glanced at the tunnel and shuddered; the wisps had become a roiling vortex of lime greens and golds with a rapidly enlarging heart of darkness.

Vincente Esteban scratched his thick black moustache and snorted through his nose. 'There has been another ten per cent increase in the last two hours,' he stated in his thick accent, peering out through the window of the buggy as if the increase in electromagnetic activity he had just reported would be visible against the darkening Martian sky.

'For Christ's sake, Vince, stop giving us minute by minute status reports,' snapped Antony McGuire, glancing over his shoulder at his Spanish colleague. 'I know you mean well, but you're not helping.' He had been looking at Esteban's overweight reflection in the windscreen for the last three hours, waiting for his Chinese water-torture pronouncements about the state of the Martian magnetic field with increasing irritation. Then again, they had provided a welcome respite from the red monotony of the Martian landscape. After five days, any distraction was welcome.

'It could be important,' muttered Piotr Kolchak, looking up from his careworn leather Bible. 'Vince is our token scientist, remember.' The cynicism was clear.

'I apologize if I am boring you, Piotr,' said Esteban. 'I am just curious about these magnetic storms. But I am glad that you appreciate me.' For a second, his expression reminded McGuire of a small child whose sweets had just been snatched from him: hurt and puzzled.

Kolchak sneered. 'You've had your nose in that tablette since we left Jacksonville.'

'And yours has been in that Bible, Piotr. You have your God and I have mine.'

McGuire sighed. The last thing he wanted on this expedition was a major falling out. They still had another day before they reached the North Pole, and he would have preferred that they got there without mutually inflicted knife wounds and plasma burns. The expedition had started so well, full of optimism that the strange energy readings Vince had detected at the North Pole indicated the possibility of supplies. But the sheer boredom of the journey had soon put paid to that. 'Go on then, Vince; how much worse?' Better to indulge him.

Esteban glanced down at the slim black tablette which nestled in the shadow of his stomach. 'The levels of electromagnetic activity have increased by eight hundred per cent over the last four days. If it carries on at this rate, well, either we're going to have the biggest electrical storm Mars has ever seen, or it will reach a point where it starts to interfere with our own nervous systems.'

'Are you suggesting that we return to Jacksonville?' asked Kolchak.

Esteban shook his head. 'No point, Piotr. The field covers the entire northern hemisphere. Jacksonville won't offer any protection at all.' He returned his attention to the tablette. 'But this is interesting –'

'To you, maybe. Perhaps we can stop and take a look at the lichen while we're at it.'

Madrigal's interjection was the first thing she'd said that day, and it made McGuire shudder. Christina Madrigal was a decorated veteran of countless campaigns, from the civil wars on the Outer Planets to the colonial struggles in the Arcturus system. Apparently she had been on Mars visiting friends when the blockade had started, and the mayor of Jacksonville had suggested – although ordered might have been a better word – that she accompany McGuire's expedition to the Martian North Pole. As far as McGuire was concerned, they were a group of volunteers looking for much needed supplies at the North Pole – with the blockade and the invasion, their regular trade routes had been cut off, and so had the colony. Madrigal's presence made the whole thing feel like a military campaign, and that made him very uneasy. All things military made him uneasy.

'Hang on, Madrigal, let Vince continue.'

'Thank you, Antony.' Esteban grinned annoyingly. 'I was going to say that the epicentre of the phenomenon appears to be the North Pole.'

'Stands to reason,' said Madrigal offhandedly. 'Poles and magnetism. Don't need to be a rocket scientist to know that, Esteban.'

'Hang on!' warned McGuire. He had been so preoccupied with preventing an argument that he had neglected to pay enough attention to what was ahead. A large hillock was coming up fast; although the ATET was designed for rough terrain, this was going to be more than rough. He turned the wheel, trying to avoid the obstacle, but knew immediately that there wasn't the time or the distance. They were going to have to go over it.

The generator strained as the caterpillar tracks tried to keep a purchase on the dusty slope of the hillock, and McGuire swallowed as he felt the vehicle shudder with the effort. He accelerated, hoping that extra speed would do the trick, and was extremely relieved when the ATET responded, painfully pulling itself up the slope. They finally reached the top of the hillock and he braked. He hoped that going down would prove a bit less dramatic.

Panic over, Esteban continued. 'Wrong, Ms Madrigal. Mars has no magnetic field. Whatever is causing the build-up is definitely not natural.'

'Someone's deliberately doing this?' asked McGuire. That changed things. 'Who? Greenies?' This was even more disturbing than Madrigal's presence, and made McGuire regret indulging Esteban's research.

'I doubt it,' Esteban countered. 'If the Native Martians had ever possessed the technology to do something like this, they wouldn't have lost the war.'

McGuire gritted his teeth. Native Martians? The bastards were Greenies, and that was that. And Esteban's bleeding-heart liberalism wouldn't bring back the thousands who had died at their hands. But stating his views would only make the situation more tense – the last thing he wanted was Kolchak preaching his belief systems at them – so he gritted his teeth even more. 'We'll deal with that when it happens. If there are Greenies at the Pole . . . well, we'll deal with them as well.' Then he saw it through the windscreen, a blazing comet that seared across the crimson sky.

'What the hell is that?' he whispered, but he already knew the answer: the slightly purple tint to the tail of the comet marked it as the discharge from a failing deuterium generator. They were watching an atmospheric shuttle plummeting down from orbit to its inevitable and fiery end. Who was stupid enough to fly a shuttle with the blockade in place? Every attempt to achieve even the lowest flight path had been met by the same hostile reaction: the orbiting invaders just shot them out of the sky.

The contrailed fireball was getting larger; you didn't need to be a rocket scientist to realize that it was heading straight towards them.

McGuire didn't hesitate; he yanked the steering wheel a quarter turn, aiming the buggy in a direction which he hoped was headed away from the crash. The shuttle's generator was leaking; the colour of the flames told McGuire that. If it went critical upon impact and they were within a klick of ground zero, they wouldn't stand a chance. McGuire hit the accelerator, watching as the buggy's own generator edged towards red-lining.

He just hoped it would be fast enough. And far enough.

'Who the hell are you?' Rachel was standing close up to the suspect, hands on her hips. What really annoyed her was the way that he was smiling at her. A charming, boyish smile that she wanted to wipe off his face with her fists.

'Adjudicator Christopher Cwej, ma'am.'

He was six three and impressively built, wearing black jeans and a padded silver jacket that could have been some sort of survival gear. His physique was obvious, even through the jacket, and Rachel could detect the smiles and glances from the female members of her team, and that made her even more angry. Blond, blue-eyed, a recruitment poster boy if ever she'd seen one. Just like her brother Michael. Rachel dismissed the memory and glared at the stranger. 'So what the frag were you doing in my Transit tunnel?' She had been prepared for anything as the tunnel resolved: little green men, brutal robots . . . anything but this.

The boy frowned. 'Transit tunnel?' And then his eyes widened. 'Transit tunnel. Of course. Yes. Transit tunnel.' She was immediately suspicious of his hesitation, but allowed him to continue. Give him enough rope . . . 'My ship broke up in subspace; your Transit beam must have caught me as the ship disintegrated.' He grinned. 'You saved my life, Ms . . .?'

'Bollocks!' As if the laws of physics were there for his benefit! 'You're one of *them*, aren't you?'

Chris shrugged. 'One of whom, ma'am?'

Rachel stepped forward and thumped him on the chest. 'Those bastards who have invaded Earth, and cut us all off from the rest of the Alliance!' Ships breaking up in subspace, indeed. If your ship broke up in subspace, you died – it was as simple as that. So who did he think he was kidding? She turned to the frightened kid next to her. 'Shoot him!'

'Professor Anders?' he asked.

'Shoot him!' she screamed. 'Before he brings his friends here!' Didn't the boy understand? The Black Fleet had been terrorizing the outer worlds of the Alliance for the last six months, and their final, unexpected act had been to invade Mother Earth and blockade the solar system. Rachel and her colleagues were now trapped on Charon, with limited supplies and the constant threat of the Black Fleet finishing off what it had started, and this bastard was one of the ones responsible.

Suddenly, Felice was next to her, her hand on her shoulder. 'Come on, Rachel. Don't you think you're over-reacting?'

Not Felice as well. 'He came through the stunnel, damn it! Shoot him!' Realizing that it was all up to her, she grabbed the plasma rifle from the pimply boy beside her and flicked off the safety catch.

And aimed the rifle at Chris's chest.

The shuttle hit like the fist of God. Roz fell to the ground as it bucked beneath her, and saw the Doctor valiantly attempting to keep his footing as she pitched to the ground. But even he couldn't fight seismology; she watched, spitting dust, as he collapsed in a plume of red. Half a klick away, a geyser of green flame ignited the Martian twilight.

Roz winced. It reminded her of the Imperial Landsknecht flitter that had been stolen by a group of joyboys; they had managed to fly it through one of the gravitic beams holding up Overcity Five, thus screwing up their antigrav drive and thereby plunging into the Undercity. By the time she and her partner Fenn had reached the impact zone, there was nothing left of the occupants and some very satisfied under-dwellers; nothing like a barbecue to please the crowds. But that was then, and this was now. Within seconds, she had scrambled to her feet and bounced over to the Doctor, pulling him up by the hood of his survival jacket.

'Are you okay?' She took in his nod and nodded in return. 'Then we're needed.' She inclined her head towards the inferno that raged in the distance.

'I just hope that there are survivors,' the Doctor muttered as he brushed himself down. Roz wondered why the Doctor couldn't wear an outfit made of dirt-repellent material, like her body armour. Then she remembered that she wasn't wearing it, and looked down at the jeans, thick jumper and silvery atmospheric density jacket that were now covered in light brown dust. Oh well. Another explosion roared through the tissue-thin atmosphere; same distance, same direction. A secondary generator, Roz mused; talk about overkill.

'Different power source,' said the Doctor, reading her mind. 'That sounded more like a cold fusion reactor ... Did you take your tablet, by the way?'

She nodded. 'Although the fusion generator's clean, the whole place'll be flooded with gamma radiation if that deuterium generator went off.'

'So let's not beta round the bush; I think there has just been a pile-up.' Two puns for the price of one, thought Roz. A bargain.

The Doctor pointed his umbrella purposely towards the crash site. 'Come along, Nurse Forrester.'

At a bouncing trot, they reached the crash site in just over five minutes. Or rather, they reached a sandbank overlooking a scene of carnage which made the flitter incident in Undertown look like a mid-air fender shunt. Thankfully, the fact that the shuttle was now ten metres of crumpled osmidium doing a very good impression of a bonfire was reassuring; if its deuterium generator had gone critical, Mars would have had another crater, approximately two hundred metres across. But the state of the shuttle didn't bode well for survivors, Roz decided.

The cold fusion detonation that they had heard had been the responsibility of the broken mess that lay about ten metres from the shuttle; from the wreckage, Roz identified it as the remains of an ATET, an all-terrain excursion transport still used in her time. One of those designs that never went out of fashion, she supposed, like Coca-Cola bottles. Its entire rear section was missing, consumed by the exploding generator. Thankfully, however, cold fusion reactors blew up with little radiation and minimal damage, although this had ensured that the ATET would never go on another excursion. She noticed that the Doctor was already at the foot of the sandbank.

Fighting a losing battle against the crumbling sand and low gravity, Roz half-scrambled, half-skidded down the bank towards the crash site, dragging up her triage-and-treatment training as she did so. But the lack of movement made her wonder whether it would be needed or not. If not, the only thing she would need would be a shovel.

'Over here!' called the Doctor, pointing towards the rear of the burning shuttle. 'I think I can see somebody.'

Roz followed, but she didn't share the Doctor's optimism.

Chris considered his options. Knocking the rifle from the woman's hands would be simple, but the armed guards might not be as green as they looked. And a plasma rifle was deadly, even in inexperienced hands. Perhaps he could grab the rifle and attempt a stand-off –

A small blonde woman wearing the same white jumpsuit as the bad-tempered harpy interposed herself between Chris and the business end of the rifle. 'This is stupid, Rachel. Shooting him won't help.' She looked round at Chris and smiled, and he couldn't help grinning back. 'If he's innocent, then you'll be committing murder; if he is one of the invaders, we might be able to find a way to pierce the jamming field.'

The older woman seemed to see reason. 'Be it on your own head, Felice.' She turned to the guards. 'Take him to one of the empty rooms in the dorm-block. But post a guard.' She scowled at Felice. 'We'll let him sweat for a few hours, just to make sure that he isn't followed. And while he's doing that, we have work to do. I want to know exactly how he ended up in my stunnel.'

Chris allowed himself a measured and secret sigh of relief. He was safe. But what about the Doctor and Roz?

* * *

Only one person had survived the shuttle crash, and even that was a miracle, given the twisted wreckage that remained. There appeared to have been only two occupants: a man – presumably the pilot – who had been disembowelled, and a woman. Roz was currently kneeling next to her, applying a dermal patch to a superficial wound while the woman wittered on and on. Roz briefly wondered whether the Doctor's survival kit included a general anaesthetic, but decided that the woman's gabbling was probably due to shock; besides, the Doctor wouldn't be too impressed if Roz started rendering everyone who annoyed her unconscious. Half the known universe would be asleep.

She looked over at the shuttle; it was still burning brightly in the thin Martian atmosphere, flickering green flames that provided some welcome warmth. Night was still four hours away, but Mars had a very protracted twilight and it was already becoming difficult to see. She returned her attention to the woman, and regretted it immediately.

'I knew it was a bad idea,' she was saying. 'I told them at Jacksonville that it was too dangerous to travel over there, what with this awful blockade, but would they listen to me? Of course not; I'm only a singer. Did I tell you that I was a singer?' Roz nodded; the woman had proclaimed her profession at least twenty times in the last ten minutes. 'I was supposed to be performing at Arcadia Planitia this evening. I don't think that's very likely now, do you, Ms – ?'

'Roslyn Forrester.'

The woman smiled with ruby-red lips, running a manicured hand through her raven hair. 'I'm Carmen Santacosta.' And then a wistful smile. 'That's my stage name, anyway. Show business; smell of the greasepaint, roar of the crowd. I was so looking forward to performing tonight.' She looked over Roz's shoulder and frowned. 'But listen to me, going on about my problems.' No thank you, thought Roz. I'd rather tear your throat out with my bare teeth. 'How are the others?'

Roz gave Carmen the once-over and decided that she was more than capable of being on her own for a few minutes. Even if she wasn't, Roz needed a break. 'Hang on, I'll find out from the Doctor.'

'Lucky that a doctor happened to be near by,' Carmen added cheerfully, as Roz gingerly scrambled to her feet, extremely conscious of the lower gravity.

Yes, very lucky. Lucky to be stranded on Mars. Lucky to have turned up in the solar system when it's crawling with Daleks. Roz walked over to where the Doctor was living up to his name, flitting between the three survivors and administering blankets and pillows he had salvaged from the ATET as needed. Apart from the green light from the ATET wreckage, illumination was courtesy of ten little wooden sticks placed in a circle around them. The Doctor had called them 'everlasting matches'; stuck in the soil and ignoring the paucity of the Martian atmosphere, they added flickering yellow highlights to the scene. A few metres outside the circle, a shrouded bump marked the one casualty from the ATET, a poor unfortunate whose chest had been virtually minced when the generator had blown – it looked as if the rear bulkhead that had separated the generator from the cabin had ruptured and torn straight through him.

'How are they?' she asked, kneeling down beside him as he took a break from tending his patients.

'Minor injuries, nothing too serious. At least, not yet.' He looked up at the sky, now a glorious blue-black. Roz followed his gaze and noticed Earth, a point of light that shimmered above the horizon. She shuddered.

The Doctor obviously misinterpreted her shudder. 'If you think it's cold now, Roz, wait until the shuttle burns itself out. By then, night will have fallen, and that will put us in real danger of hypothermia.'

Roz nodded; already she could feel the cold creeping through her atmospheric density jacket and she cursed herself. Her Adjudicator's uniform had built-in temperature control and insulation, but had she put it back on once they had left Benny's wedding? Oh no, she had raided the TARDIS wardrobe for something comfortable, and now she was regretting it. *Comfort is the best way to lead an Adjudicator into a sense of complacency*; wasn't that what Konstantine had said? And, just to rub it in, he'd delivered that pronouncement in their suite in Jackson City. On Mars.

'Why are they still unconscious?' she asked, trying to forget about her time squiring. 'Surely they should have recovered from the crash by now?' The three bodies, covered in reflective, insulated blankets from the ATET, were as unmoving as the shrouded corpse.

He squatted on the ground and warmed his hands over one of the matches. 'At a rough guess, I would say that the driver of the ATET attempted to avoid the shuttle as it crashed. Unfortunately, he overloaded the generator. This particular model of ATET was notorious for a rather nasty design flaw: under certain circumstances, the cold fusion generator had a tendency to go critical.'

'What sort of circumstances?'

'Influx of hard radiation.' He nodded over to the shuttle wreck. 'Although the deuterium generator didn't explode, the secondary engines did, briefly flooding the surrounding area with high-energy gamma radiation. The ATET was caught in it and its own generator went critical. And, as a side-effect of that explosion, there was a promethion pulse.'

As the conversation strayed into the realms of particle physics, Roz held up her hand. 'What the hell is a promethion pulse?'

'Nasty, short-lived particles caused by third-generation cold fusion reactors when they go critical,' he replied tautologically. 'They have an immediate and deleterious effect on the human brain, causing unconsciousness. No permanent side-effects, though; they should wake up soon.'

He was interrupted by a groan from the ground. The compact, olive-skinned woman with tight, curly hair was coming round.

'You're safe,' reassured the Doctor, placing a comforting hand on her shoulder. Her reaction was immediate; she grabbed the Doctor round the throat and lifted him above her.

Roz could have sworn that he gargled 'oh no, not again,' before sinking to the ground. However, she was too preoccupied to notice an enormous shape that detached itself from the shadows and lumbered away.

* * *

Christopher Cwej sipped the coffee that one of the guards had brought in and tried not to wince at the bitter, earthy taste as he pondered his predicament. He knew that he was on Charon, the oversized moon of Pluto, and from what Felice and Rachel had said, he was in some kind of stunnel research base. But where were the Doctor and Roz?

He tried to recall the sequence of events inside the TARDIS, but it was difficult; his mind couldn't seem to link them together in any logical order. He remembered the Doctor frantically operating the console, and the floating orange ball that had suddenly materialized in front of them. The Doctor had handed both of them a silver atmosphere density jacket and a survival kit – Chris's jacket was currently slung over the back of another chair, the kit on the seat – and then urged them to dive through the ball. Chris had watched as the other two vanished into the luminescence before following them, well aware of the explosions behind him as the console room broke up. But only he had arrived here.

He considered how he had arrived on Charon; according to Rachel, he had been caught in a subspace tunnel. Hadn't the Doctor called one of the two reasons for the break-up a 'subspace infarction'? Perhaps the two events were connected. Don't be stupid, Chris, he chastised himself; of course they're connected.

And perhaps the Doctor and Roz were scattered atoms, adrift in subspace.

Putting the fate of his companions to one side – he was worried sick about them, but there wasn't a lot he could do while locked in a cell on Charon – he returned his attention to the facts at hand. Stunnel technology put the date anywhere between the early twenty-first and the middle of the twenty-second century. But what else had Rachel said? Something about Earth being invaded, the blockade of the solar system... With a horrible squirming feeling in his stomach, Chris suddenly realized when and where he was. It did nothing to make him feel better.

The single pertinent fact about Charon that Chris could remember was the reason why it was still a radioactive cinder, even in the thirtieth century. It had been the target of a vicious and uncompromising nuclear bombardment by the Daleks. No, that wasn't quite right, he corrected himself; there had been two attacks. The first bombardment had destroyed the domed colonies, but the survivors had fled underground, only to be killed by the second bombardment, which took place on 7 May 2157. Chris remembered the date because it was his father's birthday, one of those odd facts which tend to stick in the mind.

He put down his mug and got up. 'Excuse me,' he called through the door. 'Being in the Transit tunnel has left me feeling a bit muddled, and I think there might have been some sort of time-slip involved as well. What's the date?'

A click and a whirr and the door opened. The guard – who looked like a kid to Chris – frowned, and the scepticism was clear as he answered, 'It's the seventh.'

Oh shit, thought Chris. Say it isn't true. 'The seventh of what?'

The kid gave him a 'what planet are you on' look, but Chris was used to that by now. 'I told you I was confused, friend.'

'The seventh of May, 2157. 11.35 a.m., to be precise. Remember now?'

Chris felt the cold sweat bead on his forehead as he turned his back on the guard. Oh yes, he remembered. He definitely remembered. Wherever the Doctor and Roz had ended up, at least they were safer than he was.

Roz leapt forward, but overshot in the lower gravity. Then again, she thought, low gravity conditions can work to everybody's advantage. Landing on the tip of her boot, she pirouetted round and kicked the woman's arm away from the Doctor's throat, before slipping and landing on her backside.

'What the hell do you think you're doing?' yelled Roz, trying to ignore the fact that she was currently sitting on her butt and in no position to argue.

'Thought he was attacking,' the other replied curtly. 'So I was defending myself. I'm Madrigal.' She sat up, dislodging the silver blanket to reveal light grey fatigues and a familiar emblem to anybody who knew the history of Earth's military forces; Madrigal was a Colonial Marine. 'Who the cruk are you?' Roz also remembered that the twenty-second century Marines were almost seventy per cent female, with a formidable reputation that had survived into the thirtieth century.

Her reverie was interrupted by the introductions. 'I'm the Doctor and this is my associate, Roslyn Forrester,' he said, doffing his hat and making it roll up his arm until it was back on his head. 'We found you and two of your companions unconscious in the wreckage of the ATET.' A sudden duet of groans indicated that the others were also waking up. 'I'm afraid one of you didn't survive.'

Madrigal looked at the other two survivors and shrugged. 'Kolchak. Oh well, he can find out about God first-hand, I suppose.'

'There are six of them. Six mammals. You assured us that we would be unmolested by these, these vermin, Abbot Aklaar!' hissed Cleece, his clamps opening and closing in a gesture of irritation. 'You claimed that the threat of aerial attack from the invaders of Earth would be sufficient to keep them in their pens.'

'They are an inconvenience, Pilgrim Cleece. Nothing more.' Aklaar gazed northwards and pointed with a bifurcated hand. 'But be assured, my son; no one will be permitted to stand in the way of our holy crusade.'

The three other Ice Warriors stared towards the North Pole in reverence, the setting sun reflecting crimson in the visors of their helmets.

Chapter 2

The Doctor picked up the china teapot that he had assembled from his survival kit and cast his gaze around the little group. Once again, fate had assembled an entourage of interesting and colourful characters against a historically significant backdrop. I really must have a word with Fate about that, he decided.

'Shall I be mother?' he asked politely, before pouring the brew into the ordered row of metal beakers in front of him. All six of them were sitting cross-legged in a circle, illuminated by ever-lasting matches and warmed by the fading heat from the shuttle, a few metres to their left. 'Anyone take sugar? No? Well, drink up before it gets cold.'

'It is cold,' whispered Roz.

'I know,' he replied irritably. 'Lower atmospheric pressure – lower boiling point. It will be at least a century before we can enjoy a decent cup of Earl Grey on the surface of Mars.' He scowled at her. 'But what did you expect? Piping hot tea and a plate of scones and french fancies? Or maybe tiffin?'

'Are you both mad?' The one called McGuire, a small, edgy man with thin, greying hair and narrow, untrusting – or were they desperate? – eyes, tried to stand, but thought better of it and slumped back to the floor. McGuire hid an inner core of distrust, tempered with hatred and bitterness, the Doctor gauged. A dangerous combination which unfortunately cropped up on his travels with alarming regularity. 'The ATET's a write-off and you're making tea!'

'We also saved your lives, McGuire,' Roz added sharply. 'If the Doctor and I hadn't come along when we did, the four of you would have frozen to death. And the tea is to help counteract shock.'

'I'm well aware of both those facts, Ms Forrester,' said McGuire coldly. 'But what the hell were the two of you doing, ten thousand klicks from anywhere?'

'You're hardly equipped for walkabout,' added Madrigal tersely. Ah, yes, thought the Doctor, Madrigal. Madrigal the warrior. In many ways, she reminded the Doctor of Ace, with all her anger, all her hostility, worn like body armour to protect – or maybe hide – whatever lay beneath. Once, lifetimes ago, the Doctor might have felt threatened by someone who embraced violence so totally. Now he found such honesty refreshing; if Madrigal were going to kill you, at least you would know about it beforehand.

'Our ship crashed about three kilometres from here and we baled out,' explained Roz with barely restrained patience. 'We've already told you that. If you're that worried, we'll show you the wreckage.'

Good thinking, Roz, the Doctor thought. Call their bluff. Any wreckage which remained from the break-up of the TARDIS would now be tumbling through the Time Vortex, fractalled pieces of outer plasmic shell and the odd roundel, no doubt.

'I am not happy being so exposed. At least the ATET offered some protection from the electromagnetic build-up,' said Esteban, the next piece on the board.

Professor Vincente Esteban was apparently a physicist, a large, bear-like man with a wonderfully childlike innocence and fascination. He impressed the Doctor: a scientist who hadn't yet lost his sense of awe at the universe's mysteries. Too many scientists of the Doctor's acquaintance had either become cynical and jaded, or drunk on the power that their discoveries offered; he thought of Maxtible, Kettlewell; even Greel and Davros had once been simple seekers of knowledge. But Esteban was the kind of person who still wanted to know where God had thrown his dice, constantly peering into irrelevant nooks and crannies for the universal truths. Of course, the Doctor could have told him exactly where the dice were, but where would the fun have been in that?

He realized what Esteban had said.

'What electromagnetic build-up?' Mars didn't have a magnetic field, a fact that the Osirians had taken advantage of seven thousand years ago – when they had enslaved Sutekh in Egypt, the stellar power relay had been placed on Mars. So how could there be a build-up? But if there was one... Once, in earlier incarnations, cogs would have turned. Now things simply *sparked*.

Esteban, warming to both the Doctor and his subject, produced a slim black notebook computer – a tablette, the Doctor recognized – and flipped it open. A small holo-field began to form above it.

'Not again,' complained Madrigal. 'Stranded in the Red Outback and the rocket scientist wants to start a lecture tour.' The Doctor repressed a smile; an honorary descendant of Ace, definitely. Then again, given the vagaries of time travel – both his and Dorothée's – it might not be so honorary.

'Look.' Esteban thrust the holographic simularity under the Doctor's nose. The three-dimensional animated display which hovered about ten centimetres above the tablette showed an extremely high magnetic flux density across the entire northern hemisphere of Mars. And if the readings were to be believed, the flux density was increasing at an alarming rate. It was almost as if someone were trying to give Mars the magnetic field that it lacked. Except that field which was blossoming across the planet was totally unnatural. It was monopolar.

'If it increases at this rate, Doctor, it will start to cause physiological damage within six days.' The Doctor nodded; the human brain was a complex electro-neurochemical sponge. Ramp up the ambient magnetic field, and very unpleasant things started to happen. Headaches were the first sign, death the last. With madness in between, of course. At least Esteban hadn't noticed the unique nature of the artificial magnetic field; the Doctor really did not feel up to explaining that magnetic monopoles – a scientific impossibility – were the province of a science far more advanced than mankind's. Currently. He frowned; shuttles crashing, buggies exploding, TARDISes falling apart and Mars suddenly deciding that it needed a monopolar magnetic field. Mix thoroughly and bake in a hot oven, then garnish liberally with Daleks. The level of coincidence was far too high, even for his liking. Then something else occurred to him.

'May I?' he asked politely, grabbing the tablette from Esteban before the physicist could respond.

McGuire stood up. 'This is getting us nowhere. The heat from the wreck's not going to last much longer, and most of the ATET's survival gear was lost when the generator blew. And you and Vince are prattling on about –'

'Wait a moment!' barked the Doctor, holding up his hand. He could sense their growing impatience, but he also sensed a major clue, something just beyond his reach. Tapping away at the tablette, he shifted the readings from magnetic flux to the third derivative of gravimetric intensity, a sure pointer to any subspace activity which might have explained the infarction he had detected in the TARDIS.

'Interesting, is it?' said McGuire sarcastically.

Ignoring him, the Doctor continued. His search for the source of the infarction fruitless, he tried another tack. Although the computer was primitive, it could still pick up the by-products of a Vortex rupture, the other disaster that had cost him his TARDIS. He started looking for reverse-spin tau-mesons with a vengeance.

'How's your comm-set?' Roz asked McGuire. The Doctor couldn't help smiling; one of Roz's greatest assets was her practicality. Reassured that she could deal with the trivia and minutiae, he returned his attention to the tablette and continued, running his analyses at speeds which left its processor gasping for breath.

McGuire shrugged at Roz's question. 'Between Vince's beloved electromagnetism and the fall-out from the shuttle, what do you think? The aerial practically lights up in the dark.'

'Of course!' Everyone looked at the Doctor, and he instantly regretted his outburst. What he had discovered was of no interest to anyone apart from himself and Roz. So it was time to improvise.

'More tea, anyone?'

* * *

Felice stared through the open door at the prisoner, watching him sitting on the chair with his square jaw resting on his palms. For all his size and physique, his expression reminded Felice of a little boy who had lost his mother, with his big teddy-bear eyes looking up at her imploringly.

'You wanted to talk to me?' she asked, walking into the room.

He stood up and frowned. It only made him look even sweeter. 'You've got a big problem, Dr Delacroix.'

'Me personally? And call me Felice. Dr Delacroix makes me feel like I'm ancient.'

'Only if you call me Chris.' He smiled, but she could see that something was really worrying him. 'I know how ridiculous this sounds, but you're all in terrible danger.'

Felice sat on the bed and crossed her legs, appreciating Chris's bashful look as she did so. 'Chris, the entire solar system is in terrible danger – you should know that. The creatures who destroyed your ship have invaded Earth, bombarded this planet – not to mention Callisto, Tethys and Nereid – with proton bombs, and blockaded the entire system, both physically and across subspace. What could be worse than that?' Felice deliberately neglected to add the rationale behind the invaders' actions; Callisto, Tethys, Nereid and Charon were the four moons – of Jupiter, Saturn, Uranus and Pluto respectively – dedicated to weapons research, if you could consider stunnels as weapons. The invaders had definitely known what they were doing.

'Surface bombardment's one thing, Felice, but I'm talking about something much worse. The Da–, the invaders have weapons of mass destruction which make proton bombs look like light artillery. They just haven't used them yet.'

Felice was confused. Who the hell was this Chris Cwej, a man claiming to know more about the invaders than Solar Security had discovered in the last eight months? 'Such as?'

Chris crinkled his nose as if weighing up whether to tell her or not.

'For God's sake, man, I thought it was a matter of life or death?' she urged.

He sighed. 'Okay. Deep penetration ion cannons. Antimatter drills. Pulsed photon impellers. Is that enough mass destruction for you?' His voice rose. 'The invasion of Earth is only the beginning, Felice. Those bastards don't stop until the entire solar system is defeated . . .' He trailed off, shaking his head. 'They're on their way. You – we've only got a few hours at most.'

Felice leant forward and grabbed his hand. 'Please, go on.' There wasn't really any harm in hearing him out. And it kept her away from Rachel for a while.

Chris hesitated. In the last few seconds, he had succeeded in breaking one of the few rules that the Doctor had specifically laid down after he and Roz had joined the TARDIS crew: *never, never try to alter your own history*. With its unspoken corollary, of course: *leave that to me*. Charon, the oversized moon of Pluto, would become a charred lump of oxidized metals within the next twelve hours, and there was absolutely nothing that he could do to stop it. And, even if there were, did he have the right to do so?

Then again, from his brief look at the base, it didn't seem capable of defending itself anyway; even if they could have outrun the real-space blockade, they didn't have a single spaceship. The initial bombardment had seen to that. Then again, given the nature of their research on Charon . . .

It was time to break the rules.

'Look, I know that you've got no reason to trust me –'

Felice chuckled. 'You can say that again. Rachel was all for carrying out a summary execution when you came out of the stunnel.'

Chris had to admit that he was on very shaky ground where his credentials were concerned. Still, it was worth a try.

'I'm an Adjudicator, Felice. Adjudication Intelligence.' At least he could be certain that Adjudication Intelligence had been around in the twenty-second century; his ancestor, Nate Cwej, was proof of that.

She frowned. 'Can you prove that?'

Of course I can, Felice, he thought. Just send a message to

Oberon. Just ask for Nathaniel Cwej and ask him about his great-to-the-nth grandson. And wait for the Daleks to intercept the signal. Reason quickly took hold. 'No ID – just in case I was captured. AI's got reason to believe that the invaders are going to strike within the next twelve hours – another bombardment, this time with photon impellers. I was en route from Oberon to here when my ship was attacked.' In Chris's time, Oberon – a moon of Uranus – was second only to Ponten IV as a shining example of the Guild, but its origins were as an underground base during the blockade. 'I came here to warn you!' That's it, Chris; just shatter the laws of cause and effect to save your own neck.

'And we just happened to be around with our stunnel safety net,' said Felice, one eyebrow arched in suspicion. 'Can't you see how improbable this all sounds?'

'I know, I know,' he shrugged. Then it occurred to him. 'Have you got a deep-scan tachyon telescope on the base?' he asked, hoping desperately that the damned things had been invented by now. Optical or radio telescopes would only tell them when the Daleks were right on top of them, given that their battle saucers travelled only a fraction slower than light.

'Of course we have. But we don't use it much now – there isn't a great deal to look at any more, and the energy it requires is needed for the stunnel experiments.'

A hope, thought Chris. A faint hope that he might be able to convince the doomed colonists of their fate, his credentials, and the need to get off Charon as soon as possible. 'Then train it in the direction of Venus. That's where the invaders are going to attack from.'

Felice rose from the bed and shook her head. 'I'm not sure –'

'They could already be on their way!' he yelled. Chris could remember the date of the attack, but not the time. Chances were, the Dalek ships had already left their orbital station around Venus; they might even be swooping down as they spoke. 'Please, Felice,' he begged. 'We don't have much time.'

She sighed. 'We haven't had much time since the blockade

started, Chris.' Then she ran her fingers through her blonde bob. 'What have we got to lose?' She got to her feet. 'I'll go and butter up Rachel.'

She reached the door and then turned back. 'I really hope you're telling the truth, Chris. I'd hate to find out you're lying.' And then she left, locking the door behind her.

Chris sat back in his chair and sighed. Proving that the Daleks were on their way was one thing; getting off Charon was another matter entirely.

'It's going to get bloody cold,' stated McGuire. Not that he really needed to remind them; the wreckage of the shuttle had been guttering for the last twenty minutes, its heat output dropping rapidly. He just felt like exerting his leadership. Two hours ago, he'd been the leader of a survey expedition to the North Pole; now he was in second place to this Doctor, this stranger who had taken over the entire thing. Then again, McGuire had to admit that he was slightly relieved; the whole operation had gone belly-up, and the Doctor did seem to know what he was talking about.

'Indeed, Mr McGuire. Bitterly cold. If we remain on the surface, you will all die of hypothermia within a couple of hours.' McGuire didn't miss the fact that the Doctor didn't include himself in the death sentence.

Then he noticed the Doctor nodding towards his friend, the hard-faced black woman, Roslyn Forrester. She wasn't wearing a uniform, but there was definitely a military bearing to her.

'Another hundred years and this would have been a balmy summer's night, Roz,' said the Doctor.

Ignoring the comment, McGuire suddenly realized the meaning of the Doctor's first statement.

'Are you suggesting that we go underground?'

'Most perspicacious of you, Mr McGuire.' The Doctor thumped his umbrella – what the hell was he doing with an umbrella on Mars? – on the ground, causing a small puff of dust that sparkled crimson in the dying light of the fire. 'Unless I am very much mistaken – and the chances of that are quite remote – we are about sixteen kilometres from a fairly sizeable Martian settlement.'

McGuire frowned; how did the Doctor know that? 'But the Greenies –'

'Indigenous Martians or Ice Warriors, Mr McGuire. "Greenies" is a little . . . crude.' The Doctor stepped forward and reached into his pocket and pulled out a crumpled and yellowing piece of paper which he proceeded to unfold. 'This is a map of the major Martian cities in this region of Mars. If we start at Ikk-ett-Saleth, and head towards Sstee-ett-Haspar –' He looked up. 'In plain English, that's from the City of the Sad Ones to the Labyrinth of False Pride; the Labyrinth then leads directly to Vastitas Borealis. Aka the North Pole, aka –' He peered at the map. 'G'chun duss Ssethiissi – the Cauldron of Sutekh. Now there's a frightening thought.'

'Why are we carrying on?' interrupted Santacosta. 'We're stranded, without food or any way of staying warm . . .' Her bottom lip started to tremble. 'Why can't we go back to Jacksonville?' she asked tearfully.

'Because Jacksonville is over ten thousand klicks away!' snapped Madrigal. 'The North Pole is only a couple of hundred klicks.'

This did nothing to reassure Carmen, who continued to cry. 'But two hundred kilometres –'

The shuttle chose that moment to finally go out, plunging them into the cold amber twilight of the Doctor's matches. The Doctor bounced to his feet. 'In the absence of any other ideas, underground it is.' He looked back at the map, before pointing into the distance with his umbrella. 'There should be a concealed entrance shaft to the city walls about five kilometres in that direction.'

McGuire gestured towards the written-off ATET. 'Madrigal, Vince, Roz; grab as much as you can easily carry from the buggy. And remember, there are six of us now.'

As the three headed towards the ATET, McGuire looked around at his expedition, so very different from the one which had set off from Jacksonville a week ago. Kolchak, who had part-funded the expedition, was dead, and the replacements appeared to be a night-club singer, a middle-aged woman with the same attitude as Madrigal, and a mystery man who not only seemed intent upon taking over the entire mission, but who seemed to know far too much about the Greenies. McGuire sighed; all they needed now were for the Greenies to show up in person, and everything would be just perfect.

'Perfect,' breathed Cleece. With a final glance at the vermin encampment, he set off for the cave in which his fellow pilgrims had chosen to rest. As he walked across the dusty scree, he considered what he had overheard. The mammals were also heading towards the Cauldron of Ssethiis; surely even Abbot Aklaar would have to agree that they should die?

He sighed, and adjusted his visor to penetrate the darkness that lay beyond the encampment. As the infra-red sensors cut in, the vague shapes that surrounded him resolved into flattened boulders and rivened ground, an endless vista of lifeless red. Cleece vaguely remembered an areography lesson years ago: Scholastor Heelek and his endless maps of the Martian surface, comparing the rolling plains of Jull-etteskul – the Garden of Oras – with the dried-up sea-bed of Ssken-dass-giis – the Dead Ocean of the Forsaken – through which Cleece and the others currently found themselves trudging. Dead . . . and depressing, he decided.

A cliff face suddenly loomed out of the darkness, a twenty-metre high wall of unbroken beige rock. Cleece felt a disturbing combination of relief and dread. Relief, because the honeycombed interior of the cliff offered food, comfort and company. Dread, because it brought him back to the lifestyle that he had come to hate: six months of endless marching across the plains and deserts and desiccated remnants of a planet that old Heelek claimed had once been verdant and rich, accompanied by constant prayers to Oras for good fortune and safety from predators . . .

He sighed, stopped, and instructed his visor to surrender to the darkness. As the boulders, scree and cliff face melted back into the blackness, he inclined his head and looked towards the stars that filled the clear night sky. The ancient myths told many tales about the stars; Ssethiis and Oras had brought their fraternal war to Mars from the stars, providing a basis for Martian culture into the bargain. And the archaeologists believed that the Great Death – the curse which had withered the vegetation and wiped out the strange and alien people who had once populated the planet – had also come from the stars, laying waste Mars before heading towards Earth. Cleece snorted: if only the Great Death had been as effective there! He grudgingly realized that he owed the mammals a debt of gratitude: at least their arrival offered a diversion from the constant sermons of Abbot Aklaar.

The stars were out of reach, as far as Cleece was concerned; he had only been a clutchling during the holy war against the Terran infidels, but he could remember the lights in the sky, the caved-in tunnels, the dead and the dying and the young whose nests had been destroyed and would become Unclean unless they were adopted. Huddled under the thick hide blankets, he had dreamed of being up there with his brother, of piloting a fighter, attacking the vermin . . . Instead, he had been adopted by a pacifist caste after his parents had been murdered. And now, decades later, he was on a pilgrimage to the Cauldron of Ssethiis, preaching a message of peace and understanding that he wasn't sure he believed in any more. If he ever had.

Up there, a new war was in progress; another race from the stars had crushed the mammals on their own homeworld, just as the mammals had done to Cleece's people. A glorious battle was happening and he longed to be part of it.

But Cleece was stuck on Mars, while the rest of his race were either dead, in hiding, or starting again on Nova Martia, beyond far Arcturus. Turning his visor back on, he left his dreams behind and walked the last few metres towards the cliff face.

Tapping the signal device that had been stitched into the hide belt around his carapace, he waited as the Chameleon field melted away like mist. The solid rock coalesced into a pattern of flickering lights before vanishing completely, and Cleece walked into the tunnel, leaving his dreams behind him.

Dreams of glory.

* * *

'Crap!' hissed Rachel. 'He told you that the invaders were coming back and you believed him? Obviously your doctorate included an advanced course in gullibility.'

Felice sighed. Rachel's reaction was hardly unexpected. 'What harm can it do?'

'It diverts us from getting a bloody stunnel, that's what. Then again, if Earth had sent me a proper scientist like Gregory Ketch, rather than a girl who doesn't know a Higgs's generator from a quantum resonator –'

Felice snorted. 'That's low, Rachel, really low.' She nodded towards the work-station on the far side of the room, a low table covered with readouts and monitors. 'I've checked; the 'scope isn't even being used at the moment. It hasn't been used for the last three months.'

Rachel leapt from her chair and made a growling noise. 'Do you realize how much power the 'scope needs? Why the hell do you think we haven't been using the damned thing?' She stormed over to the 'scope station and thumped it. 'For every hour that we use the 'scope, we lose ten minutes of stunnel access.'

Got her, thought Felice. 'But you aren't planning to try another stunnel attempt!'

'Not till tomorrow, no.' She groaned. 'Oh, go on. Use the bloody thing. See if I care.' She reached into the pocket of her white jump-suit and retrieved a small cube: the trisilicate key for the 'scope station. 'Let's see if lover-boy is telling the truth, or just trying to save his skin.' She inserted the key into a depression in the station, and beckoned Felice over as the readouts and monitors lit up.

'Aim it towards Venus; that's where Chris reckoned that the invaders would set off from.'

'Oh, Chris is it now?' She could have curdled milk with *that* look. 'Okay, okay, Venus it is.' She tapped away at the keyboard for a few seconds. 'Co-ordinates locked, bringing up visuals . . .' A large viewscreen faded into life on the nearby wall, patiently waiting for the tachyon beam to return from its exploration of Earth's neighbouring world.

'I know that you're going to find this hard to believe, Rachel, but I really hope that Chris is lying.' Felice thought back to the initial bombardment; the jet-black saucers had swooped down out of the sky, clearly visible through the transparent geodesic domes. She had been one of the fortunate ones, working below the surface in the stunnel lab when the ships shattered the domes.

Most of those who survived the sudden vacuum – the paranoid people who kept environment suits handy, in the once-thought-pointless fear that the domes would rupture – failed to survive the directed energy weapons that followed the bombs and turned the carefully thought-out cities and elegant buildings from architecture into so much radioactive dust, sparkling in the feeble reflected light of cold Pluto.

Here, a thousand metres below the frozen crust of Charon, the fifty-four survivors soon imagined themselves safe from the horrors that were being inflicted upon the solar system, a bastion of freedom with their subspace researches and supposed invulnerability. But if Chris's horror stories were true, the invaders were returning with weapons that could penetrate the surface and finish off what they had started.

'Oh, shit.' Felice looked round at Rachel's whispered expletive, and felt her stomach drop through the floor as she took in the grainy images on the screen.

Three of the terrifyingly familiar saucers were just passing the orbit of Jupiter at near lightspeed. On a direct course for Charon, according to the overlaid telemetry.

'All techs to the stunnel room,' barked Rachel into the comm unit. And then she turned to Felice. 'Your boyfriend was right, Felice; those bastards are on their way. Let's just hope that we can create a decent, two-ended stunnel before they arrive.' She set off for the stunnel room. And then paused in the open doorway. 'Because, if we can't, we're on a direct road to hell.'

Felice followed; her pleasure at Chris's honesty being proved was well and truly soured by the knowledge that the invaders were on a return visit.

In a little over two hours, the invaders would start bombarding Charon. And this time, there wouldn't be any survivors. How prophetic that in Greek mythology Charon was the ferryman to the Underworld.

Taal-Iis Esstar looked up from her meditations as the sound of heavy footsteps came from the hidden cave entrance. Cleece was back from his spying mission, brimming over with talk of killing and death, no doubt. She turned her attention to the Abbot. Aklaar was deep in prayer, sitting cross-legged on the uneven floor next to the portable lightbox, and Esstar wondered why such a Martian – a Martian who had devoted his two centuries of life to peace and the disciplines of Oras – had chosen a bully and a thug like Cleece for their pilgrimage to G'chun duss Ssethiissi. But she knew why: Aklaar wanted her to accompany him, and her betrothal meant that Cleece would have to come along as well.

Instinctively, she glanced at the other pilgrim in the cave: Sstaal G'Hur-Tiis. Even for a member of the pacifist caste, Sstaal was lightly built, his green-ridged carapace and helmet at odds with his slender frame. Within the high walls of the buried seminary, Esstar and her brothers and sisters dispensed with the protective armour that characterized her race: it symbolized an aspect of the Martian psyche that the Holy Order of Oras despised. But their pilgrimage would have been foolhardy without some sort of defence against the hostile terrain that they would encounter on their long journey, so the ancient armour-incubator vats had been fired up for the first time in millennia. The thick green shells, augmented with cybernetics, had taken a week to grow, and she and Sstaal had been decidedly uneasy when they had been fitted onto their bodies. Not so Cleece, who appeared to thoroughly enjoy wearing the heavy carapace and helmet. Esstar and Sstaal had felt slightly more comfortable once the Abbot had reminded them of the perils that they would face on their pilgrimage: the rock snakes and the spider-lizards – not to mention the venom-moss – that inhabited the wastelands of Mars would have proved fatal to an unprotected Martian.

She wasn't surprised to see that Sstaal was indulging in his favourite pastime: reading. Sstaal was a Martian who had wholly embraced the teachings of Oras upon which their order was built; he was a nervous but pious young Martian who embodied the spirit of Oras to a degree that was extraordinary, even in the cloisters of the seminary. She thought back to their early days at Jull-ett-eskul during their long childhood; she and Sstaal would spend hours in the stone labyrinth of the library, reading, discussing, arguing the finer points of philosophy, while Cleece would play juvenile and distasteful war games in the walled grounds. Usually on his own, a pariah amongst his adopted brethren who found his attitude odd at best, and repulsive at worst.

If only the complex interrelationships of the pilgrim caste had allowed her friendship with Sstaal to develop in the way that they both desperately wanted, she thought bitterly. But no; the Abbots in the seminary had decided that the combination of her bloodline – a descendant of Priest-Queen Lataar – and that of Cleece – an adopted warrior who could trace his lineage back to the time of Tuburr – would be an important asset to their holy cause, so they had been betrothed. Esstar felt a spasm of nausea at the knowledge of her entrapment which intensified as *he* walked into the cavern: Cleece Ett'Shturr. Her mate.

She looked him up and down and felt a dichotomy of emotions overlaying the nausea. True, Cleece was a magnificent specimen of the Martian male: over two metres tall, with the heavy build which characterized his true birthright as a member of one of the warrior nests. For a brief moment, she imagined him in the full battle armour of an Exalted Warrior; pictures danced in her mind, pictures of Cleece marching against the humans, or fighting during one of the Primal Wars when legends had been forged and myths had been made.

She found herself suddenly repulsed, both by Cleece's latent militarism, and her own sensual fantasies over it. 'How did the spying go, Cleece?' she asked without affection.

He smiled. Without warmth. And ignored her. 'My suspicions were correct, Abbot Aklaar. The mammals are heading towards G'chun duss Ssethiissi.' He let out a venomous hiss.

Aklaar interlocked his clamps in a gesture of prayer. 'The writings of Oras teach us many things, Pilgrim Cleece. In this situation I would refer you to the Book of Oras; in particular, the Sermon of Liis –'

'"The Universe is wide enough to encompass all its children",' Sstaal interrupted. 'The humans have every right to travel where they will, Cleece.'

'They have no right, Sstaal – Mars is our world!' Cleece smashed his clamps together. 'Another few months, and the Eight-Point Table would –'

'Silence!' barked Aklaar. Esstar was taken aback; in all the years that she had known the Abbot, she had never heard him raise his voice. Cleece had, as usual, touched a nerve. 'The Eight-Point Table led our people into a war that they could not possibly have won, Pilgrim Cleece. They were barbarians and butchers, followers of Ssethiis and Claatris . . .' He trailed off, as if exhausted by the exertion. 'Never speak of the Eight-Point Table again, Cleece. Never.'

Suitably chagrined, Cleece cast his gaze to the ground. 'The verm–, the humans are leaving their encampment and heading towards the surface shaft to Ikk-ett-Saleth. They are planning to defile our cities, Abbot!' Esstar sighed; once Cleece started arguing, he never gave up. He was like a spider-lizard toying with a rock-snake. Relentless.

Aklaar rose from his meditative crouch. He was small, wizened, even; thanks to the complicated genetic structure of the Martians, Abbots of the religious caste were physically similar to the Lords of the Warrior caste; Esstar could remember hearing about an Abbot who had masqueraded as a Lord in order to convert an entire nest to the faith of Oras; he had actually succeeded. Aklaar's armour was thinner and smoother than the others – but just as protective – in reverence to his position, and his green helmet was a smooth grey-green dome.

'Our cities were defiled a century ago, Pilgrim Cleece. By Martians, fighting a pointless war that tore the soul from our race and left us all steeped in the blood of thousands. The humans cannot do any worse than we did ourselves.' He smoothed down his cloak. 'But I do find myself in agreement with you. The humans must not be permitted to wander through the graves of our ancestors without a care. There are ghosts in Ikk-ett-Saleth; ghosts that should not be awakened.' He gestured towards the lighting unit and their supplies. 'Pack everything up. We leave for Ikk-ett-Saleth in half an hour.'

But Esstar was close enough to Cleece to hear his whispered retort. 'Even Oras forgives the killers of heretics.'

How long could she continue, feeling as she did? How long could she stay trapped in this abomination of a betrothal? As she started to pack her meagre belongings, she glanced over at Sstaal, and felt the warmth of his attention as he smiled at her with feelings which honour and culture insisted she should feel for Cleece.

Chapter 3

'It doesn't look like an entrance,' said Carmen miserably. Roz had to agree; the collection of boulders looked like, well, a collection of boulders, a metre high and two metre wide pile of reddy-grey rubble. Although night had fallen on Mars, they were all carrying powerful torches, except for the Doctor who was relying on a bundle of everlasting matches which also provided a small amount of extremely welcome warmth. Martian night was well below zero, and even the jacket and gloves were insufficient protection against the cold.

The light from the torches illuminated an area of about thirty metres in all directions, revealing the cracked and desiccated evidence that Tharsis Plain had once been a wide and deep ocean. Millions of years ago, Roz remembered, Mars had been as habitable as the Earth, but then some global catastrophe had wiped out virtually all life on the planet. It was a miracle that the Ice Warriors had managed to survive.

Millions of years, only to be bested by Man. It was sad, it was ironic, but it was yet another law of the universe: survival of the fittest. It was a law that Roz wasn't sure she felt comfortable with any more.

'Are you sure this is the entrance?' asked McGuire. 'Perhaps your map is a bit out of date.'

'Looks can be deceptive,' protested the Doctor, folding his map away. 'The Ice – the Martians prided themselves on their secrecy.' He nodded at the boulders. 'I believe this is called a Chameleon field.'

Esteban trotted over to him, and Roz felt another wave of

irritation; like the others – including Carmen Santacosta, for the Goddess's sake! – he was wearing gravity boots, allowing him to enjoy the benefits of a full Earth gravity on Mars. The Doctor, of course, had no need of technological support. Roz had considered suggesting that she 'borrow' Piotr Kolchak's boots, but, deciding that such a suggestion would have been in rather poor taste, she had endured the eight-kilometre bounce from the crash site to where the Doctor's crusty old map claimed the entrance to the Martian city lay.

'A Chameleon field?' Esteban asked. 'Of course, the Martians used them to pack out their fleets. An advanced form of solid holography,' he stated for the benefit of the others. Roz had learnt that Esteban was actually quite a Martian enthusiast; what a shame that he wouldn't get the chance to meet Benny – they would have got along tremendously.

'Indeed they did.' The Doctor clapped his hands together, cleverly managing to avoid burning himself with the matches as he did so. 'A very, very deceitful device that mankind will inevitably invent and undoubtedly find a deadly use for, Professor Esteban.'

Esteban pulled his tablette from within his jacket and pointed it at the nearest boulder. 'I find it difficult to believe that this is nothing more than a clever simularity.' He knelt down and felt the rough surface. 'The tablette registers it as solid rock, even down to the traces of trisilicate and iron.'

For a second, Roz was confused; in the thirtieth century, solid holograms were an everyday occurrence. She brought up her history lessons, and remembered that solid holography had been invented in 1998 and suppressed soon after; the furthest mankind had reached by 2157 was the simularity, a primitive holographic system. Not for the first time, Roz was amazed that mankind had ever reached the thirtieth century. Survival of the fittest indeed.

'I'm freezing,' muttered Carmen Santacosta, hugging her metallic blue survival jacket. 'Can't we go underground?'

The Doctor cocked an eyebrow. 'Carmen is right; it is time that we made our way to the City of the Sad Ones.' Roz agreed; all of them were wearing some sort of thermal jacket – Carmen and the buggy people were wearing standard issue insulated numbers, while she was in the atmospheric density jacket that the Doctor had flung at them as the TARDIS broke up – but neither type of jacket was designed for long-term use. Unless they found somewhere with a temperature that didn't have a minus sign in front of it, they would soon become very well acquainted with cryogenics.

'How do we get in?' asked McGuire. 'Presuming that this is an entrance and not a scientific curiosity,' he added pointedly.

'Chameleon fields are, as Professor Esteban pointed out, nothing but clever-dick holograms,' replied the Doctor. 'And they can be switched off.' He reached into the pocket of his silver jacket and pulled out his sonic screwdriver, a twenty-centimetre silver cylinder. 'It's times like this when I'm really glad of my sonic screwdriver,' he said cheerfully. 'I'm just thankful I sued the Terileptils for criminal damage.' He aimed it at the cluster of rocks and pressed a contact with his thumb.

After a few seconds of high-pitched buzzing from the screwdriver, the boulders faded from sand-blasted rock to glitter, and then, finally, to nothing. In their place, a five-metre-wide hole had appeared, with roughly hewn steps leading into the darkness below.

'The City of the Sad Ones awaits, ladies and gentlemen,' the Doctor announced, waving a theatrical arm towards the hole. The others filed past him, showing various degrees of nervousness. Once they had started to descend, the Doctor turned to Roz. 'Before we follow, I have a present for you, Adjudicator.' He reached into his jacket once more and pulled out a filigree bracelet that appeared to have been woven from hundreds of silver-red strands.

'Jewellery?' she questioned. 'Not really my style.' What was the Doctor playing at?

'A gravimetric adjustment device, Roz, courtesy of the Nimons.' He slipped it over the sleeve of her atmosphere jacket, and she immediately felt herself become three times as heavy. A trifle disconcerting, but a relief when all was said and done. He grinned as she tried to force her face muscles to adjust her mouth from what felt like a desperately sour look into some semblance of normality. 'Why didn't you give me this earlier?' she mumbled through spastic lips.

'A little suffering is good for the soul,' he said cheerfully, then nodded towards the abyss. 'Into the underworld, then? Charon awaits.'

Chris walked into the stunnel room to discover a frantic and frenetic hive of activity, threaded with an atmosphere that was a tangible mixture of terror and panic. About twenty technicians were running around from station to station with all manner of equipment in their hands, while at the centre of the chaos Felice and Rachel were focusing their attention on the main control console. In front of them, the tunnel beyond the oval throbbed and pulsed up and down the visible spectrum in peristaltic waves of jarring light.

Not sure of the best way to attract attention, Chris fell back on the tried and trusted method. 'How's it going?' he called across the room. When the guard had opened the cell door and told him that he was wanted in the stunnel room, Chris guessed that Felice had persuaded Rachel to check out his prophecy of doom. Under other circumstances, he would have been rather pleased with himself; but the knowledge that a fleet of Dalek saucers was heading his way had a decidedly sobering effect. He realized that Felice was beckoning him over.

'They're coming, aren't they?' he asked rhetorically, dodging technicians as he walked over to the central work-station.

'Too right, Nostradamus,' snapped Rachel over her shoulder. 'Telemetry reckons that we've got about an hour and a half before the bastards are breathing down our necks. Know anything about subspace engineering, Mr Adjudicator?'

Chris shook his head; although he had built toy warp engines for the spaceships he had modelled as a boy, subspace drives had been superseded by hyperdrives centuries before he had been born. 'Sorry –'

'Never mind,' said Rachel dismissively. And then she looked down at one of the monitors and tutted. Little red LEDs were flickering. 'Bugger! Higgs's Generator four is fluctuating outside safe parameters, Mr Khan!' she yelled across the room. A young Asian jerked his head in surprise, nodded, and began adjusting the controls on his station. Rachel growled. 'One and a half hours to generate a stable stunnel! We haven't managed to achieve it in six bloody months, but we've got to sort it all out in the next couple of hours or else we burn in our boots.' She thumped the work-station and elicited an aggrieved bleep. 'Oh, sod it. I came here to further the cause of science, not to perform miracles.'

'Are you okay?' Despite Rachel's generally unpleasant demeanour, Chris couldn't help but feel sorry for the woman. Unless she could perform a scientific miracle, they would all die.

Like they were supposed to, a nasty little voice murmured in his mind. By warning the Charon survivors of their imminent demise, Chris was altering history – assuming they succeeded, of course, and the way things seemed to be going, that was far from a certainty. But if they did manage to generate a stunnel, over fifty human beings would live who should have died eight hundred years before Chris's version of reality. Who knew what effect that would have on the web of time? Chris paused; where had he heard that term before? Then he remembered, and stray thoughts collided and coalesced and gave birth to an even more horrifying idea.

The TARDIS had been destroyed when it was caught between a subspace infarction and a Vortex rupture, according to the Doctor's hurried explanations as the time vessel started to break up. The infarction, well, Felice and Rachel's stunnel experiments – and Chris's presence on Charon, come to that – probably explained that. But a rupture in the Time Vortex . . .

Chris was a learner: he listened, he read, he watched, and he took it all in. He had spent months in the strangely organized TARDIS library, learning about subjects that he had not even heard of. And that included a knowledge of the bizarre dimension through which the TARDIS travelled: the Time Vortex. From what he had gathered from his months in the TARDIS, if the Doctor's precious web of time were damaged, the feedback could cause anomalies in the Vortex; the greater the damage, the worse the anomaly. What if the survival of the fifty or so Charonites changed history? What if Rachel, or Felice, or any one of the others survived, only to totally change Chris's past? A seemingly innocent technician, forced to lend his talents to the Daleks' war effort, could ensure that their aborted attempt to mine Earth's magnetic core succeeded and guarantee their sovereignty over the planet. Or five hundred years in the future, the descendant of one of the colonists could become a worse tyrant than Hitler, Green and Williams all rolled into one. Was the survival of Chris and the others worth the risk to history? His theorizing was interrupted by an excited shout.

'The Thornley-Ramsay Ramping Law!' yelled Rachel. She typed furiously, and nodded as the monitor displayed a complex wave formation. 'It's perfect! Why the hell didn't I think of that before?'

'The effect of adrenalin on the brain, perhaps?' hissed Felice.

Chris frowned; despite his basic attraction to Felice – and Rachel's general belligerence – he found himself on the chief scientist's side this time. 'Hey,' he intervened. 'We're all working together here, Felice. What's the Thorn-Rampling Law, then?' Time was short, and there definitely wasn't enough of it to spare on personal rivalries.

Felice glared, and Chris tried very hard to fight off his embarrassment.

'The Thornley-Ramsay Law concerns the penetration of subspace,' she stated coldly. 'It's never been applied, because we've never needed to use it. It applies to situations when the subspace boundaries are non-aligned.' She nodded towards one of the monitor displays, which showed an oscillating web of purple lines.

'What is that supposed to be, then?' he asked.

'The matrix which lies beneath subspace,' Felice explained. 'The invaders' jamming field works by shifting the boundaries of that matrix slightly out of phase, making it impossible to shift between the real universe and subspace. Explanation enough, or should I repeat it in words of less than one syllable?'

His ears just short of ignition point, Chris nodded. 'Sort of. Will this law help?'

Rachel answered as Felice picked up her tablette and started keying in data. 'We've been looking at this the wrong way, Mr Cwej. We've been trying to counter the invaders' field with brute force. They've flooded subspace with strange icarons, and we've been trying to punch through the interference – force our way through the non-aligned boundaries – by ramping up the strength of the stunnel carrier wave.' She looked over towards a ruddy-faced man and beckoned him over. 'Oi, Whiteley, get your arse over here.' And then she busied herself at the keyboard.

Felice continued the explanation, pulling Chris over to one side as she did so, mainly to prevent him from being run over by a technician with a trolley. 'With the subspace boundaries out of phase, we can recalibrate the stunnel transjector and go underneath the jamming field. And the data that we got when you entered our earlier stunnel attempt will tell us exactly what energy levels to use. At least, that's the plan.' She grabbed his hand. 'I'm sorry about that, Chris. Rachel and I, well, we don't really get on.'

'I'd gathered. But we haven't got much time.' Another twinge as Felice's words sank in; his arrival on this base might be the direct cause of their escape. What the hell was he going to tell the Doctor if he ever saw him again?

She sighed. 'I know. And I know that you know a hell of a lot more about what's going on than you're telling me.' She gave him a pleading look.

What was he supposed to say? 'Felice –'

She held up her hands in mock surrender. 'Okay, okay; you're an Adjudicator. Loose talk costs lives and all that.' Chris felt like throwing up; deceit wasn't his strong suit. But the truth – that he was a stranded time traveller from the thirtieth century – wasn't really the best way to gain the scientists' trust, was it?

'Felice?' It was Rachel, head down, reading a monitor. 'Can you work on the transjector arrays with Appleby? If we're going to use Thornley-Ramsay, we need to carry out quite a bit of recalibration.'

Felice shot Chris a smile, and he felt a quiver that he really didn't want to feel: he liked her, but their lives were on the line. 'Time to go to work, Chris. Make yourself useful and get me some coffee.' She nodded towards the door. 'There's a replimat just down the corridor. White, no sugar, please.'

Chris walked off with a mixture of emotions; he managed to identify them as lust, guilt and impatience. But not necessarily in that order. As he reached the door, he turned round, but Felice was deep in conversation with a thin, nervous man with a beard.

He felt jealous.

Roz suppressed a yawn as she continued trudging down the seemingly endless carved steps. Although the temperature had risen noticeably as they descended further below the surface, Roz was well aware that she was in danger of falling prey to another problem – exhaustion. Still, at least they weren't going to freeze to death.

But she also had other concerns. The Doctor's blithe decision to travel to the North Pole using the Ice Warriors' own cities and tunnels might have seemed a sound idea, but what if those cities and tunnels weren't as abandoned as the Doctor thought? According to Benny, there had never been any absolute proof that all of the Martians had left for Nova Martia; for over a century after their exodus, there had been stories and tales that suggested that Man was still sharing the planet with his old foe. What if this Ikk-ett-Saleth was actually inhabited; would the Ice Warriors take kindly to a group of humans simply walking in as if they owned the place? The Ice Warriors hardly owed mankind any favours, did they?

Any further speculation was cut short by a sharp increase in illumination from just below her. From what she could see, the stairwell had, thankfully, come to an end. Even with the comfort provided by the gravity bracelet, it had still been an uncomfortable slog.

'Where are we now? The city?' asked McGuire, peering over the Doctor's shoulder.

'Not quite, no; the staircase was basically a service

shaft, Mr McGuire; this is the corridor proper.' The Doctor stepped forward, beckoning them all to follow. As he did so, he blew out the everlasting matches. Walking out from the base of the stairwell, they found themselves in a wide corridor, hexagonal in cross-section. Each side was about ten metres in length, and each side was made from an almost translucent amber rock, polished to almost mirror smoothness apart from the decoration on the two upper walls.

'It's beautiful,' hissed Santacosta. 'I didn't realize that the Greenies lived like this.'

'The Ice Warriors pride beauty and aesthetics above everything – apart from war, of course,' said the Doctor. 'This is one of what was an extensive network of tunnels which run under the surface. Of course, the Thousand Day War destroyed most of them.'

'And a good thing too,' muttered McGuire.

'Mr McGuire,' stated the Doctor coldly. 'The Ice Warriors may be many things, but might I remind you that we are reliant on their hospitality to survive this current ordeal. Your prejudices are not welcome.'

McGuire fell silent, but his face displayed his anger. It was clear to Roz that the man had some unfinished business with the Ice Warriors, something which was fuelling his hatred. She decided that it might prove wise to keep a close eye on Antony McGuire.

'Ikk-ett-Saleth is a couple of kilometres in that direction,' said the Doctor, nodding towards the left. 'We should reach it in just over an hour.'

'Why so long?' asked Madrigal.

The Doctor pursed his lips. 'Because the Ice Warriors do not take kindly to unexpected guests,' he said mysteriously. 'Keep together – and do not touch anything,' he warned.

As they set off, Roz looked around at the corridor, agreeing with Santacosta's earlier comment. It really was quite breathtakingly beautiful, and the fact that it was only one of thousands of similar corridors, a network that circumnavigated the whole of Mars, was a humbling thought.

The lower three sides of the hexagonal tunnel were smooth

55

and featureless, but the other three were anything but. Illumination was courtesy of the thick cables of brilliant yellow that threaded above them on the ceiling, complex interwoven patterns that covered the high surface and stretched the entire length of the corridor. Roz guessed that it was some sort of bio-engineered fungus; she had seen something similar – but far less ornate – on the planet Igrillius 6. Such a light-source had the advantage of being both low-maintenance and long-lasting, ideal for a tunnel such as this one which would presumably have been busy when the Martian civilization had been at its height.

Then there were the walls. As they proceeded down the tunnel to whatever reception awaited them in Ikk-ett-Saleth, Roz realized that the patterns that she had initially thought were merely decoration were in fact carvings; an endless line of engraved Martians, no two the same. Some wore the standard reptilian body armour that marked them as Warriors; others the smoother, more dignified costumes of Lords, and the odd one or two were in an ornate version of the Ice Lord armour. Roz guessed that they must be the Grand Marshals, the rulers of Mars when they had been a warrior race. The poses in which they were depicted were formal and stiff, and Roz racked her brain to work out why they looked so familiar. In her time, the new Martian homeworld – the inventively named Nova Martia – was still off limits to everyone; the Martians of the thirtieth century valued their privacy above everything, especially war. So what did this frieze of carvings remind her of?

After minutes of irritating blankness, it finally occurred to her. The unrealistic poses, the angular symbols carved underneath each Martian – they were the Martian equivalent of Egyptian hieroglyphics. Each figure or collection of figures probably told some complicated and detailed epic that Roz would never understand, stories of an ancient culture that had fascinated so many archaeologists. Thinking of archaeologists, she really wished that she had some sort of recording device handy; Benny would have killed to see what Roz was seeing.

She stopped her examination of the carvings at the sound

of raised voices. The Doctor and McGuire were arguing, and she walked faster to catch up with them.

'If there are still Martians in Ikk-ett-Saleth – and I very much doubt that there are – we are not going in with all guns blazing, Mr McGuire.'

'They'll shoot us as soon as look at us, Doctor – don't you understand that?'

The Doctor closed his eyes and sighed. 'I do understand that Earth has been invaded; surely it will not be long before the invaders turn their attention to Mars? A Mars on which the only two sentient species are still at loggerheads would prove far easier to conquer than one on which they pool their resources; do you not agree?'

McGuire turned away with a look of disgust, and Roz was sure that he had muttered 'Greenie-lover' as he did so. 'You do what you bloody well want to, Doctor.' With that, he carried on walking down the corridor.

'What was all that about?' she asked, watching as McGuire carried on alone.

'McGuire is carrying an awful lot of emotional baggage, Roz. I was trying to act as a psychological porter, but it all went a little bit wrong.' He rubbed his forehead. 'I'm not the Time Lord I thought I was.'

Before Roz could comment, a loud cry rang out – it was McGuire. Roz looked round, but the man was nowhere to be seen.

'Damn!' snapped the Doctor. 'I thought that the *Ga'jur-ett-Lii'is* would be much closer to the city.' He broke into a run.

'A *Ga'jur-ett-Lii'is*!' exclaimed Esteban. 'I must see this.' He ran off after the Doctor. With a shrug, Roz followed.

McGuire was hanging by his fingers over what might as well have been a bottomless ravine; a metre-long chasm had opened up, reaching from wall to wall.

'The Martians call it the *Ga'jur-ett-Lii'is* – the lure for the unfamiliar,' explained the Doctor, seemingly unaware of McGuire's predicament. Roz wondered whether this was some kind of twisted psychological torture on the Doctor's part, revenge for McGuire's xenophobia. A little voice inside her reminded her of her own attitudes before she had come on board the TARDIS, but she silenced it.

'Get me out!' yelled McGuire, but the Doctor carried on as if he had not heard him.

'In Ice Warrior terms, we are approaching the city boundaries. The *Ga'jur-ett-Lii'is* ensures that only those who are welcome to enter may pass. Somebody familiar with the ways of Ikk-ett-Saleth would have seen the warning signs' – he pointed at the hieroglyphics on the wall to their left – 'and known what to do.'

The Doctor reached over with his umbrella and waved it over the carvings, before finally shoving it at an Ice Warrior figure with its arms outstretched.

With a low rumble, a slab of amber stone began to slide across the gap.

'Oh dear,' said the Doctor, as the slab closed in on McGuire's fingers. 'I didn't expect that.'

With breathtaking speed, the Doctor threw himself forward and grabbed McGuire's wrist. The slab was about five centimetres away from consigning McGuire to a very long drop as the Doctor dragged him out of the chasm.

McGuire lay on the floor, looking extremely shaken. But he was still able to look up at the Doctor and smile hesitantly. 'Thank you.'

The Doctor didn't return the smile; instead, his eyes narrowed as he answered, 'Just remember, Mr McGuire; the Martians should never be underestimated.'

A simple enough statement; so why did Roz find herself translating 'underestimated' as 'trusted'?

Rachel knew that she was taking it out on everyone around her, but for once she felt it was justified. Not that the justification was retrospective enough to forgive her for the countless other displays of both general and specific bad temper, but she knew that the time for confession and absolution would be at the other end of the stunnel.

If she could create the stunnel.

If it had another end.

The faint smell of scorched fibre optics assaulted her

nose, and she looked around the chamber for the source. It was obvious from the commotion surrounding the tall, thin cylinder to the immediate left of the stunnel mouth that her underlings were quite prepared to turn it into a major crisis. And, given the importance of that particular cylinder, that was a definite possibility. Grunting, she slammed her tablette on the work-station surface and barged over to the three technicians who were doing their best impressions of wastes of space.

Ignoring their witterings, Rachel examined the tall, grey pillar. A long thin panel had been removed, exposing the delicate circuitry within. The pillar was one of the eight Higgs's generators arranged along the length of the stunnel generator, equipment which created the elementary particles whose unique properties could open the subspace meniscus and rip the fabric of the continuum apart, granting them the access to subspace that they desperately needed. Losing even one of the generators would make their current predicament a dead end. Very dead for all of them.

'The primary trunk shows signs of overloading, Professor,' mumbled a mouse of a girl called Dortmun. Rachel shook her head in disbelief. Signs of overloading? Couldn't she be more specific? Rachel tried to be understanding – her research staff was mainly culled from the survivors of the Black Fleet's attack, and most of their knowledge of subspace engineering came from Rachel and Felice's informal teach-in sessions – but Erica Dortmun had no excuse for her crass stupidity: she was here as a graduate in subspace mechanics from the University of Greater London, and her father was apparently a renowned scientist back on Earth. Assuming he was still alive, that was.

A single glance at the insides of the Higgs's generator told Rachel volumes; one of the minor relays was having trouble handling the increased throughput from the generator and was causing a feedback into the subtrunk – a side-effect of the rewiring that they had been doing to take advantage of the Thornley-Ramsay Effect. Ironically, although they were no longer trying to penetrate the blockade using brute force, they needed even more power to operate that deep in subspace. The answer was simple: the relay needed to be replaced by one of the sturdier models from the depleted stores. And soon. Another five minutes and the entire generator would be slag.

'Rachel!' She looked round, but she needn't have; Felice Delacroix was the only person on the Charon base – apart from the newly arrived Chris, of course – who ever addressed her so informally. Quickly ordering Dortmun to replace the relay, she walked over to her deputy. Felice was intelligent, but intelligence was more than a matter of a first-class degree and a doctorate from Cambridge. Given time, the girl would grow and learn, but time was the one thing that Charon didn't have. Rachel just hoped that Felice could handle the strain that they were all under.

'What's the problem?' she asked as she walked over to her deputy.

Felice smiled. 'There isn't a problem, Rachel – everything checks out at this end. Once the Higgs's generator is back on line we'll be ready to generate the stunnel.'

'How long have we got?' Chris loomed up behind Felice, smiling in that ingratiating way of his. Why the frag did he look so much like Michael, she wondered, before registering what Felice had said.

'You've installed the feedback sink?' Her earlier doubts about Felice were quickly evaporating – she was good, when all was said and done; especially since the motley crew helping her were less a help than a hindrance. 'I'm impressed. We've got –' she glanced at the image from the 'scope, and saw from the telemetry that they had less than forty minutes before the saucers were in range. Five minutes less than when she had last checked. 'Forty minutes. If Dortmun over there remembers to put her brain in, the relay will be recalibrated in about five minutes . . . Bloody hell, after the safety checks, we'll have less than twenty minutes!'

'Screw the safety checks, Rachel,' said Felice enthusiastically, 'let's just make a stunnel and to hell with it!'

Rachel threw her head back and roared with laughter. Perhaps Felice had learnt something from her after all. 'Good thinking. No, *excellent* thinking. Start the primaries – they don't need the Higgs's. And as soon as Dortmun gets her butt in gear, we'll get going. Okay?'

Both Felice and Chris grinned back at her, warmly.

And for the first time since she had heard the news of Michael's death, Rachel felt accepted, felt that she belonged. That felt good.

'Welcome to Ikk-ett-Saleth, ladies and gentlemen!' The Doctor threw his arms open and bellowed his greeting across the entire Red Planet, or so it seemed to Madrigal. 'The City of the Sad Ones awaits us.'

Christina Madrigal looked over the Doctor's shoulder and was grudgingly impressed. She'd seen alien cities before, of course; being in the Colonial Marines had broadened her outlook considerably. Born on Earth, in one of the ghettos that leeched off the Massachusetts Conurb, she had escaped the poverty and depravity as soon as she could. Signing up with the Marines, she had toured the Alliance and the worlds of its neighbours: dawn on Kentaurus one day, nightfall on Arcturus the next. Twin suns setting in a purple sky, followed by a bloated red giant rising over the horizon, while Arcturan cities shrouded in methane gave way to the elegant and oxygenated turrets and pillars of Alpha Centauri.

Ikk-ett-Saleth was something else.

Madrigal estimated that the city was approximately seven kilometres across, lying at the bottom of a huge deep bowl smoothed from the Martian rock – the result of the Greenies' fabled sonic technology, no doubt. She wondered how long it had taken them to excavate a space this large; the engineering effort must have been astronomical. You had to hand it to the Greenies, she thought; when they built cities, they really built cities.

Realizing that the cavern was even brighter than the corridor, she looked upwards for the source. The illumination was courtesy of a small but concentrated area of what she assumed was the same bio-luminescent fungus from the tunnel, high up in the centre of the roof. But what a roof: the translucent amber rock was inlaid with a darker material like jet, forming a mosaic that must have been over five kilometres across. It was a triangle overlaid with a jagged lightning bolt, with an artificial sun burning in its centre.

'What is that?' she whispered.

'Martian planetary identification glyph,' said the Doctor. 'Their flag.'

Shaking her head in amazement, she looked around. She and the others were in the wide gallery that had opened up from the corridor, a circular, three-metre-wide ledge that ran round the entire circumference of the bowl. Other doorways were just visible at regular intervals around the gallery, and Madrigal guessed that they led to other parts of the corridor network. A metre-high lip of a green, onyx-like material, carved with an assortment of angular glyphs, provided a degree of security from the gentle thousand-metre slope of smooth grey rock which led to the city: Ikk-ett-Saleth, City of the Sad Ones.

From where they were standing, the entire city was laid out below them, its distance making it look like some townplanner's model; at its centre – exactly below the false sun – was a thin golden pyramid, about five hundred metres tall, while the other buildings – low, flattened cylinders – were laid out in concentric circles around it. But the main impression was one of space, of room; the majority of the city was devoted to parks and woodland. True, they weren't made of grass and trees but orange moss and purple bushes, but a park was a park on any planet.

'That is an areothermal geyser, I would wager,' muttered the Doctor, pointing at the pyramid with his umbrella. 'The reason that we managed to avoid hypothermia.'

'It is deserted, isn't it?' asked Santacosta. 'If there are Greenies still around . . .'

'Ikk-ett-Saleth is deserted, Ms Santacosta,' said the Doctor. 'I can assure you of that.'

Madrigal wasn't convinced. Like the others, she had heard the stories, the rumours. The briefly glimpsed figures lumbering through ruined Martian cities; the travellers who strayed from the recommended routes and never arrived at their destination; the short snatches of radio signals, being broadcast in a language that definitely was not one of Earth's. Madrigal wouldn't have bet her wages on Mars being deserted, that was for sure.

If they encountered Greenies in Ikk-ett-Saleth, they would have to be dealt with. She automatically checked that her plasma pistol was still holstered at her hip; although she didn't want to enter Ikk-ett-Saleth with all guns blazing, if there was a possibility that the expedition was threatened, she was prepared. The Mayor of Jacksonville had asked her to accompany McGuire's expedition to provide protection, and, being a Marine, she knew the meaning of duty.

'The main causeway to the city is just over there,' said the Doctor.

'Can't we just bed down here?' asked Roz. 'It's warm, protected . . .'

'Why do that, when there are beds and blankets down there,' said the Doctor. 'Come along, Roz: not long now.'

As the extremely weary travellers began the last stage of their journey, they were totally unaware of the four shadows observing them from the far side of the city bowl.

'They passed through the *Ga'jur-ett-Lii'is*!' whispered Cleece. 'How?'

Aklaar reached up and placed a clamp on Cleece's shoulder. 'Since the Thousand Day War, some humans have made a detailed study of our ways; of our culture and our customs. The trap of the unfamiliar way was laid wide open for us, since we are pilgrims, and privy to the secret signs. The humans obviously have a man of learning in their party, and he could prove more dangerous than an entire battalion of warriors.'

Cleece shook his head. 'The result of the lax security of a civilian nest. If this had been Liis-arrat-Ixx, or another of the military nests, the *Xssixss* would have been their downfall.'

Esstar sighed. Cleece's obsession with military history was wearing. An *Xssixss* – the path of easy virtue – was a false entrance corridor into a Warriors' nest, one which ensured that any intruders were picked off well before reaching the Queen's chamber. In essence, it was exactly the same as a *Ga'jur-ett-Lii'is*, the unfamiliar way. But to Cleece, a *Ga'jur-ett-Lii'is* was naturally inferior to his Warrior traps. Anything the Warriors did, anything the Warriors built, was superior. The fact that the Warriors' actions had cost them their home planet did not seem to worry him.

'This city is abandoned, Abbot,' added Sstaal. 'What harm would there be in the humans enjoying its comforts, when there are comforts to be spared?' Esstar had to agree with him; Oras had always welcomed all comers to his table, even his treacherous brother Ssethiis and his sister-wife Netysss.

'They are vermin!' spat Cleece. 'Vermin who dare to infest Ikk-ett-Saleth! This city is disgraced, that is true; but they will bring an even greater disgrace upon it by desecrating it with their presence.'

As always, Sstaal tried to be conciliatory. 'But Oras says –'

Cleece smashed his clamps together. 'Oras be damned!'

The shocked silence was electric. Cleece's outbursts were habitual, but this time he had gone too far. Far too far. This was blasphemy of the first order, and Esstar could not help but feel the shame that her accursed mate brought upon her.

Cleece obviously realized the magnitude of his insult. Then again, he would have been an even bigger fool to remain silent. 'Abbot, I beg forgiveness,' he murmured, bowing his head.

Sstaal stepped forward. 'Oras says –'

'Peace, Pilgrim Sstaal,' hissed Aklaar, holding up a clamp. 'Pilgrim Cleece speaks from concern for the memories that are buried in Ikk-ett-Saleth. Such concern provokes deep passions, and his outburst must be forgiven. I suggest that we spend some time meditating over the Ninth Book of Oras: the Rebirth of the Father.' He reached into his thick hide belt and retrieved a small book, bound in green leather. 'Be seated,' he gestured, 'and let us pray.'

Aklaar and his pilgrims sat down in a circle, cross-legged, their copies of the Book of Oras in their clamps. 'Let us repledge our souls to Oras.'

Speaking as one, the Martians began. 'Through your teachings, sacred Oras, may we find the path to heaven.'

Meanwhile, on Charon, all hell was breaking loose.

'Check the software!' screamed Rachel over the even

louder screaming which bellowed from the stunnel mouth. According to the master work-station, the Higgs's generators were doing their job; indeed, the swirling vortex in the stunnel mouth was proof that the subspace meniscus had been penetrated. But the stunnel itself simply refused to obey the laws of physics and resolve at the other end.

Although none of their previous attempts had been any more successful, this situation was different. They were taking a radically different approach, and all the indications were that they should have managed it this time; indeed, from the readouts in front of Rachel, there should have been a stable subspace tunnel between Charon and the Ultima relay, sixteen million kilometres beyond Cassius and well outside the blockade – their escape route. But there wasn't. There wasn't anything apart from a bit of ineffectual subspace penetration.

Felice looked up from her own station. 'I've checked the Matterbase program; it's running okay.' She shook her head. 'Damn it, Rachel, it should be working!' She tapped on her work-station keyboard and frowned. 'The glitch must be coming from somewhere, but where?' She glanced over at the telemetry relay from the telescope. Rachel followed her gaze and froze.

The three saucers were assuming orbit around Charon, ebony disks that bristled with gun-ports. Chris had been right so far: the ships had set off from where he said, and had arrived when he said. So his prophecy of ion cannons, photon impellers and anti-matter drills bombing them into oblivion was a very real threat. Rachel estimated that they had about ten minutes before the surface of Charon began boiling into space.

'Got it!' yelled Dortmun. 'The quantum resonators need recalibrating – they're not working properly this deep into subspace. It'll take about five minutes.' Rachel was relieved; even Dortmun was living up to her responsibilities.

'We haven't got five minutes,' said Felice, hurrying over to the other woman's station to give her a helping hand. Rachel re-evaluated Felice yet again; she really did know what she was doing. It just needed the right circumstances to bring it out of her. It was a shame that those circumstances involved death raining down on them from the sky.

The floor suddenly trembled beneath them, and everyone in the stunnel chamber simultaneously turned to look at the screen. One of the saucers was spitting purple fire at the pitted grey surface of Charon, and Rachel recognized it as the discharge from an ion cannon. Trust the Black Fleet to be early: she guessed that the base now had about three minutes before the real earthquakes began.

'Done it!' Felice shouted. 'The stunnel must resolve now.' And, confirming her words, the banshee screaming from the stunnel mouth transformed into a mellow hum, while the green and red void beyond the meniscus deepened to turquoise.

'We've got to get out of here now!' insisted Chris, appearing behind Rachel. 'Charon won't stand a chance with the sort of ordnance they're bringing to bear on us.'

'Don't you think I know that!' She entered the instructions into her station and watched as the simularity – an out-of-scale map of the solar system – showed a straight green line between Charon and Ultima – the stunnel. Meanwhile, in the huge, oval, peristaltic waves of phosphorescent blue pulsed up and down the infinite tunnel.

Despite the attack, Rachel couldn't help grinning. After all this time, after all the false starts, they'd finally succeeded. 'That's it, everybody. The stunnel's open and stable. So get your arses into gear!' Another tremor – a damned sight more violent than the last one – almost knocked them all to the floor. Rachel grabbed the work-station for support. 'And get a fragging move on!'

As the fifty-odd colonists filed up to enter the stunnel, Rachel glanced back at the simularity and gasped. The green line suddenly wasn't connecting with Ultima any more; it was bending back, deep into the solar system, in a sweeping hairpin arc. 'Belay that! What the hell's going on?'

Felice was next to her. 'We die if we stay here, Rachel.'

'But the other end –' The stunnel's exit terminus was hurtling back through the solar system, past Neptune, Uranus, Saturn . . .

Chris added his support to Felice. 'Any destination is better than here.' He pointed at the 'scope screen, where all three saucers were firing incandescent streams of orange light at Charon: photon impellers, capable of reducing a planetary crust to ionized plasma within minutes.

'We'll end up as frozen corpses floating in space if we go through now,' Rachel protested, but she knew that their current predicament had only two solutions: possible death or certain death. And even the slightest chance was better than being buried under a million tonnes of molten rock.

'The stunnel's being dragged off course by something,' said Felice thoughtfully. 'And that something might be a safe haven.'

'And it might be the invaders' base,' Chris pointed out. To drag a stunnel away from its destination required a massive source of electromagnetic, gravitic and subspace radiation, all in one handy package. Mankind hadn't created anything like that, so the invaders were the logical culprit. Not only were they bombing Charon to hell, but they were grabbing the survivors into the bargain. But what choice did they have?

The explosion that erupted outside the main doors threw them all to the floor: Rachel didn't like to think what the surface of the planet looked like now. As she pulled herself to her feet, she realized that only the osmidium walls and doors which enclosed the sealed stunnel chamber were protecting them from the inferno which Rachel's instruments told her now engulfed the base.

'We haven't got a choice,' said Chris, echoing her thoughts. 'If we don't go through now, we're all going to die.'

That was it. Only one option. 'Into the stunnel, everyone!' she called over to the colonists. It was stable, but that was all that could be said for it. The other end was currently somewhere in the asteroid belt, passing by Ceres on its route to who knew where.

Rachel, Felice and Chris watched as her fellow colonists filed through the pulsing blue corridor into subspace. But where would they materialize? Was she saving them from one death, only to condemn them to another?

Another tremor. Rachel picked up her rucksack and made her way towards the stunnel, supporting herself by swinging from work-station to work-station. She looked at the 'scope screen as she passed: it was a square metre of interference, the aerials of the 'scope having disintegrated along with most of the surface of the planet. The temperature had risen to unbearable levels over the last few minutes, and Rachel knew that Charon's life expectancy could be measured in seconds. With relief, she saw that the last of the colonists was passing through the meniscus – but where were they all going?

'Come on!' Rachel grabbed Felice's arm and pulled her towards the stunnel entrance, impressed that she had stayed her ground. Felice was followed by Chris, and they all ran towards the blinding glare of the entrance.

As Rachel prepared to enter the stunnel, she gave the chamber a final once over – and saw Dortmun, unconscious under a toppled work-station. Rachel was horrified; she hadn't even realized that the woman hadn't been with them.

'Dortmun!' she yelled.

'Leave her!' shouted Felice. 'We've got to go.'

'No,' said Chris, running over to the prone woman.

'Chris!' shouted Felice, but her protest was cut short as part of the ceiling cracked open into a wide crevice. The osmidium shell of the stunnel chamber was buckling; the molten rock that was all that remained of Charon would come raining down in moments. One of the stations burst into flames as a slab of ceiling hit it, and that was the last thing that Rachel saw as she dragged Felice into the stunnel to their unknown destination.

No, not quite the last thing. The last thing was Chris, sweeping Erica Dortmun into his arms and running towards them. And then she was through the subspace meniscus and into the stunnel, and whatever lay beyond.

A second later, the chamber was crushed like a wet cardboard box as a billion tonnes of lava pressed in from all sides, obliterating the last bastion of subspace research in the solar system. Charon had reclaimed its own, its surface now a radioactive and roiling mass of liquid metals, shot through with the faintest traces of osmidium alloy.

For thirty thousand years, the wafer-thin inhabitants of cold Pluto had crawled across the frozen ammonia surface, edging their crystalline bodies cell by cell towards the thin veins of methane ice that they called food. Distant Charon was nothing but a dim light in the dark sky, glowing with the reflected light of a sun too far away to be of any use.

When Charon ignited like a new star, its fatal radiation washed over the day-side surface of Pluto. The population died en masse, screaming as their delicate bodies ruptured and boiled along with the ammonia and methane. It took less than a second for the ancient culture to become nothing more than ionized gases, leaving nothing to mark their passing.

Their mission accomplished – Charon was nothing more than a globe of radioactive slag – the three saucers spun out of orbit and headed back towards Venus for refuelling and new orders. They had completed their mission; they were now the undisputed masters of subspace, Earth, the solar system . . .

And, when they claimed the GodEngine, they would be the masters of the galaxy as well.

Chapter 4

The giant steps of the causeway led the Jacksonville expedition from the high parapet to the suburbs of the City of the Sad Ones; the vast staircase, cut into the amber of the huge bowl, was inclined at a comfortable angle towards what Roz Forrester hoped was their long-deserved rest. Okay, so she was an Adjudicator, combat-trained to deal with most things; she was also human, and totally exhausted. Then again, she could still be impressed, and the walk to Ikk-ett-Saleth was definitely impressive.

The walls that towered above them on either side of the causeway were decorated with detailed carvings, illustrating what she could only guess were episodes from the history of the city. At the top of the stairs, it had shown the founding of Ikk-ett-Saleth, with hundreds of caravans ferrying thousands of Martians through the labyrinth of caves and tunnels beneath the surface – from the look of them, they were natural caves and tunnels; this was well before the extensive tunnel network had been established. Twenty steps later, the pictures showed the area around the aerothermal geyser being carved out with sonic cannons; the pyramid was built some little time – about five steps – later.

As the illustrations recorded the growth of the city, Roz compared them with what lay before them at the foot of the staircase. At the height of its glory, Ikk-ett-Saleth had borne no relation to the collection of uninspiring low hexagons that now made up the majority of the city; half a million years ago, if the carvings were to be believed, it had been a place of stunning architectural beauty, with spires and minarets reaching to the very roof of the cavern, almost touching the inlaid symbol.

'A tragic loss,' muttered Esteban, gazing at the same picture, his voice reverential. 'T'Ran-ikk-Liis – the Dwellings of Triumphant Majesty – was the largest and most glorious city in the Northern hemisphere, but a tactical strike with a burrowing thermonuclear warhead soon put paid to that. Still, modern Ikk-ett-Saleth is a perfect example of Giis-lon dynasty architecture – dull as that might appear. Those hexagonal dwelling units afford optimum space while –'

'Are we liable to see any of the older cities before we reach the Pole?' Roz interrupted, not really that interested, but even less interested in hexagonal dwelling units.

'Wait until we reach Sstee-ett-Haspar; I have not seen it myself, but according to Professor Furniss's research it is truly magnificent,' he sighed.

Roz smiled; Esteban's obsession with Martians and their culture counterpointed her own feelings about aliens. Only her travels with the Doctor had tempered her xenophobia, but she still felt the occasional twinge of unease in the company of extra-terrestrials. Then again, the Martians she had met at Benny's wedding had been charm personified, and, in a way, she was hoping to meet more of the race – after a good night's sleep, though. Travel really does broaden the mind, she concluded. Then she thought about the TARDIS, and wondered how much more travelling she would be able to do without it.

'This is the pivotal period in the city's history,' Esteban pointed out, and Roz returned her attention to the murals. Wars, alliances, famines, plagues; all of them had cropped up in the carvings up till now; half a million years of history, condensed into a series of detailed pictures which encapsulated each episode in the lengthy and often dramatic saga of the city.

But ten thousand years ago – and currently alongside them in mural form – a civil war had begun, and the illustrations changed dramatically and accordingly. The carnage was like nothing the city had faced before; through the murals, Roz observed the city burning after bombardment from the

Proud Warriors, the bacteriological backlash, the execution of the Eight-Point Table . . . and then the rebuilding – this time, as Ikk-ett-Saleth – in the disappointing form that lay before them. All of this accompanied by Esteban's ongoing travelogue.

'These pictures are horrid,' squealed Carmen Santacosta, and Roz shook her head; the Goddess knew how the singer would react if she was faced with a real crisis. She turned to Esteban.

'Did the city ever recover from the civil war?'

'No. According to the oral traditions, it lost its soul after the Eight-Point Table was executed. A city without a soul; one of the saddest traditions in Martian culture,' he said sadly.

Like the Overcities, she thought bitterly. Their souls were sold for material gain, leaving the heart of the Empire empty and meaningless. Something that she would eventually deal with. Then again, if she was stranded in the twenty-second century, what hope did she have of reaching her own time again?

Esteban suddenly frowned, and seemed to have read her thoughts. 'Martians and humans have so much in common,' he sighed. 'Things could have been so different.' He fell silent, and remained that way until they finished their descent.

As they reached the foot of the staircase, Roz was able to appreciate the city better. What there was of it. The majority of Ikk-ett-Saleth was devoted to parkland: beds of orange lichen, adorned with copses of lilac shrubbery and skeletal red trees. But there was still room for thousands of clusters of hexagons, red-stone buildings laid out in what, at first glance, appeared to be no particular pattern. But closer inspection revealed that there was a pattern; one of aesthetic beauty that spoke directly to the soul. Roz was pleased; it proved that, unlike the city, she still had one. And it reinforced the feelings that she had had about the Martians at Benny's wedding, feelings that the Doctor had reinforced earlier; they were creatures whose passion for warfare was only matched by their passion for beauty.

The staircase finally ended, depositing them in one of the parks. Roz noted that the lichen was spongy beneath her feet; a pleasant relief after the stone steps, the stone tunnels, the dusty surface . . . She knew that she could hardly keep her eyes open, she was so exhausted.

'We should head for the nearest buildings,' advised the Doctor, pointing at a group of the red-brick hexagons about three hundred metres away. 'And then bed down for the night.' And it was night; the output from fungal sun had diminished considerably since they had commenced their descent, and it was now a dull, orangy glow that populated the city with deep, dark shadows.

'Although one of us should keep watch, naturally.' The Doctor nodded at Madrigal, who nodded back. Roz was puzzled; hadn't it been the Doctor who had assured them that Ikk-ett-Saleth was completely deserted? Perhaps he knew something that they didn't.

'Keep watch against what?' asked McGuire, saying what she had thought. 'Are you suggesting that there are still Greenies about?' He looked around the park suspiciously.

Esteban interrupted any reply that the Doctor might have been composing. 'From my researches, this city was definitely abandoned, Antony. An expedition came here in 2115 – they didn't find anything.'

'It may have been deserted forty years ago, but what about now?' asked Santacosta. 'It could have been reoccupied since then.'

The Doctor coughed. 'Excuse me, but you are all very tired. With Madrigal on watch, we can all be tucked up safely in our beds without a care. If any Ice Warriors do turn up – and that really is very unlikely – I am sure that we can deal with it.'

Taking the lead, he set off for the nearest hexagonal dwelling, jauntily resting his umbrella over his shoulder. 'Off to the land of Nod,' he muttered.

Roz couldn't be quite as nonchalant; from virtually promising that Ikk-ett-Saleth was deserted, the Doctor was definitely backtracking. Was the city abandoned, or did the Doctor – as usual – know something that he wasn't telling them? Ever since the destruction of the TARDIS, he had been distant, distracted, as if the problems of mere human beings were below him.

Deciding that she was so tired that she didn't really care whether she slept with an Ice Warrior or not, she followed him into the hexagonal dwelling. She hoped that even the Doctor would benefit from a good night's sleep.

While studying for her doctorate, Felice had experienced most forms of matter transmission – Travel-Mat, Transit, stunnel – but this was nothing like any of them. With them, you were there, and then you were somewhere else, end of story. Felice had never been one of those people who found the concept of having her body reduced to elementary particles anything to worry about; understanding the science that lay behind the technology took the mystery out of it.

This was different.

The moment that Rachel had dragged her through the weakened subspace meniscus and into the stunnel, Felice had known that something was wrong, and her entry into subspace had proved it.

Immediately she had been immersed in the dimension, she had felt as if her hands and feet were at the ends of million-kilometre-long arms and legs, her body smeared across subspace – but that was not what it was meant to be like! From her degree and doctorate in physics, she knew that human beings couldn't survive for more than about fifteen minutes in the warped reality of subspace before their molecules flew apart, but she no longer had any sense of time; she could have been in subspace for minutes – or hours, come to that. All she knew was that this wasn't what she had expected.

Perhaps she was trapped in subspace. Perhaps they were all trapped. She laughed; or rather she tried to laugh. But since her mouth felt as if it were sixteen light-years wide, and her brain had no control over her body – a peculiar quirk of subspace meant that the human body was in stasis but the consciousness remained active – it was a rather pointless exercise. But the possibility remained: had they escaped the destruction of Charon, only to suffer a lingering disintegration in subspace?

Actually, that possibility was far too acute; Felice couldn't see anything, she couldn't hear anything, she couldn't feel anything ... For all she knew, Chris's dissociated body could have been floating next to her, or even mingling with her, atom to atom. Ironic, she thought: what if the closest they ever got to sex ended up as a quirk of subspace physics?

She suddenly sensed a change, a twisting, nauseating change that rushed along her infinitely long limbs before exploding in her brain like a thunderbolt. Felice discovered that she had eyes again, and those eyes revealed that she was hurtling down a tunnel of light towards a blindingly bright destination, a rainbow maelstrom that pulled and tugged at her barely corporeal form.

And she wasn't alone. She didn't know how, but she could sense the others alongside her, spectral figures falling towards what she assumed was the other end of the stunnel. But her relief at the presence of her fellow survivors was tainted by a sickening foreboding. Had the stunnel resolved properly? If so, what would they find there? The vacuum of space, the inner sanctum of the invaders? What was waiting for them?

She hit the incandescent exit point of the stunnel.

Every particle of her being – and Felice knew the scientific name of each and every single one of them – turned inside out and collided, transforming her from a vague subspace shadow into –

Whatever it was, it hurt. It seared every nerve ending with microscopic red-hot pokers, taking her to a level of pain that she had never imagined existed. Any thoughts about the other end of the stunnel were overridden by an excruciating agony that seemed to last for an eternity.

When she finally stopped screaming she was back in the real world.

After her brain connected with her body, she felt the rough ground beneath her, and the cold air around her. She peered through the gloom and saw that she was not alone. She just hoped that they had all made it.

'Is everyone okay?' It was Rachel, on her feet and counting the others to make sure that they were all there, although it was difficult to see much in the dimness; the only light came from a few hand torches that some of the more alert colonists had pulled from their backpacks. Felice jumped to her feet, only to stumble; the gravity was considerably less than the Earth-normal of Charon's gravitic web. She tentatively stepped forward, only to discover that her bloody gravity boots weren't working. Then she cursed herself – she hadn't turned the bloody things on. She reached down and pressed the contacts on both boots.

'Rachel!' she called out, standing up. 'We made it!'

'Go to the top of the class, Dr Delacroix,' Rachel retorted. And then, more warmly, 'How are you feeling? Pretty rough ride, wasn't it?'

Felice began to answer, and then tripped over a lump that she realized was Maxwell and slowly fell onto him. She felt sick, and that wasn't entirely due to the vertigo of the low gravity. Maxwell was a grade-A creep.

She felt hands rescuing her from Maxwell's expectant expression and realized that it was Chris. 'Thanks,' she muttered.

'Anytime.' He looked embarrassed. And cute. 'Rachel's done a count, and we're all here,' he told her. 'Was it as bad as I thought it was?'

Before she could answer, Rachel called her over. Gingerly stepping over the disoriented colonists – and refraining from stamping on Maxwell's head – Felice shut her eyes as light erupted from near by and almost stumbled again. She assumed that someone had broken out the emergency lighting from the supplies, and stood still until she became accustomed to the brightness.

'Oh shit,' she whispered in awe as her surroundings resolved. She was staring into a carved stone face that looked back at her from the far side of the vast chamber. The image was unforgettable, and made their location obvious. It was the notorious alien Sphinx.

They were on Mars.

Unable to ignore the commotion, Sstaal looked up from his book – the third chapter of the Book of Oras – and frowned.

Cleece was bullying Esstar again. Shouting and ranting, he obviously got a great deal of satisfaction out of belittling his mate. Sstaal held his ground; despite his feelings for Esstar, he would not – could not – interfere between them. It wasn't his place to come between a betrothed couple. Shoving the book in his hide belt, he stood up and walked over to the Abbot, who was standing next to one of the purple Lakk-tiis-Pertum bushes.

'Abbot Aklaar?' he asked meekly. 'Are we planning to hurt the humans?' The Martian pilgrims had waited patiently in one of the parks as the humans had descended the causeway to Ikk-ett-Saleth, watching them ignore the Holy Seal of Oras that protected the city from all but anointed pilgrims. The pilgrims themselves had entered the city via the *Fississ-cal-oon*, The Way Reserved For Pilgrims, a more direct route. Thanks to the *Fississ-cal-oon*, Aklaar, Cleece, Esstar and Sstaal had reached Ikk-ett-Saleth well before the humans, and had watched and waited once more as the humans defiled the city without a soul, occupying the dwellings without regard for the spirits who begged forgiveness for the atrocities of their ancestors.

But, despite their heresy, Sstaal couldn't agree with Cleece's decision to exterminate them. Then again, it was not Cleece's decision to make. The Abbot was in charge of the pilgrimage, and his decisions – wise decisions, based on his years of service to Oras – were the ones that counted, not the racist cant of Cleece.

Aklaar laid a clamp on his arm. 'The humans are on this planet by virtue of superior force, Pilgrim Sstaal. But they would not have been on this planet had it not been for the hubris of the Warrior caste; the same hubris that Pilgrim Cleece feels. He must be tolerated for the good of us all. It is my hope that this pilgrimage will open his eyes to the greater truth.'

They both looked over at Cleece, just in time to see him attempt to grab Esstar's clamp; obviously reason had deserted him, and he was resorting to the only other tactic he knew: violence. But Esstar was having none of it; she pulled her clamp away and hissed at him like a nest mother protecting her clutch. Which, in a way, she was. Sstaal felt a small warmth within him, a warmth which intensified when Esstar glanced at him and smiled.

'If you have finished conducting your courtship, we must return to the matter in hand,' said Aklaar quietly. Cleece looked embarrassed, but that was more to do with his humiliation by Esstar than his earlier behaviour towards her: Sstaal knew that Cleece never learnt from his mistakes. 'The humans will undoubtedly sleep for another four hours,' Aklaar continued, 'but one of their kind is taking watch. Given their current state of exhaustion, our appearance now might prove disturbing to them.'

Cleece squeezed his clamp; Sstaal realized which clamp it was, and Cleece's intentions. 'Best to strike while they are asleep, Abbot Aklaar,' he said. 'Six humans will prove no match –'

'Enough!' bellowed the Abbot, his fury unrestrained. He strode up to Cleece and punched him in the chest. Despite the difference in size – Cleece's warrior frame against Aklaar's wizened body – Cleece stumbled backwards. 'The humans are not to be harmed. They are travellers, pilgrims in their own right. The teachings of Oras are specific on this point.' He turned away, the anger dissipating rapidly.

But Sstaal knew that Cleece wouldn't leave it there.

The hexagonal dwellings were fully furnished, single rooms, with beds and chairs and ample blankets in relaxing russets and browns. Roz was surprised; she found it difficult to reconcile the fearsome Martians of myth and legend with what appeared to be futons and duvets. Soft furnishings and Ice Warriors – a bizarre combination.

She sighed with exhaustion, but still looked carefully around the room for anything which could have been hiding an Ice Warrior; she was still unconvinced – as, she was sure, was the Doctor – that the city was as deserted as he claimed.

'This was a civilian nest, Roz,' said the Doctor, as if he had read her mind. 'Even Ice Warriors like their creature comforts.' The Doctor threw his backpack and jacket onto the nearest Martian futon and sat on the thickly carpeted floor in the lotus position, his eyes closed. Roz began to wonder exactly how tired the Doctor was. More importantly, perhaps, what damage had been done to him by the destruction of the TARDIS?

'This isn't right,' Roz muttered as she divested herself of her own rucksack and jacket and sat down on – although in was a better word – one of the Martian chairs, a huge thing covered in what looked like green fur. 'It's like the entire city population just got up in the middle of what they were doing and left.'

Without opening his eyes, the Doctor answered. 'That's exactly what they were supposed to do, Roz. When Mars surrendered at the end of the Thousand Day War, the UN team that arrived to beat out the peace terms couldn't find a single Martian left on the planet, only the bodies of the members of the Eight-Point Table – their ruling assembly. They had been executed according to Martian tradition.' He frowned. 'Actually, only six of the eight were executed; Falaxyr and Abrasaar managed to escape.' He yawned, and Roz was taken aback; she couldn't remember the last time the Doctor had done something so human. 'As we now know, the majority of Martians had already left for Nova Martia, a suitable planet on the edges of Arcturan space.'

Feeling slightly more certain that she wasn't going to wake up in the middle of the night staring down the muzzle of a Martian disruptor, she decided that the time had come to say it. 'I'm going to ask you one question, and I want an answer. Agreed?'

'It depends on the question.'

'Agreed?' she hissed.

'Agreed,' he said with resignation.

It had been bugging her for hours, but she had been biding her time, waiting for the right moment. And this – almost asleep in an abandoned house in an abandoned Ice Warrior city – was as near as she was going to get to the right moment.

'What the hell happened to the TARDIS, Doctor?'

He opened his eyes and smiled, but it was a smile so empty, so devoid of emotion, that Roz felt for him. 'The TARDIS was destroyed, Roz. Torn apart because she was unlucky enough to be caught between two incredibly rare phenomena: a Vortex rupture and a subspace infarction. The former is incredibly rare; I've only ever encountered two of them. One was quite soon after I got the TARDIS, the other, well, that won't occur for another nine thousand years.'

'What is a Vortex rupture?' Roz knew that the questioning was hurting the Doctor, but she had to know what was going on. First rule of Adjudication: be prepared, or be prepared to die.

The Doctor cradled his fingers. 'On certain occasions, forces come to bear on the fabric of the Time Vortex, ripping it apart and allowing the substrate – the poly-dimensional foundation of the Vortex – to erupt. TARDISes – well, Type Forties, like mine – cannot cope with these events very well. But they can cope. Normally. But coupled with a subspace infarction . . .' He sighed.

'Go on.'

'Goodness knows what caused the rupture, although I have my suspicions. But the cause of the infarction is pretty straightforward if you apply a little reasoned deduction. The Daleks have a strange-icaron generator on Mercury, and it's fouling up subspace across the entire solar system – an effective blockade which prevents starships from getting even close to Earth.'

'Why?' Starships and FTL-drives were more Chris's area of interest, but it didn't hurt to have too much information.

The Doctor tutted at the interruption, but answered. 'Strange icarons are the black sheep of the icaron family, Roz, because they have no harmful effects on organic life.' Roz remembered icarons only too clearly; the presence of an icaron generator on Earth had been the trigger to the events that had led to her and Chris teaming up with the Doctor. 'But they have a most deleterious effect on starship jump-engines. Any ship attempting to either enter or leave subspace within a blockade field of strange icarons will explode.' He chewed his bottom lip. 'The only place still capable of attempting to break that blockade was Charon, the moon of Pluto: it was one of the few places where research into subspace engineering still continued after the Transit project was dropped. If I remember correctly, they spent the few months between the initial attack and the final assault – which killed them all – trying to bore through subspace. And if they ramped up the power a few thousand per cent – a likely stratagem – and tried to open a stunnel using brute force, it would undoubtedly cause an infarction.'

He closed his eyes once more, then continued.

'The infarction engulfed the TARDIS, effectively causing her to stall. And then the rupture blew directly beneath her. She lasted about two minutes before the outer plasmic shell disintegrated.'

Roz could feel sleep making unreasonable demands upon her, but she needed to know the answer to one last question. 'You said you had your suspicions about the cause of the rupture. Care to elucidate?'

'The Time Vortex is virtually indestructible; it is the fundamental reality which supports all of creation. In many respects, the physical universe is nothing but a shadow of the Vortex. But the link is two-way: do something unimaginably nasty in the real world, and it might just affect the Vortex.'

Roz frowned. 'But what could be so unimaginably nasty?'

The Doctor's voice was sepulchral as he replied. 'A Jonbar Hinge: an event which shatters the Web of Time, rewriting history on a major scale.'

This did not bode well. 'Such as?'

'Such as the destruction of Earth.'

She shook her head. 'But Earth's still there. We saw it.' And the obvious defence. 'It's still there in the thirtieth century!'

'The Vortex isn't answerable to the laws of cause and effect, Roz. The destruction could happen tomorrow, or it could happen in thousands of years. But history has been or will be altered. Earth was or will be destroyed. Excuse the ambiguous tenses – this is a very ambiguous concept.'

'Can't you be less ambiguous? This is my planet you're talking about.' Roz felt a coldness, an emptiness, which had nothing to do with her exhaustion.

The Doctor looked at her, through her, with infinite eyes. 'At a rough guess, from the location and intensity of the rupture, some time in the next week.'

The next week? But what of her future? What of the thirtieth century? It may not have been the most golden of eras, but . . . But it may not have been. Period. She swallowed.

'I'm sorry, but you did ask.' He got up and walked over to a transparent cone, about a metre high, that stood next to a green and black tapestry-covered wall.

'But my world!' she exploded. 'And what about me and Chris? We won't be born! Why haven't I ceased to exist?'

The Doctor tapped the cone and watched as currents of pink fluorescence swam through the clear liquid interior. 'Because you have travelled in the TARDIS. It protects the worldlines of its occupants; in many respects, you exist outside of time. The effect wears off after a while, otherwise it would disrupt the normal operation of the Universe –'

'Wears off?' The meaning behind the Doctor's casual phrase hit her immediately. 'So, how long have I got before I just fade away?' she shouted. After all she had been through, the thought that her life would end with her being surgically removed from reality on account of some bit of cosmic book-keeping was almost more than she could bear.

'Long enough for us to get to the bottom of this conundrum and find a way out, I hope. While I was playing around with Professor Esteban's tablette, I learnt one, salient fact.' He cocked an eyebrow. 'The rupture was instigated at the Martian North Pole.' With that, he reached out with his umbrella and tapped the contact on the light switch by the door, plunging the room into darkness.

'Pleasant dreams, Roz,' he whispered.

Pleasant dreams? How could she even think about sleep at a time like . . . and then she felt her exhaustion batter her into submission, and she closed her eyes gratefully and sank back into the fur of the chair.

But just before she surrendered to the mercies of sleep, her eyes opened almost reflexively, and she found herself staring out of one of the slit-like windows set into the walls at regular intervals. She could have sworn that she saw a ghostly TARDIS floating past, a gossamer-thin police box that bobbed along for a few seconds before vanishing.

She wanted to tell the Doctor, but her tiredness finally

won, and she fell into a deep sleep, haunted by floating, ghostly TARDISes.

Now that emergency lighting had flooded their current location with its antiseptic glare, Rachel could see they had materialized in some sort of a temple. The chamber was about two hundred metres across, an octagon of tall sloping walls which met at a vertex some half a kilometre above them. Each wall of polished amber stone featured a tall carving of the same figure in slightly different poses; dressed in robes, and adorned in jewellery, it looked exactly like an Egyptian pharaoh, except that it had the head of a jackal.

A table stood in the dead centre of the chamber; a huge, black stone table about a metre and a half tall and three metres across. It was shaped like an eight-pointed star.

But the chamber had been violated. A massive hole had been carved out from two adjoining walls, revealing an equally large antechamber beyond. And the Martian Sphinx . . . Rachel had heard of it, she had seen simularities, but nothing could have prepared her for its sheer majesty and grandeur. Its similarities with its namesake on Earth were obvious: it appeared to be about the same size, with the leonine body and paws of its counterpart. But instead of a pharaoh's face, it bore the helmeted visage of a Martian Lord.

'Quite a sight, isn't it?' said Lebrun, one of the junior technicians on the project. Rachel suddenly remembered that he was a bit of a Mars buff, and wondered whether he could clear up one problem.

'What the hell's it doing here?' she asked. All of the simularities she had seen had shown the Sphinx as an impressive structure that lay beneath the pink Martian sky. So why was it sitting in the antechamber of a deserted temple?

Lebrun shrugged. 'It was moved during the Thousand Day War, Professor. For reasons that aren't very clear, the Greenies devoted a sizeable force to defend the transport, and it was brought here. It was all recorded by the satellite network in orbit around Mars. Nobody knows why, though.'

'So where's here, exactly?' Mars was a big place, thought Rachel. And far too near Earth – and the invaders – for her liking.

'Vastitas Borealis, Professor. The Martian North Pole.' He pointed towards the grand table in the centre of the chamber. 'And, unless I'm mistaken, that is the Eight-Point Table. The meeting place for the entire military high command on Mars.'

Felice had come over by this time, and Rachel considered her deputy. The last few hours had shown Rachel that the woman was far more than the arrogant upstart that she had first appeared to be; she was a fine scientist with a cool head, and Rachel couldn't think of anybody else who she would rather have had backing her up.

'What do you think, Dr Delacroix? Any suggestions?'

Felice frowned. 'There has to be a reason for us being here, rather than on Ultima, so what is it? Unless . . .' She slapped her forehead. 'Christen me an idiot! Of course, there must be a subspace attractor near by!' She reached into her jump-suit pocket and pulled out a micro-tablette which she then aimed around the cavern, allowing its sensor grid to soak up the ambient radiation.

Rachel did the same, and examined the readings. And swallowed. The sensors were indicating something that she would never have expected on Mars; in fact, she would never have expected it anywhere in the solar system. 'According to this, there's a subspace attractor near by that goes off the dial. Of course it would interfere with our stunnel, draw it off course. That's exactly what we were seeing when the stunnel bent back from the Ultima relay. But why would the Martians build a subspace attractor?' She looked down at her micro-tablette. 'Is it some sort of a weapon?'

'There's a problem there, Professor,' forwarded Lebrun. 'The Greenies never developed subspace technology; that's why we won the war. After those bastards dropped that asteroid on Paris, they thought that they had a couple of days until we retaliated because they were expecting the counter-attack to come in a fleet of spaceships. Instead, we arrived via Transit beam within hours and . . .' His face crumpled as the memories surged back, and Rachel felt another part of her soul shrivel and die as she thought about the personal repercussions of the Earth–Mars conflict. Michael's death tried to revisit her mind, but she repelled it. She was getting good at doing that.

Chris sidled up to them. 'So there's technology here that the Martians couldn't possibly have developed?' A brief but noticeable expression of fear crossed his face. 'It might be the invaders.'

Rachel weighed up the options. They definitely couldn't stay where they were; despite the acceptable temperature and the thin but breathable air – Rachel remembered reading a paper on the terraforming programme which had followed Man's conquest of the planet in the middle of the twenty-first century – they would very soon die of thirst, or eventually starvation, when the meagre supplies which they had brought with them from Charon ran out. But the presence of unexpected subspace technology suggested that there might be others near by, and that could mean food and water.

Or something.

As she saw it, there were four alternatives: the subspace attractor was a natural phenomenon; such things were known – Rachel had read of such a thing on the sixth moon of Clavidence, the result of a high concentration of rare and peculiar minerals. Or the attractor was the responsibility of the Martians, humans, or the invaders. The fifth possibility – that another race was involved – was instantly dismissed. Things were complicated enough without involving another set of aliens. For a second, she thought about their options. And then she decided.

'We do a recce,' she announced.

'All of us?' asked Lebrun.

She shook her head. 'I'm going, and I'd appreciate Chris and Felice tagging along.' She looked at them both, and smiled inside; both were nodding, and she felt strangely proud of them. They were her team; it was that simple.

Addressing the crowd of colonists and scientists, she assumed her most authoritative tone.

'It looks like there might be some sort of complex not too

far away, and I'm going to take a look. Adjudicator Cwej and Dr Delacroix will accompany me. If we can verify that it's safe, we'll come back and get you.' She began to turn towards the direction which Felice's micro-tablette had indicated, before remembering one last thing.

'Give us twenty-four hours.' She stabbed a finger at Mitchell, a young, auburn-haired Welsh woman sitting cross-legged against the wall. 'Ceri-Anne – you're in charge now. If we're not back by then, use the emergency transceiver and try to contact the Bureau on Oberon.' She caught Chris's look of surprise – did he really think that the head of the Charon colony wouldn't know about the support which the Adjudicators were providing from that godforsaken moon of Uranus? – and smiled. 'Any questions?'

The group of survivors nodded and grunted, but nobody seemed to have any objections. 'Right then. Chris: grab a survival pack and four plasma rifles. Felice: bring that micro-tablette. We're going hunting.'

Rachel just hoped that they were armed for bear; something told her that humans were the last race that they were going to find guarding the mysterious Martian subspace attractor.

Vincente Esteban carefully eased himself out of his sleeping bag, stood up, and looked around the Martian dwelling. Antony McGuire was fast asleep on the low hard bed, twitching with bad dreams in the dim twilight of Ikk-ett-Saleth, and Esteban stared at him with pity. Esteban knew of the death of McGuire's family, and felt for him. But he didn't share his hatred of Martians; he couldn't. There was no proof that the Martians had been behind the terrorist attacks, only ideograms carved into the wall of the Montreal monorail terminus. The assumption that they were responsible was nothing more than a leap of false reasoning by a planet still living in fear. The Martians simply didn't behave like that – terrorism was an insult to their racial honour, he thought, as he put on his environment jacket.

Sleep had completely eluded the scientist; the knowledge that he was in the fabled City of the Sad Ones was too overwhelming for him to relax, despite his exhaustion. He smiled; Juanita had always said that he lived, ate and breathed research.

He reached into his rucksack and extracted a torch and his tablette, automatically checking the power levels on the small palmtop and tutting when he saw how low they were. The spare battery pack had been in the storage area of the ATET, vaporized along with the majority of his equipment, and the solar recharging facility hadn't been very useful given the feeble sunlight on Mars; the illumination from the roof of Ikk-ett-Saleth wouldn't be much use either.

Still, he reassured himself, he had survived, and was participating in the greatest adventure of his life; compared with this, his expedition to the methane falls on Sinope, that fascinating moon of Jupiter, had been as interesting as a walk in the countryside. Pocketing his tablette and switching on the torch, he tiptoed out of the dwelling and into the dawn.

Shining the torch around him, he tried to decide what to look at next. From the fragmentary information he possessed about the city, he knew of at least twenty places that were vying for his attention, and that was just his first port of call. Esteban doubted that he would get any sleep at all; there was just too much to look at. For a brief second, he thought of his friends and family on Earth, suffering under the invasion – if only he could tell them of what he had seen. He hadn't spoken to them for over eight months, and the longing within him was a constant, nagging pain. And then his wife's face appeared in his mind for a second, gutting him with pain: Juanita was on Earth, millions of kilometres away, and there was absolutely nothing that Esteban could do about it.

Heading off in the direction of the central plaza, he still couldn't help remembering the last time that he and Juanita had seen one another. Esteban had been off to Mars, hoping to mount an expedition; Juanita was committed to a lecture tour, and was planning to join him on Mars as soon as it was over.

And then the Black Fleet had arrived.

Esteban shuddered with a chill of horror: he didn't even know whether Juanita was dead or alive – he knew about the plague decimating whole cities, but had no idea whether Madrid was affected or not. Part of his soul was displaced, lost, and there wasn't a damned thing he could do about it. Apart from focusing on the job in hand.

Pocketing the torch – the overhead illumination was increasing as dawn broke over Ikk-ett-Saleth – he checked the rough map of the city stored in his tablette and set off in the direction indicated, towards the central plaza. As he walked, he brought up his files on the city, hoping to spot some new line of research that he had missed, something which would give him a better insight into the mysteries of Ikk-ett-Saleth and the complexities of the Martian psyche. Anything to take his mind off Juanita.

He was so preoccupied by his researches that he never noticed the figure which approached purposefully through the shadows. He never saw it come up behind him. And he never felt the blow to the back of his head which shattered his spinal column.

As Esteban fell, he twisted around and saw his murderer. Shock and confusion mingled with the pain and surprise as he recognized them.

'You?' he hissed, unable to understand why they had done it.

Then the emptiness hit him, and his assassin meant nothing. For a final moment, his wife's face floated in front of him, centimetres away and yet too far to hold, too far to rescue him. Too far away to say goodbye.

Chapter 5

'Impressive, isn't it?' muttered Rachel as she and the others attempted to squeeze past the left-hand side of the Sphinx towards the back of the antechamber; there was a gap of less than half a metre between the sand-blasted yellow surface of the ancient statue and the satin-smooth polished walls, and she was finding it a bit of a tight fit. Even the half-rations that had been imposed on Charon had done little to reduce her fearsome backside, she thought ruefully.

'Why the hell did they build a Sphinx?' she wondered out loud. 'Jealous of the one on Earth?'

Felice, leading the way with the heavy-duty torch and her tablette, shrugged. 'No idea,' she called over her shoulder. 'History's never been my strong point.' She stopped, and touched the sensor probe of the tablette against the statue's side.

'Now that is odd,' she muttered. 'Look at this.'

Rachel forced herself further along the narrow passageway until she was wedged next to her deputy. Felice proffered the tablette's screen to her.

Frowning, Rachel looked from the screen to the Sphinx and back again in surprise. 'There has to be some mistake,' she protested.

'No mistake, Rachel; this tablette's loaded with the latest surveying software – the dating program has an accuracy of ten years either way.'

'What is it?' said Chris, craning his neck to look over Rachel's shoulder.

'According to these readings, the Martian Sphinx is over a

thousand years older than the one in Egypt.' She shook her head. 'Didn't anyone date it when it was on the surface?'

'I doubt they had the chance,' said Felice. 'It was heavily guarded during the Thousand Day War, and when we finally had the chance to have a look at it, it was gone. Brought here, presumably.'

'You're saying that the Martians had an Egyptian-like culture *before* Egypt itself? That's unbelievable,' said Chris.

'A mystery for another time,' Rachel stated. 'I want to find that subspace attractor.'

The party continued their uncomfortable journey past the Sphinx.

Quiet and cross-legged in the small clearing, Abbot Aklaar contemplated their current position. Their pilgrimage to the North Pole was almost over; Sstaal estimated that they would reach their destination in a little over three days. But the presence of the humans was worrying. He knew that they would only have attempted such a journey if they were desperate, but the invasion of their homeworld and the blockade of the solar system meant that their struggling colony at Jacksonville was slowly being starved of supplies. And hunger and fear were common causes of desperation.

Aklaar needed to meet the humans; he needed to ascertain the reason for their expedition. If they came in peace, then he could offer them protection against the perils that could still confront them as they approached the Pole. If, however, their intentions were hostile, he would have to find some way of dissuading them. The importance of his own mission could not be greater, offering a chance for his people to cleanse their collective souls of guilt and blood and step forward into the dawn of a new age of understanding. As an Abbot of Oras, he was loath to tarnish his pilgrimage with bloodshed, but he knew the weight of the greater good was on his shoulders. If only force would stop the humans from interfering, then force would be necessary. He made a brief, silent prayer to Oras that such measures would not be necessary.

But to talk to the humans, he and his pilgrims would have to make themselves known, and Aklaar was uncertain of the reaction they would encounter. As far as the humans knew, there were no Martians left on Mars. How would they behave when they were confronted with their old enemies?

He stood, and beckoned the others over.

'The time has come to reveal ourselves to the humans, my children.' He looked at Cleece, whose reckless nature could very well be their undoing. 'I urge you all to practise the greatest of restraint; their reactions may be unpleasant, but they will be understandable. Violence is the last resort, and proof that we have failed to behave as Oras taught us.'

They all nodded, and Aklaar could see that Sstaal and Esstar saw the truth of his words.

Sadly, Cleece's expression was indecipherable.

Working from the centre of the rear wall, Felice and Rachel had scanned every square centimetre for some sign of a door. Felice moved to the left, Rachel to the right, their tablettes humming in unison. Until Rachel's tablette began to whine loudly.

'Got something!' she called out, but it was unnecessary; Felice and Chris had come running over as soon as the noise had started.

'What have you found?' asked Felice.

Rachel pointed at the smooth, unbroken amber rock. 'There's a discontinuity in the crystal matrix of the wall; there's a door, but it's absolutely seamless.' She whistled. 'Absolutely amazing.'

Chris frowned. There was something about this chamber – specifically the eight-pointed table on the far side of the Sphinx – that reminded him of something. He racked his brain to remember, but nothing came.

Felice stepped forward and placed her palm on the centre of the invisible door and pushed, but, unsurprisingly, nothing happened. 'What about a plasma burst?' she asked.

'Not with this molecular structure,' said Rachel. 'A plasma burst wouldn't have the slightest effect. The mineral is laced with an alloy that the tablette doesn't recognize, but its composition is such that it absorbs directed energy and virtually superconducts it across the entire wall.'

'Of course!' shouted Chris. He knew why he'd forgotten; there had been an almighty hangover in between then and now. He had been with Roz and a group of Martians at the bar during Benny's wedding reception, downing Martian ale like it was about to be rationed. As the wonderful – but eventually costly – effects of the ale had started to set in, the conversation had moved on to the subject of battle anthems. He and Roz had regaled the group with ballads and stirring songs enshrined by the Guild of Adjudicators, while the Ice Warriors had sung some wonderful military tunes from their less-friendly past. One of the songs had been about the glories of the Eight-Point Table – and Chris could only assume that that was the item of furniture they had seen earlier. They had also sung of the secret entrances that protected the chamber from attack, entrances that could only be opened by those that knew the correct procedure, such as the Grand Marshals and their adjutants.

Walking over to the wall, Chris tried to visualize the movements that the Ice Warriors had made, bold sweeping gestures that apparently dated back millennia. The left arm was held horizontally at forehead level, the right at neck level, and then they were slowly moved up and down to symbolize the opening of some great eye – at least that was how one of the Ice Warriors had slurringly explained it afterwards.

As Felice and Rachel watched him with looks of puzzlement – and amusement – on their faces, Chris felt himself redden. But the thin sliding noise from in front of him made up for his embarrassment; as they waited, a three-metre square of wall retracted inwards before swinging upwards.

'How on Earth did you know how to do that?' asked Rachel suspiciously.

'An Ice Warrior – I mean a Martian – told me,' he said without thinking. Then he cursed himself; in this era, the Ice Warriors were still feared and hated – and they weren't even called Ice Warriors. By revealing that he had actually talked to one, he was immediately coming under suspicion.

But the odd smile on Rachel's face made him uneasy; far from suspicion, it was almost as if he had just gone up in her estimation. A shout from Felice made him look round.

'Whatever that wall was laced with, it also blocks subspace readings. I'm going to have to recalibrate the tablette to find the exact source of the emissions. If we thought that attractor was powerful, we'd better think again.'

She paused, then added, 'It's unimaginable.'

Running into the dwelling, Roz was surprised to see that the Doctor was still asleep. Surprised, because she had never known him sleep for more than an hour or so; if he had nodded off when she had, he had been asleep for over five hours. He was twitching slightly and giving plaintive low moans, as if being visited by bad dreams; she was very glad that she wasn't sharing them. She knew that he had been telepathically linked to the TARDIS; the severing of that connection must have cost him dearly. She wondered whether nightmares were the only side-effect of the TARDIS's destruction.

Because of that, she was loath to wake him, but she had no other choice. He had to know what had happened.

Laying a gentle hand on his shoulder, she shook him slightly. The shout that resulted made Roz jump. For a second, his face was a mask of desperate fear, but his flexible features soon assumed a look of irritated enquiry. 'I'm sorry – I must have overslept,' he said hesitantly, as if it was the first time he had ever uttered those particular words.

'We've got a problem,' Roz stated. 'Esteban's dead.'

'What?' The Doctor jumped to his feet. 'How did it happen?'

'Well, it wasn't suicide, unless you know of a way to shatter your own spine. Madrigal found him about five hundred metres away, hidden in some bushes.'

The Doctor sighed. 'I was worried something like this might happen.'

Roz didn't understand. 'You knew Esteban was going to be murdered?'

'No, not the specifics. But I suspected that there might be an incident of some kind.'

'Why?' she called after him as he set off for the door.

'Because we're not alone,' he muttered.

'Great,' mumbled Roz as she followed after him. 'This is all we need.'

The door from the antechamber had led them into a wide, square corridor with mirror-polished stone walls, their amber surfaces engraved with impressive carvings of battles and wars. A vivid reminder of who they were dealing with, as if they needed one. As far as anyone in the twenty-second century was concerned, the Ice Warriors had deserted Mars after losing the war. The seemingly operational base that Chris, Rachel and Felice now found themselves in definitely suggested otherwise.

Chris stopped them as soon as they passed through the door into the corridor. He didn't want to frighten them, but he knew that he had to give them some warning.

'I know I might be telling you the obvious, but I don't think this is an abandoned base,' he said.

'Really?' said Rachel sarcastically. 'I would never have guessed.'

'Aren't you surprised?' he asked.

'What, that there are still Martians on Mars?' She shook her head. 'I've known for a long time. My brother told me.'

'Your brother?' said Felice.

Rachel held up her hand. 'It's a long story, and I don't really want to go into it at the moment. But yes, Chris, I knew. So we'd better be on our guard.'

Chris pondered her words. There was some link between her brother and the Ice Warriors – but what sort of link was it? Did she share her time's hatred of the race, or was it something more complicated? Knowing the way his life was going, Chris guessed that it was something more complicated.

A sudden noise made them all look round; the secret doorway was sliding back in place.

'Oh shit!' exclaimed Chris. He'd been so pleased with himself about opening the door, he hadn't thought of the consequences. If there were still Martians about – and it was best to assume that there were – they would now know that there were intruders in their base.

'Let's find that attractor and get out of here,' he stated. 'Before we get caught.'

They moved quietly and vigilantly down the corridor, the silence only broken by intermittent chirps and bleeps from Felice's tablette as it scanned for the emissions characteristic of a subspace attractor. Suddenly it started screeching, a banshee wail that echoed up and down the corridor before she could shut it off.

'Got something!' she snapped, ignoring Chris's urgent 'shush'. 'We must be right on top of the attractor to get readings like this.' She showed the display to Rachel. 'Wouldn't you agree?'

Rachel nodded. 'Somebody is playing around with subspace, all right.' She gave a low whistle, infuriating Chris even more – didn't these women have the word 'stealth' in their vocabulary? 'Actually, a damned sight more than playing around,' Rachel continued. 'From these readings, I'd say that they could punch a stunnel through the blockade without breaking into a sweat, and probably reach the other side of the galaxy before they ran out of steam.'

Chris exited the conversation as Rachel began to talk about subspace inertia and quantum drag and looked around, hoping to see some way of getting the group out of the corridor where they could be spotted at any moment. He had no intention of being apprehended by whatever was running the base; the Daleks notwithstanding, in the twenty-second century the Ice Warriors were particularly nasty.

And nasty meant nasty; despite the friendly demeanour of the Ice Warriors he had met at Benny and Jason's wedding, he knew that their forebears were generally some of the most belligerent, unreasonable and downright vicious bastards in the galaxy. The probability of a friendly reception was, at best, remote.

And that was just the Ice Warriors; there was still the chance that this was a Dalek base, one which history had never recorded. Indeed, it was far more likely that they were the culprits, given their advanced technology. Although history gave the date of the Dalek invasion of Mars as much later in 2157, Rachel and her colleagues were living proof that history wasn't immutable.

'Rachel,' he hissed urgently. 'We've got to find a hiding place. The presence of the attractor is a pretty damned big pointer to somebody still being around.'

Rachel nodded. 'According to the readings, the attractor's about five hundred metres behind this wall. Then again, the wall's laced with that peculiar alloy, and that's distorting the readings.' And then she chewed her bottom lip. 'Odd; not even a trace of trisilicate.'

'Is that important?' asked Chris.

'Probably not. Anyway, there's got to be some way of getting through this wall; a door, or something.' She strode off with the others in tow. Chris just hoped that he wouldn't have to dredge another Martian song up to get them in. Not for the first time since they had arrived on the planet, he cursed the fact that Benny wasn't with them. It wasn't that he resented her wedding; of course he didn't. But why did the TARDIS's resident expert on all things Martian have to choose this precise moment to take a temporary leave of departure? Even a copy of her seminal work on Mars – 'Down Among the Dead Men' – would have been welcome, but his was sitting on a bookshelf in his bedroom in the TARDIS – not that that was much use to anybody any more.

About three hundred metres down the corridor, the amber rock was interrupted by an inset square of embossed bronze about ten metres across, a doorway – presumably – decorated with a bas-relief of the Ice Lord features of the Martian Sphinx.

'So how the hell does this one open?' Rachel complained. 'More Martian aerobics?'

'I'm not sure about this,' said Chris. 'And this isn't what I meant about getting out of the corridor. I can't believe that they'd leave the subspace attractor unguarded.' Although checking out the attractor was their main purpose, Chris had hoped that they would find a way of investigating it without a frontal assault. Before he could say anything, however, Felice stepped forward and gave the door a hard shove. He tried to stop her, but it was too late; without a sound, the door began to move.

The square opened in exactly the same way as the previous

one – backwards and up – but unfortunately revealed very little: the room was dimly lit and details were difficult to make out. At the same time that the doorway had opened, a duet of high squeals issued from Rachel and Felice's tablettes, confirming their theories about the attractor being shielded.

They stepped into the gloom, and Chris switched on his torch and cast the beam around the room – any Ice Warriors would have been warned of their entrance the moment the door had opened, so he was hardly advertising their presence. The beam caught the far side of the room, and suddenly the chamber was flooded with reflected light.

It was the subspace attractor.

Chris looked at the attractor, frowned, and then shook his head. This was not the sort of thing he would have expected to encounter on Mars. Then again, after the Sphinx, Chris realized that he should have expected anything.

'From the degree of bone splintering to his spine, I'd say that Professor Esteban was killed by a blow far in excess of that capable by a normal human assailant,' said the Doctor as he rose from his crouch over the corpse. 'Mr McGuire; we need to talk.'

No, thought McGuire, we don't need to talk. Vince had been killed by the Greenies, and that was all there was to it. Ikk-ett-Saleth was probably infested by the reptilian bastards, and they had made the first move. He turned to Madrigal.

'Madrigal; organize a recce across the city. Arm them with that stash of plasma pistols that you have been hiding in your rucksack.' Did she really think that he wouldn't realize that she was packing? 'Shoot to kill.'

A hand suddenly descended on his shoulder. He looked round to see the Doctor. 'Aren't we over-reacting a tad, Mr McGuire? It was indiscriminate bloodshed which led to this current situation; hasn't the time come for humanity to think first and act a tiny bit later?'

Bleeding-heart liberal! McGuire's wife and children were dead because the Martians had acted first. A group of Greenies had infiltrated the Montreal monorail company, waiting until rush-hour to detonate a series of small fusion bombs on a large number of tracks. Small fusion bombs, but enough to derail three hundred and ten trains. And enough to consign his wife and two children, off to do their Christmas shopping, to their graves. Although the murderers had never been caught, the presence of Martian ideograms carved near the bomb site was definite proof of who was responsible as far as McGuire was concerned – they were inhuman reptile bastards who deserved to die. He suddenly realized that everybody was looking over his shoulder. He followed their gaze.

And saw the four Martians who had just walked out of the grove of twisted blue trees and felt his hatred collapse into a super-dense black hole of sheer, vicious anger and hatred. 'You –'

Roz's arm was around his throat, the pressure firm on his Adam's apple. 'Make a move and you'll end up like Vincente here.' She moved closer and whispered into his ear, 'Don't make any rash decisions, Antony; wait and see what's going on, first.' He tried to sigh – rather painfully – but realized, not for the first time, that the strength of his dislike of the Martians could sometimes prove to be a hindrance. He forced himself to rein back his anger and wait. If he waited, an opportunity might present itself.

The Martians stopped about five metres away. 'May the beneficence of Oras rain down upon you,' hissed the smallest of the four, a slightly stooped figure in the tabard, cloak and pointed helmet of a Martian Lord. He was supporting himself with a thick, gnarled branch – almost a small tree – surmounted with a pearly sphere trapped between the stumps of two truncated branches. 'I trust that the hospitality of Ikk-ett-Saleth has left you refreshed?'

'Why did you kill him?' McGuire growled with some considerable effort. Roz increased the pressure in response.

The Ice Lord walked forward, flanked by the others. They were dressed in the ridged green carapaces and helmets that marked them as Warriors, but something wasn't right ... With a frown of disbelief, McGuire realized that one of them was female, with the slighter body and the characteristic dorsal spine of her gender. As he watched, she moved past him and over to Esteban's body, kneeling to examine him.

She looked up and stared at McGuire through her glassy visor. 'We overheard your conversation. This was not of our doing. We are pilgrims, taking the holy path to G'chun duss Ssethiissi. Why would we harm fellow travellers?' She stood. 'That would be an affront to our order.'

'You must admit, though,' said the Doctor, stepping forward and staring up into the female's face, half a metre above him, 'a mysterious death and your sudden appearance would seem to be a remarkable coincidence.'

The largest of the three Ice Warriors waved a clamp at the body. 'Had he faced us in combat, his head would have been cleaved from his neck. This trifling wound would be an insult.'

'Be quiet, Cleece,' snapped the female. 'Your posturing will not help this situation.' She turned back to the Doctor. 'Are you the leader of this group?'

The Doctor shook his head and nodded at McGuire. 'That honour goes to Antony McGuire over there.' McGuire gave an inward sigh of relief; given the Doctor's previous behaviour and knowledge of the Greenies – not to mention his friend's arm round his neck – McGuire had briefly entertained the possibility of some sort of arranged ambush, engineered by the Doctor to deliver them to his allies.

The Ice Lord executed a deep bow in McGuire's direction. 'I am Abbot Aklaar, spiritual guardian of these children.' Returning to his full height, he pointed his staff at each of the Ice Warriors in turn. 'Cleece, Esstar and Sstaal.' McGuire noticed the final Martian, a decidedly small specimen who lurked nervously in the background. A nervous Ice Warrior? That was a first.

'If you are from a religious nest,' said the Doctor suspiciously, 'why are you all wearing Warrior armour?'

'During our pilgrimage, we have faced many dangers – the wilds of our home planet are brutal and unforgiving. Without the protection of Warrior armour, we would have perished,' explained Aklaar.

Roz released her grip, and McGuire rubbed his bruised throat. 'Can you prove this?' she asked.

Aklaar looked round the group of humans. 'We have been observing you; your actions – and your success in reaching Ikk-ett-Saleth – suggest that you have an expert in our culture in your party.'

'He's the stiff,' Madrigal pointed out with her usual lack of tact. 'What are you getting at?' But McGuire couldn't help looking at the Doctor; if anyone in the expedition could be considered an expert, it was him.

'A student of our ways would recognize this.' Aklaar reached into his hide cloak and pulled out a small silver-blue object, not dissimilar to a melted treble clef symbol. 'This lies at the heart of our faith.'

The Doctor snatched it from the Abbot's clamp and held it up to the light of the artificial morning. He raised an eyebrow. 'Utet-Sak-Oras . . . the Divine Sight of Horus. Then again . . .' He leant down and irreverently snatched the tablette from Esteban's death grip. With a brief tap on its keyboard, he held the symbol up to its sensor port and examined the readings. Clearly satisfied, he pocketed the object and replaced the tablette in Esteban's unfeeling fingers. 'The metallurgy readings show it as genuine – hand-drawn from an Osirian star-sapphire. I believe you.' But McGuire couldn't help but notice a worried tone in his voice.

The Doctor unexpectedly voiced McGuire's own concerns. 'But if you didn't kill the Professor here . . . who did?' Then again, the Doctor couched it in considerably friendlier terms than McGuire would have done.

'Just because these ones are pacifists, it doesn't mean that their relatives aren't around here somewhere,' said Carmen Santacosta nervously. 'This horrid vile city could be crawling with them, hissing away with their nasty sinister voices.'

'This city is under the Interdict of Oras,' intoned the Abbot, ignoring the singer's insult. 'No Martian, be they pilgrim or warrior, builder or serf, would dare to transgress its holy boundaries.'

'But you're here,' Roz pointed out.

Sstaal raised his clamp. 'The – the importance of our holy mission is such that the Abbot was able to obtain permission from the Parliament of Seers,' he stammered. 'No interdict can prevent our holy passage.'

McGuire suddenly noticed the Doctor's expression. He was staring at Sstaal, or rather, at Sstaal's backpack. Sstaal and Cleece were both carrying large backpacks, fastened across their chests with two black leather straps. But Sstaal's was different: a large serrated sword with an ornate hilt was strapped to the top.

'So what is a group of pilgrims doing with the Sword of Tuburr?' the Doctor whispered. 'Unless I've mistaken Pilgrim Sstaal's sword for the legendary symbol of the Martian military ethic.' He raised an eyebrow. 'Or has the law forbidding the forging of copies been revoked in the last few years?'

The chamber was about five hundred metres across, with a circular floor enclosed by a hemispherical bowl of similarly polished light brown rock, brightly lit by a knot of fluorescent fungus at its summit. To the left and the right of the doorway, banks of controls were set into the smooth walls; and, from the preponderance of translucent amber inlaid into the metal surface, Rachel immediately recognized the technology responsible – Michael had gone on about it in his letters frequently enough.

Martian.

But the identity of the agency behind the subspace attractor itself wasn't quite as clear as that. The attractor took up an entire quarter of the floor space, a pyramid half-buried in the farthest wall. A pyramid of ancient Egyptian relics.

'Tell me I'm seeing things,' muttered Chris, mirroring her own thoughts. He had walked up to the attractor and was staring at the incongruity. 'Tell me this isn't what it looks like.'

Felice shrugged. 'Come on, is it that unexpected? We know that the Martians had a Sphinx; it's obvious that whatever influenced the ancient Egyptians also influenced the Martians. This is just another example.'

The attractor was basically a glass pyramid with a polished golden frame inscribed with tiny glyphs, although the top third was a solid block of gold. Within the glass walls, there were three levels; like some bizarre museum exhibit, each of the levels was packed with Egyptian artefacts. Rachel recognized statues of the jackal-headed god Anubis, and guessed that some of the others were gods such as Isis and related members of the Egyptian pantheon. There were smaller pyramids, canopic jars, scarab beetles and carvings of hounds, as well as needle-shaped pillars like the one that stood on the banks of the Thames. Rachel doubted that a better collection of Egyptian relics existed outside of the British Museum or the exhibition on the Moon.

'Incredible!' Felice exclaimed, waving a hand around the chamber. 'In subspace terms, this place is so hot you could fry an egg. I never picked up any of this outside. The readings are off the scale – and that's the recalibrated scale.' She turned to Rachel. 'Scratch what you were saying about this having the power to reach across the galaxy, Rachel; this beauty could drop someone off in Andromeda before paying a visit to the next Local Group.'

'But what exactly is it?' asked Chris. 'Is it like your stunnel projector on Charon?'

'Not exactly,' Felice replied. 'On Charon, we could only weaken the boundaries between our dimension and subspace, create an entry and an exit point, and project matter through the tunnel we had created. This is far beyond anything mankind is capable of.' Her voice was reverential, and Rachel didn't blame her. The technology in front of her was at least two centuries beyond their own researches on Charon, and that had been a state of the art installation. The only scientist in the Alliance who ranked above Rachel was her old mentor, Doctor Ketch, the Emeritus Professor at Alpha Centauri; and Gregory had vanished from the scientific arena about the time of the Black Fleet's first attacks on the outer planets.

She nodded. 'From the readings it's giving out, I'd say that it could manipulate the fabric of subspace itself.' She thrust a finger into the simularity that Felice had brought up. 'Look at the level of Higgs's radiation. Creating a stunnel would be child's play to apparatus like this.'

'So what's it doing in a Martian city?' was the obvious question from Chris. 'Lebrun reckoned that they had never developed subspace technology.'

'I think we'd better suspend the discussion,' whispered Felice, nodding towards the doorway. The huge figure of an Ice Warrior stood framed within it, the sonic disruptor attached to its clamp aimed unwaveringly in their direction.

Rachel caught a slight movement to her left, and realized that Chris was reaching for his plasma rifle. She grabbed his arm to stop him.

'If we're going to get any further with this, we need more information. Perhaps the Martians can provide it,' she explained.

Chris snorted. 'And I'm the Empress's handmaiden,' he replied.

Ignoring his odd remark, she stepped forward and addressed the Martian. 'We surrender.'

'That was never in doubt,' it hissed.

Oh well, she thought. Perhaps Chris will look good in a dress.

'You are very well versed in our ways, Doctor,' said the Abbot. 'Pilgrim Sstaal does indeed carry the holy Sword of Tuburr.' Roz tried to tell whether Aklaar was angry or impressed, but the Ice Lord's carefully measured tones revealed nothing.

'And disgraces it with his pacifist ways,' mumbled Cleece breathlessly. Roz was puzzled; weren't these supposed to be that ultimate oxymoron, peaceful Ice Warriors? She wondered whether she was confusing the word pilgrim with pacifist. Why the hell did Benny have to pick this moment to get married, for the Goddess's sake – her knowledge of Martian culture would have proved invaluable in this situation. Normally, Roz would have relied on the Doctor's mental encyclopaedia to furnish her with the information she needed to be one step ahead, but his recent behaviour worried her; since the destruction of the TARDIS, he just wasn't the Time Lord that she had signed up with. She suddenly realized that the Abbot was talking.

'The Sword is the symbol of our warlike past, Doctor, but we are the nucleus of the new future of Mars. We follow the teachings of Oras, not the warrior paths of Ssethiis or Claatris. Our possession of the Sword – and our pilgrimage – marks a new beginning for Mars.'

'Albeit a little late,' he snapped. 'Anyway, why are you heading towards the North Pole?'

'A pilgrimage to the holy lands of Oras,' Sstaal answered hesitantly. Roz couldn't help smiling; stuttering, stammering Ice Warriors weren't exactly common. 'With so many of our brothers and sisters having chosen to seek sanctuary on a far distant world, we have a duty to preserve the faith. By walking in Oras's footsteps, we can renew the vows of all our people, wherever they might be.'

Roz had an idea. Stepping forward, she held her arms out. 'Why don't we join forces? The Martians are familiar with the route we need to take, and we can share our supplies – as far as I know, we can eat one another's food.' She saw the critical looks on some of the others' faces. 'It's the logical solution,' she insisted. 'Without them, our expedition isn't really viable.' She caught McGuire's look and decided that further explanation was desirable. 'There's one more city between here and Vastitas Borealis –'

'G'chun duss Ssethiissi,' interrupted Sstaal. 'The – the Cauldron of Ssethiis.'

'Whatever, the assistance of our Martian... colleagues could prove invaluable.' She looked around at the others, but nobody seemed convinced. She gazed imploringly at the Doctor, but he was staring impassively into the distance. 'Well? What does anybody else think?'

'The question is, why should we pool our resources with you?' asked Aklaar. 'Despite any previous... misunderstandings, Mars is our world. You are the trespassers.'

'We won that bloody war!' shouted McGuire. 'This planet is now part of the Earth Alliance. It's ours!'

Aklaar bowed his head. 'Some might see it that way. Yet some of us took no part in the "war", as you call it. Some of us have always argued for a peaceful accord with our terrestrial neighbours. Can you not see the truth of the path of Oras?'

McGuire stepped up to the Abbot, shaking with anger. 'I don't give a damn about Oras. And I don't give a damn about you!' He held up his fist just inches in front of Aklaar's helmet, but the Abbot didn't flinch. 'You cost me everything I ever cared about, you reptile bastard, everything! You killed my wife and children!' And then it all drained away. Closing his eyes, he turned away. Roz had seen the reaction countless times; people who had carried a hatred around for so long, who had wrapped it in such fantasies of revenge, only to discover that, beneath the wrapping, the hatred no longer existed. People like her, for example, she realized. In all honesty, could she have suggested teaming up with a bunch of aliens before she had met the Doctor?

The Abbot threw his arms open and addressed McGuire's back. 'I see that such prejudice cannot be countered by the wise words of an Abbot of the Order of Oras. If this is your opinion, Antony McGuire, then we will leave you and your associates to your fate, although I should point out that my people have not committed any acts of violence against your people since the end of the war: given your age, it is not possible that your family died at Martian hands.' He locked his hands together in a gesture that Roz took as one of prayer. 'Helping you reach G'chun duss Ssethiissi would bring us the benevolence of Oras, according to our beliefs. But if your personal feelings cannot be put aside, then I wish you all well on your journey. We shall pray for your souls when we encounter your corpses on the return to our seminary. Then again, Antony McGuire, since you believe that your soul died long ago, I shall pray for you now.'

Roz was impressed: an Ice Warrior with a perfect understanding of the human psyche. And McGuire reacted in suitable textbook style.

'I'm, I'm... You have a point, Abbot,' he mumbled. Clearly, the Abbot's penetrating analysis had shaken him badly. Eventually he collected himself and looked round at Santacosta and Madrigal. 'Well, how do you feel about it? Joining forces?'

Madrigal shrugged. 'What have we got to lose?'

'We haven't really got much choice, have we?' Carmen

whimpered. 'I don't like it, but if we're to stand any chance of reaching the Pole . . .'

McGuire stepped forward and tentatively stretched out a hand to the Abbot. Roz could see the effort that this was taking, and she understood it perfectly; only the Doctor's guidance had allowed her to let go of her own prejudices, she realized. She watched as the wizened Abbot's clamp grasped McGuire's hand, a gesture of peace that would have been unimaginable under different circumstances.

A joint expedition to the Martian North Pole, Roz pondered. Ancient Humans and Ancient Martians together, exploring the abandoned cities of Mars; now *that* would have been a honeymoon for Benny! Thinking about her adopted family, she looked over at its paterfamilias. The Doctor was staring into the distance, but his expression was obvious.

He didn't trust the Ice Warriors one little bit.

Interlude

From their command base – a supersaucer that had landed upon and subsequently crushed the insignificant urban collection that the humans had called Luton – the invaders were now monitoring the entire planet. Every signal, every transmission, was intercepted and analysed according to standard invasion strategy, and computer simulations developed to determine any courses of action. The situation on Earth was totally predictable and totally under control.

Resistance levels were high, but that was to be expected; from what they had learnt about the human species, they were brave, tenacious and now desperate. They had developed a large number of colonies throughout this quadrant of the galaxy, and had exhibited character traits that the invaders could understand: subjugate if necessary. In many respects, they were two very similar species. But the invaders did not need rivals.

Once the expanding human Alliance had become a threat to the invaders' own empire, it therefore had to be crushed, as their futile city had been crushed beneath the command saucer. For 10.6 human years, they had watched mankind's fledgling empire before finally determining the optimum time to act: seemingly random attacks which had a complex pattern – generated by the central battle computer – that the humans had missed until it was far too late. The fleet had reached the original star system of humanity without effort and had seized it in an unbreakable grip, ready to rip the heart from mankind's empire and watch it die.

Then the message had arrived: humanity was not the only

intelligent life form in the star system. The inhabitants of the fourth planet had something to offer the invaders, and for such a small price. They offered a power that was centuries beyond that of the invaders, and all they wanted was the return of their home.

The Supreme Council had decided to accept the gift that the Martians offered; with it, they could conquer the galaxy. The puny efforts of mankind's empire would wither and fall as the new masters of space conquered star system after star system without effort.

Whether they subsequently paid their debt to the Martians was another matter, and one that would be decided by the battle computers – it depended upon the future usefulness of the race. All they knew was that they would now have to neutralize Earth's magnetic field in preparation, and that meant extracting the planet's magnetic core.

The human beings on Earth would die as a result, but that was not a problem; the invaders would utilize them for as long as possible and then discard them; such beings made an ideal disposable workforce.

All that mattered was that the Martians deliver the God-Engine to them. After that, the galaxy would belong to the Daleks.

For eternity.

Chapter 6

Rachel, Felice and Chris – their weapons lying behind on the floor, the result of a less than gentle body-search – walked out of the chamber. Two more Martians, waiting outside the door, covered the party with their inbuilt disruptors.

Felice had watched Rachel's efforts to engage them in conversation fall on deaf but cybernetically advanced ears as they were herded from the chamber along the seemingly endless corridor, and began to wonder about this mysterious Michael. He had obviously influenced Rachel's feelings towards Martians, but how, why?

'They're quite impressive, aren't they?' whispered Felice to Chris. 'I've never seen one in the flesh before. Then again, I didn't think that there were any left here any more.' She shrugged. 'Obviously I was wrong.' Then she remembered what Chris had said earlier. 'When you opened the door, you said that a Martian told you how. Have you been to Mars before?'

Chris sighed. 'I have, but it wasn't then. The ones I spent most of the time talking to were really nice people. But then again, they were from some considerable time in the future.'

'You're a time traveller?' Felice found the idea exhilarating; there had been some advances in temporal physics – it was almost a sister science to subspace mechanics – but nothing concrete. Then again, there was always the possibility that Chris was lying. Felice just hoped – for all manner of reasons – that he wasn't. 'I thought you were an Adjudicator.'

'I am. Both, that is. I'm an Adjudicator from the thirtieth century. That's how I knew about the assault on Charon. But please –' his face screwed up into an adorable grimace of pleading, 'please don't ask me anything else. Just my telling you that, I might have totally buggered up my own future.'

The laws of causality were as well known in the twenty-second century as they presumably were in the thirtieth; and Felice had no desire to see her gorgeous Chris fade away into a time paradox. 'Fair enough. But answer me just one thing: do you know what's going to happen here?'

Chris shook his head. 'Truth be known, Felice . . . I don't think we were ever meant to be here.'

Felice suddenly felt all goosepimply as the hidden meaning in Chris's words sank in. If they were never meant to be on Mars, well, were they ever meant to have survived the destruction of Charon? Changing the subject to something more mutually comfortable, she continued. 'Do you think they're going to kill us?' It was a pity that she had to change the subject to something just as gruesome, though.

Shrugging, Chris nodded towards the Martian in front of them. 'The Ice Warriors – that's what we occasionally call them; it's a bit more polite than Greenie – the Ice Warriors of this century are a pretty brutal lot. But whether they'd shoot us on sight . . . They're extremely proud of their caste system, Felice. In a military nest, you've got the grunts – like this lot – the senior grunts, the Lords, and a Grand Marshal. And sometimes a Queen, but she tends to manipulate from behind the scenes. And lay eggs.'

Felice was impressed. She began to wonder about how useful he was going to be to them. 'So these grunts can't do anything without the say-so of the head grunt, then?'

Chris shrugged. 'The chances of this place meriting a Grand Marshal, given the current state of the planet, are remote – especially since most of them were executed after the War, apparently. And this might not even be a military nest: it could be a civilian one. Sometimes it's difficult to tell them apart.'

Rachel, obviously tired of her failure to communicate with the Martians, slowed down to allow them to catch up.

'Nothing, I'm afraid – still, it was worth a try. Anyway, this is all rather unexpected, isn't it?' she asked. 'What I wouldn't give to look at the design specs of that attractor.'

Felice found herself slipping back into scientist mode. 'You and me both, Rachel. I haven't read a single theory which could account for the radiation levels coming from that, that thing – what's the power source, for one thing? The most energetic reaction I know of is orders of magnitude below this! Then again, there's Lebrun's claim . . .'

'That the Martians never developed subspace technology?' Rachel shook her head. 'If they didn't, who did? And the fact that we're being frog-marched to God-knows-where by a bunch of Martians does tend to put the icing on the cake, doesn't it?'

Felice looked at their escorts and felt a shudder of nervousness. 'For once, Rachel, I'm totally in agreement with you.'

The Doctor was scurrying around the Martian dwelling, looking for the various rucksacks and holdalls that contained their supplies, when Roz entered.

'Busy?'

He didn't look up. 'The others are busy. I am preoccupied.'

'You don't like this idea, do you?' she said, picking up a flashlight which had rolled under the bed. 'If I didn't know you better, I'd swear that you think that the only good Ice Warrior is a dead Ice Warrior. But xenophobia's my province, isn't it?' That's it, Roz; be provocative.

He stood up and gave her an indecipherable look. 'Xenophobia is an irrational hatred of alien life forms. At this point in time, I have never felt more rational. I just don't trust them. One day, far in the future, they will become valuable members of the Galactic Federation. But now, in the twenty-second century, they have just lost a futile and pointless war with mankind.'

'The pilgrims seem happy to team up with us.' Roz was feeling more than slightly put out; after her self-satisfaction at actually being the one who suggested the inter-racial expedition, the Doctor's obvious unease was unsettling – and disappointing.

He knitted his brows. 'Logic dictates that we join forces with the Ice Warriors. Logic dictates that they are pilgrims, not warriors.' He paused then said, 'So who killed Vincente?'

Roz knew that he had a point. 'You, me, McGuire, Madrigal, Carmen, the Ice Pilgrims, or some other party. That sums it up.'

'Spoken like a true Adjudicator,' he murmured, and she wasn't sure whether he was being insulting or not. 'Well, you can rule two of those out straightaway, can't you?' But the way that he said it, it didn't sound like a rhetorical question.

'I'll assume that you mean me and you. That leaves McGuire, who had no motive – and the idea that he could overpower Vincente is rather far-fetched; Carmen – well, I won't waste my breath on her, and Madrigal.' She thought for a second before continuing. 'Madrigal is a Colonial Marine; she could have killed him without breaking into a sweat. What do you think?'

The Doctor hoisted the rucksack over his shoulders. 'I think we should continue the expedition. Vincente died for a reason; the longer we draw this out, the more likely it becomes that the murderer will show his hand.'

'Or his clamp?'

The Doctor gave her a wounding stare. 'Come along, Roz; we don't want them to set off without us, do we?'

Roz picked up her own rucksack and watched as the Doctor walked through the door. For the first time in ages, she realized exactly how alien he really was, and it wasn't a feeling that she relished.

'We're on Mars, we're surrounded by Ice Warriors, and the TARDIS has been destroyed. Business as usual, I suppose?' she shouted after him. But his retreating back was mute.

After ushering them through an impressive set of huge bronze doors, the Ice Warriors followed, striding over to the sides of the room in some kind of honour guard position. Room? – no, definitely a chamber, Chris decided. Actually, room didn't seem to do justice to any of the Martian structures they had seen; the Ice Warriors obviously built as they lived: grandiose and overstated, full of pomp and ceremony. They didn't have rooms, they had chambers, amphitheatres, halls and throne-rooms.

This chamber was no different; about two hundred metres wide, the floors, walls and ceiling were of the ubiquitous amber rock. Bright tapestries hung on the walls, tapestries of battles and conquests. Chris frowned; although that suggested a military nest, he knew that even the religious caste took some pride in their military history, so he was still none the wiser. They had been shown to the front of the chamber, standing before a big stone table made of what seemed to be black marble, with a throne-like chair behind it.

A door suddenly opened with a slight grating noise; locating the source, Chris watched as a slab of rock slid back in the farthest wall.

Two more Ice Warriors stepped through. Then Chris corrected himself. These weren't common or garden grunts; they were members of the Martian aristocracy. The one on the left wore the smaller armour – more of a green tabard, really – and smooth helmet of a Lord. But the other . . . His armour was considerably more ornate, a light purple in colour inset with gold. And, centred on his chest, was an embossed representation of the face of the Martian Sphinx. The shoulders of the body armour were distinguished by two sets of three gold arches, and a third set of arches graced the metallic violet and gold helmet. The entire ensemble was finished off with a voluminous cloak, so dark a purple that it was almost black.

The ceremonial armour of a Supreme Grand Marshal, one of the eight ultimate rulers of Mars. And, presumably, one of the two Marshals who had escaped execution at the end of the Thousand Day War.

'Welcome to G'chun duss Ssethiissi,' said the Grand Marshal. 'I am Supreme Grand Marshal Falaxyr-Ett-Halat, and this is my adjutant, Supreme Lord Draan-Utt-Slaar.' He gestured to the other with a clamp. 'Your arrival here was something of a surprise.'

Chris stepped forward. Given the Grand Marshal's terms of address, his reply required full name and title to prevent offence. 'Adjudicator Christopher Rodamonte Cwej, Professor Rachel Jean Anders and Dr Felice Rebecca Delacroix,' he stated, and then wondered whether he had done the right thing. He had given their full names and titles because Martian culture respected that, and he was trying to ingratiate himself and the two scientists. Too late, he realized that he had admitted that he was an Adjudicator – the bloody skirmishes between the then Bureau of Adjudicators and certain Martian factions in the twenty-first and twenty-second century were required learning on Ponten IV – and betrayed the others' scientific expertise. Still, tradition – Martian tradition – meant that he had to identify them all. 'We meant no disrespect at our trespass, Your Excellency.' A slightly blurry memory of a particular midnight drinking session with Benny came to mind; the topic had been the correct terms of address for Martian rulers. Funny; he never thought it would come in useful. Especially after the hangover. Was he always going to associate Martians with alcohol, he wondered.

'We are the only survivors of an attack by the invaders,' Rachel began. 'We attempted to escape the destruction of Charon in a stunnel.' Chris barely suppressed a groan – that was one thing he hadn't intended for them to give away – yet. Still, Rachel had told them, and it was too late now. She continued, and Chris just hoped that she didn't get them any deeper into it. 'The stunnel was aimed beyond the blockade, but an equipment malfunction brought us here.' Chris was slightly relieved; a succinct summing up that hadn't given away the presence of the other survivors – although Rachel had given virtually everything else away.

Falaxyr nodded gravely. 'These are desperate times, Adjudicator Cwej. We suspect that the party responsible for the invasion of Earth will soon mount an attack on Mars, and we are currently preparing to leave this planet for the Nova Martia colony. Such an exercise must be carefully planned and executed in order to escape the blockade, and the entire nest is now busy with the preparations. Of course, you are welcome to enjoy our hospitality until we are ready to leave;

we will then make arrangements for your safe return to one of the human colonies on Mars.'

Chris wasn't reassured by the Marshal's friendly manner in the slightest; the whole thing stank of a trap. But they weren't exactly in a strong position to argue, were they?

'That is most . . . kind of you, Your Excellency.'

'*Professor* and . . . *Doctor* are terms of scientific expertise, are they not?' asked Draan. Chris was puzzled; there was a belligerence in the Ice Lord's voice that was uncalled for. 'In which fields are you competent?'

'We're all subspace engineers, My Lord,' said Rachel. Chris was impressed by her knowledge of Martian culture. 'We were members of the Charon subspace research team until the colony was destroyed.'

'Subspace. Fascinating,' hissed Falaxyr. 'Perhaps – after you have rested, of course – you might care to discuss the subject with our own scientists?' And that sounded more like an order than a request.

Rachel gave Chris a sideways, questioning look, and he nodded slightly, allowing her to continue. She smiled at the Grand Marshal. 'I'd be more than happy to.' Not that they had much choice.

'Excellent,' said Falaxyr, folding his arms across his armoured chest plate. 'Then my personal guard will escort the four of you to somewhere more comfortable. I look forward to talking further when time permits. Meanwhile, please enjoy your resting place.'

With that, the Ice Warrior guards led them from the chamber. Chris was even more concerned than ever; the Martians were in possession of a subspace manipulator beyond anything his resident experts had ever seen, and Falaxyr seemed rather too keen to talk about subspace with Rachel and Felice.

They were being set up, Chris decided grimly. He just hoped that he could put them all in a better position to fight back before the jaws of the trap sprang shut. Not for the first time, he wished that the Doctor was around.

The abandoned city of Ikk-ett-Saleth was now many

kilometres behind them, its secrets safe once more. The party of humans and Martians had left the city through a hidden passage revealed to them by the Abbot, who had warned them that the more obvious exit that the party probably would have taken would have sent them on a one-way trip to the molten core of the planet – Roz wasn't impressed by Martian hospitality, given the trap they had faced upon reaching the city as well. They were currently passing through a cramped service tunnel heading north; Aklaar claimed that this was the most direct route to the next city they would need to enter on their journey to the Pole.

The atmosphere was one of nervous co-operation; two species, held apart by mutual distrust, forced together by a common need. So it wasn't any surprise that the level of conversation between Martian and human – or Martian and Time Lord, come to that – was restrained to the odd platitude and grunt.

After about four hours of this irritating, unbroken uneasiness, Santacosta decided to throw another meaningless question onto the fire in her normal annoying manner. 'How long before we reach the North Pole?'

Roz shrugged. Although her tolerance level was now strong enough to allow her to stomach the woman, she had no intention of getting pally. Unfortunately, it looked like the nightclub singer had singled her out as her special friend on the trek. 'About two days, according to the Doctor. One more city, and then a direct route straight to the Pole.' And she had stopped just short of thumbscrews to get that information out of the increasingly taciturn Doctor. His attitude just seemed to be getting worse and worse. He was currently walking at the head of the party, but there didn't seem to be very much inconsequential chit-chat going on between him and Aklaar. As far as Roz was concerned, they looked like two ancient old Guild Interlocutors, leading the Adjudicator acolytes to prayer.

For one horrible moment, Roz wondered whether the strain of recent events was actually getting to the Doctor. Despite all that she knew he was capable of – manipulating entire cultures before breakfast, that kind of thing – she found it hard to reconcile that Doctor with the almost paranoid one at the head of the party. Had the destruction of the TARDIS been the final straw; was he cracking up on them? She sighed; even if he was, there was absolutely nothing that she could do about it.

'Two days,' Santacosta whined. 'This is the most exercise I've done in years, Roslyn. I could have been relaxing in a jacuzzi in a private suite in Jacksonville if that blasted shuttle hadn't come down.'

I don't doubt it, thought Roz. Then again, I could have been sunbathing in the arboretum if the TARDIS hadn't blown up.

'Fascinating,' muttered the Doctor suddenly from up ahead, giving Roz the perfect excuse to increase her stride and catch up with him. And escape from Santacosta.

'What is?' She had decided to seize any chance to engage him in conversation; anything was better than his furious silence.

He waved his hands at the tunnel walls. They were grey, and lacked the sonically carved smoothness of everywhere else. Indeed, the surface looked gouged. Not that she would have noticed; geology was not her strong point. 'This rock should be rich with trisilicate,' he explained.

'And it's not?' Geology was definitely not her strong point. She knew of trisilicate, but that was about all.

'Look at the irregularities; the veins have been mined.' He turned to the Abbot. 'Any idea why, Abbot Aklaar?'

The Abbot shook his head. 'Something to do with the war effort, perhaps?' But his voice was hesitant, unsure . . . From the look on the Doctor's face, he obviously thought so as well.

'Whatever the reason,' he said with an arched eyebrow aimed towards the Abbot, 'it's a fascinating discovery, Roz; it looks like somebody has strip-mined all of the trisilicate from these tunnels.'

'Is that important?' Obviously it was, but given the Doctor's current reticence to engage in conversation, such questions were necessary, just to keep him talking.

The Doctor shrugged. 'All Martian technology is based on

trisilicate, in the same way that twenty-first-century Earth relied almost exclusively on silicon and germanium. I suppose that it could have been something to do with the war, and yet . . .' He frowned. 'To remove this amount of trisilicate would take well over a thousand days. Although some of the surface degradation of the rock is consistent with the time of the Thousand Day War, the rest suggests that it was mined much more recently. Why would the Martians need so much trisilicate in the last few years?'

'The exodus?'

'No, Roz; the majority of the population would have left well before most of this mining took place.' He tapped his nose. 'Oh well, a mystery for another time. Eh, Abbot?' he finished pointedly.

The Martian's expression was inscrutable, but that wasn't surprising given that most of his face was covered by his helmet. Even so, Roz felt certain that the Doctor had touched a raw nerve.

A sudden groan made Roz turn round. Esstar had stopped, and was leaning against the rough wall, doubled up in pain. Her clamps were pressed against her lower stomach. Surprisingly, Santacosta was next to her, offering support by putting her arm around the shoulders of Esstar's green carapace.

'What's wrong back there?' asked McGuire, stopping the party.

'It is nothing,' wheezed Esstar. 'I am experiencing a little . . . discomfort. It will pass in a few minutes,' she hissed, clearly in agony.

'Well, make sure it does,' snapped McGuire without sympathy. 'We haven't got time to waste on sick Greenies.' Suddenly, Cleece's clamp was on the human's shoulder.

'She is my intended mate and the future mother of my clutch, McGuire. If she is in pain, then we should wait.'

McGuire ran a hand through his thinning grey hair. 'Mother of your clutch?' he said softly, shaking his head. 'You're saying that she's pregnant?' He grunted. 'That's all we need. Little Greenie sprogs.'

Uh oh, thought Roz. She glanced at the Doctor, but his face was impassive. McGuire blamed the Ice Warriors for the death of his wife and children; discovering that one of the party was preparing to give birth to a new generation of Martians probably wasn't the best news that he could have received.

Cleece raised his voice in pride. 'Our clutch will be born in G'chun duss Ssethiissi – the first of a new era for our race, the first of many. The few of us who remain on Mars seek a new direction, and they shall be the vanguard.' Noble words, but Roz just didn't believe them. Cleece lacked the – the spirituality, for want of a better word, that the other three pilgrims virtually radiated. In its place was the barely caged belligerence that she associated with the Warrior caste.

'Then we'll leave her here,' snapped McGuire. 'If she wants to lay her eggs, then let her. We're not running a bloody nursemaid service.' McGuire looked at Cleece. 'And if you want to stay with your brood mare, then that's fine by me.'

The Pilgrim's reaction was immediate: he grabbed McGuire round the throat with his other clamp. 'Your disrespect is becoming irritating, vermin. I should tear your spindly carcass apart and leave the pieces here as an example.' As McGuire's flashlight clattered to the floor, the Doctor and the Abbot moved in to separate them. As far as Roz was concerned, it was nothing more than a display of machismo, and she actually found it rather amusing.

She turned her attention from the macho posturing and looked at the female Ice Warrior. Esstar was clearly feeling a lot better, but what she was saying to Santacosta was extremely interesting. And worrying.

'Your assistance is most welcome, Carmen. Far more welcome than the misdirected concern of others.' And then she stared at Cleece. 'I need no assistance to continue the holy pilgrimage.'

Perhaps Cleece and Esstar weren't exactly a match made in heaven. And then Roz caught the subsequent exchange between Esstar and little Sstaal. Oh dear, she realized, a Martian love triangle; just the sort of thing to make the expedition go with a bang. Literally.

Looking around, she was pleased to see that Aklaar and the

Doctor had somehow managed to persuade Cleece to release McGuire, but the result was going to be an atmosphere that could only get worse. Could they manage another two days without tearing one another apart?

And then she caught a movement some fifty metres in front of them, in a direction in which only she was looking. In the distant dimness of the tunnel, she could have sworn that the familiar shape of a blue police box, its roof light blinking, was caught in the light of McGuire's discarded torch. As she watched, the hovering TARDIS floated through the wall and vanished.

Another ghostly TARDIS? The first she had dismissed as fevered imaginings on the verge of sleep, but this one? Did dead TARDISes rise like the phoenix, or was this connected with the Martian North Pole?

With such concerns nagging at her, she and Carmen helped a recovering Esstar to her feet. Roz knew that she ought to ask the Doctor about it, but she decided to wait until he was in a better mood. If ever.

Chris's eyes carefully scanned the route from the Grand Marshal's chambers to their 'resting place' – couldn't Falaxyr have chosen his words more carefully? – with all of his fledgling Adjudicator skills, creating a vivid mental map of the Martian base. If they were walking into a trap, he needed to know every last hiding place and possible chance of concealment; he wanted to memorize the layout so that he could later determine the best location to draw the Ice Warriors into an ambush. He also wanted to work out the relative positions of the rooms he had seen so that he stood the best chance of leading them back to the others in the abandoned parliament.

He was relieved that the other two were making his task easier by staying quiet, giving him a chance to think things out before they arrived. But arrived where? Chris didn't trust Falaxyr or Draan in the slightest; underneath their almost philanthropic words lay the battle-hardened Martian psyche that Chris had learnt about in school history lessons and – more entertainingly – from Benny. Because, despite his friendliness, Falaxyr was a Grand Marshal, which meant that they were in a military nest.

The idea that a military nest would offer them shelter out of the goodness of their hearts was as alien as the Ice Warriors themselves. And just as dangerous.

Chris noted that they had descended a sloping walkway to a lower level. The corridors were narrower, the lighting less intense, and he got the feeling that they were approaching their 'resting place'. That made him uneasy. Even the knowledge that Rachel and Felice might prove useful to the Ice Warriors wasn't that reassuring; with their skills in subspace engineering, they might be, but Chris – an admitted Adjudicator – couldn't be anything but a threat. He needed time to formulate a plan of action, but he doubted that the Ice Warriors would be so accommodating.

They came to a halt. 'Here,' hissed the lead Ice Warrior, pointing a clamp at a grey square door set in the rock. 'You will rest here until the Grand Marshal demands to see you.' Bashing the door with his forearm, the Martian stepped back as the door swung inwards. Shrugging, Chris took the lead.

The room was well lit and – in contrast with the rest of the rock-carved base – artificial. The walls, floor and ceiling were interlocking white sheets of some kind of heavy-duty polymer, and strangely lacking in the usual illustrations of war and conquest. Eight low cots were arranged against the farthest wall, but there was something not quite right about them...

As the Ice Warrior pulled the door closed, Chris walked over to the row of beds and threw his backpack down. 'Everybody all right?'

'They don't seem so bad,' added Felice, slipping out of the thick jacket that she had been wearing over her jump-suit. 'I was expecting... well, I don't know what I was expecting. I definitely wasn't expecting to be treated like a houseguest.'

Chris put a finger to his lips before reaching into his pocket and retrieving a small grey orb. Standard Adjudicator kit – a bug-catcher. He aimed it around the room in wide, sweeping arcs, listening for the bleeps that would reveal that their hosts were watching their every move, listening to every word. A sudden chime from the orb confirmed what he had already suspected: they were being bugged. He pressed another contact on the device, and placed it on the table.

'There, that should jam the surveillance devices, although I suggest that we still watch what we say.'

'What do you think we've been doing?' said Rachel, sitting down on the edge of one of the cots.

'You let slip about the stunnel,' said Chris.

Felice frowned. 'Is that important?'

'It's obvious now that the Ice Warriors are the ones behind the subspace manipulator. How coincidental that a couple of subspace engineers just drop in.'

'You think that they deliberately brought us here?' Then she groaned. 'Of course they did. They must have been waiting for us to generate a stunnel; as soon as we did they grabbed it.'

'Anyone mind if I have a quick nap?' asked Felice. 'I don't know about you, but I'm exhausted.' She lay back on the bed – and that was when Chris realized what had been staring him in the face: the cots were far too small for Martian use, a clear indication that they were meant for humans.

More proof that Falaxyr had been expecting visitors – human visitors.

'Then this is a trap,' stated Rachel. 'Either that, or they were pretty desperate for company.' She shook her head. 'Come on then, Adjudicator; what's the plan?'

'I need just a bit more time,' he said evasively. He considered their options. Falaxyr wouldn't have had them taken to quarters so far away from his chambers – or the subspace manipulator – if he had an immediate need for them, so it was fairly safe to assume that they had at least a couple of hours before they were disturbed – unless, of course, their hosts took umbrage at Chris's jamming their surveillance devices.

He began unpacking the rucksack onto one of the beds, hoping that it contained something that might prove useful. Without their plasma rifles, they were unarmed; even Chris didn't know how to turn a flashlight into a directed energy weapon. He pulled out a small white box: the first-aid kit that the Doctor had thrust into his hands just before the

TARDIS had been destroyed. Although he couldn't really see how dermal patches and headache tablets could help them out of this situation, he might be able to make some sort of explosive if there were any useful chemicals inside. He opened the box.

Chris whistled through his teeth as he examined the contents of the kit. If this was the Doctor's idea of first aid, he had a very weird bedside manner. With renewed hope, he began an inventory.

Falaxyr stood in front of the holographic cylinder, waiting impatiently for his allies to respond. Despite the usefulness of the alliance, the Grand Marshal hated to be kept waiting; military success depended upon precision timing, and he found it hard to believe that the new masters of Earth had managed to carve out an empire when they couldn't even reply to an urgent communiqué promptly.

The cylinder suddenly began to sparkle.

'Incoming transmission from Earth, Your Excellency,' said the technician redundantly. And then, without needing to be told, he stepped away from the control panel and left the communications suite.

The image resolved, and Falaxyr stared at the holographic form of his ally.

'Report,' it intoned.

Falaxyr repressed a sigh of irritation. Even when he made the first move, the invaders always took the credit. If the stakes weren't so high, he would have dissolved the alliance months ago. Unfortunately, Falaxyr needed them – for the time being, that was.

'My technical staff report that the *Ssor-arr duss Ssethissi* approaches completion, Commander.' No such report existed; the device was little closer to becoming operational than it had been when Falaxyr had first contacted the invaders a year ago. But the Grand Marshal knew the importance of keeping his allies interested; and besides, the presence of the human scientists made true completion of the *Ssor-arr duss Ssethissi* a very real possibility. He decided to take a calculated risk.

'At the current rate of progress, Commander, the *Ssor-arr*

duss Ssethissi will be operational in less than a year.'

The Commander stared back impassively from the cylinder. 'Progress reports are of no value, Grand Marshal. Your excuses and delays are irrelevant. Our only concern is the GodEngine. Unless you fulfil your obligations, it will be necessary for us to oversee the project directly.'

The cylinder emptied, leaving only the threat behind. Falaxyr shook his head. These invaders lacked the passion for war; they were soulless machine creatures whose conquest of the galaxy was due to nothing more than a set of logical imperatives. The GodEngine – a cold, unfeeling translation of *Ssor-arr duss Ssethissi* – was nothing more than a single equation in the positronic net of their battle computer. There had been no threat from the Commander, only a statement of fact. Unless Falaxyr could present them with a demonstration of the GodEngine, they would annex Mars without hesitation.

His mood growing fouler by the second, Falaxyr left the communications suite, his purple robes sweeping behind him. Until recently, he had left the day-to-day management of the technicians to his adjutant, Draan, deciding that such matters were beneath a Grand Marshal of the Eight-Point Table. But the remarkable lack of progress had finally prompted Falaxyr to take action.

According to Hoorg, the lead scientist on the project, the GodEngine should have been operational six months ago. Unfortunately, he lacked the knowledge of subspace engineering necessary to locate the exact reason why this was not actually true, and Falaxyr couldn't really blame him. Mars had only started pursuing subspace technology in earnest when they realized that their lack of it put them at a strategic disadvantage compared with the humans. As thousands of troops poured onto the surface of Mars through subspace Transit tunnels from Earth, the Eight-Point Table had sequestered the cream of the Martian intelligentsia and set them to work at the North Pole, where ancient alien technology offered a possible solution.

Unfortunately, the war had ended in defeat before the *Ssor-arr duss Ssethissi* could be completed – indeed, before it could really be started – and the majority of the scientific elite had subsequently been reassigned to the exodus project. When Falaxyr had gone into hiding, he had only been able to take a handful of scientists with him.

Over the last seventy years, the collection of scientists – overseen by Falaxyr and bullied by Draan – had obeyed the Eight-Point Table's last direct order. Despite the conquest of Mars, despite the exodus to Nova Martia, the GodEngine was still to be completed. Because, once operational, it would finally give the Martians the bargaining power they had lost when humankind had raped their world.

The opportunity had finally presented itself in the form of the invaders. They were willing to pay highly for the use of the GodEngine, and that payment would justify the seven decades of isolation.

Unfortunately, they wanted a fully functional GodEngine, not the temperamental and unreliable device that was all that Falaxyr had to show for seventy years' work. It was clear that Falaxyr needed external help; and the presence of the invaders on Earth and their subspace blockade made this somewhat problematical.

And then, some months ago, Hoorg had detected subspace emissions from the moon of distant Pluto. Falaxyr consulted his intelligence reports and was pleasantly surprised to discover that Charon housed a research base, the last bastion of subspace technology in a solar system which had all but abandoned the idea. From the readings, Hoorg suggested that the base was attempting to bore a stunnel through the invaders' jamming field. And then Hoorg had made another suggestion. Under other circumstances, Falaxyr would have had him disciplined for not following the normal chain of command, but the suggestion was a remarkable one.

The jamming field was extremely effective, but posed no hindrance whatsoever to the unparalleled might of the GodEngine. And although the device wasn't fully operational, it would still act as a powerful subspace attractor. And so Falaxyr had given his orders.

When the scientists had made their final – and finally successful – attempt to breach the blockade (and Falaxyr had ensured that they did by informing the invaders of the continued presence of humans on Charon; the invaders' response had been immediate and totally predictable) the GodEngine had been more than capable of seizing the stunnel and dragging the end-point to Mars. It hadn't taken long for the survivors of Charon to make their presence known to Falaxyr, and their obvious interest in the GodEngine was a direct vindication of his plan. His thin lips formed a cruel smile.

As the Grand Marshal entered the GodEngine Chamber, his mood was far more positive than it had been earlier. Despite the incompetence of his own scientific staff, it looked like the two Earth women would deliver the GodEngine to him. Which, considering the reason why the Daleks wanted the GodEngine, was the ultimate irony.

Chapter 7

Aklaar held up his clamps to stop the party, although that wasn't really necessary: they were approaching a solid rock face which McGuire suspected was another bloody irritating trap. The idea that they could only reach the North Pole with the Greenies' help was gnawing at him, although not as much as he would have thought. 'What's the problem now?' he groaned. The corridor had no other obvious means of passage, although 'obvious' was not a word he associated with Martians – they were too damned secretive for their own good.

The Abbot gestured to the face, a barrier of blurred and molten rock that was obviously artificial. It wasn't completely unbroken: there was a large plug of the same material set into it. 'Can any of you identify this?' The question was obviously aimed at his pilgrims, but it was the Doctor who answered.

'*Utt-keth-Johith*, perhaps?' he said in a bored tone. Not for the first time, McGuire found himself confused by the Doctor; the man possessed an encyclopaedic familiarity of Martian culture, and yet he seemed to view them with almost as much distrust than McGuire did.

Aklaar nodded. 'Once more, I am impressed by your knowledge, Doctor. For those unfamiliar with the High Tongue, this is a Plague Seal. The city of Sstee-ett-Haspar – the Labyrinth of False Pride – has been cut off to prevent further infection.'

Sstaal stepped forward and examined the molten rock, paying special attention to a small carved glyph in the centre.

'Our information was correct, Lord Abbot; the city was sealed over five centuries ago,' he explained hesitantly. 'An outbreak of sleeping fever.'

'Oh, great!' snapped McGuire. 'Your bloody traps weren't bad enough, were they? Now we've got to expose ourselves to some Greenie disease.'

'Is it catching?' asked Carmen.

Aklaar sighed. 'Sleeping fever is a purely Martian infection, Miss Santacosta. Even if the disease were still virulent, it would pose no threat to your kind. But fever is not the problem.'

'After five centuries, the disease will have died out completely,' explained Cleece. 'Our geneticists chose sleeping fever as the basis for many bacteriological weapons because it burns itself out in less than a decade, leaving the city intact but uninhabited.'

'Chose?' Roz was frowning. 'Are you saying that this city was the target of germ warfare?'

McGuire felt something hard tightening in his stomach at yet another example of the Martian obsession with death and killing. Then the female Greenie stepped forward.

'Once again, Pilgrim Cleece's fixation with our race's military exploits both confuses and confounds,' explained Esstar. 'Cleece refers to such events as the bacteriological attack on the Dwellings of Triumphant Majesty, over a hundred thousand years ago. He wishes that he could have been there,' she added, her tone making it quite clear that she wished he had been there as well. 'The sleeping fever still occurs naturally, despite the Warrior caste's attempts to subvert it for their own purposes. This benighted city is an example of the harshness of nature.'

'You knew it was sealed, then?' asked McGuire.

'Naturally,' replied Aklaar. 'I would never have begun the pilgrimage without careful preparation.'

McGuire turned to the Doctor. 'So why didn't your map show it?'

The Doctor shrugged. 'It's a very old map, Mr McGuire. Anyway, I would wager that the Abbot here has a solution. Don't you, Aklaar?'

'We can enter the city,' agreed the Abbot. 'However, although there is no risk of disease – to either of our races – there will undoubtedly be other hazards to face. After five hundred years, the city will have partially reverted to wilderness – without Martian habitation to keep it tamed, it will undoubtedly have proved an ideal location for some of the less friendly native flora and fauna.'

'Since we are so far north,' said Sstaal, 'the most dangerous threat will be the rock-snakes. Our body armour will provide defence from their vicious attacks, but you do not have such protection.'

Madrigal hefted her plasma rifle. 'Rock-snakes? No problem.'

'And what about venom-moss?' the Doctor pointed out. 'Or spider-lizards? Or those metre-wide amoebae that secrete sulphuric acid?' He seemed to delight in pointing out how inhospitable the Martians' home planet was, as if it were their fault.

'Venom-moss is confined to the southern hemisphere of this planet, Doctor, and the plasma vampires are all but extinct. We may encounter the odd spider-lizard, but they are timid, reluctant creatures.' Aklaar turned to the rock face.

McGuire watched as Cleece and Sstaal started pushing the Seal, but not inwards; they were trying to rotate it. McGuire realized that the Seal was a screw, plugging the entrance to the city. As he waited, the plug turned in its socket and retreated until it finally toppled backwards with a thump of stone on stone. Only gloom awaited them beyond the open doorway.

Cleece aimed his clamp at the doorway and clenched it. A warbling noise was followed by a dull explosion as the remains of something grey and nasty flopped from the lip of the entrance and landed on the floor. About a metre long, what was left of its body appeared to consist of spherical grey boulders linked together, with a scorpion-like sting at one end.

'A rock-snake,' said the Doctor, poking the smouldering remains with his umbrella. 'How fortunate that you were armed, *Pilgrim* Cleece.' The meaning behind the Doctor's words was obvious to McGuire: these were pilgrims; so why was one of them armed with a sonic disruptor?

Aklaar raised a clamp. 'We are all pilgrims in the sight of Oras, but it would be a foolish pilgrim who set off into hostile territory unarmed,' he explained, clearly understanding the Doctor's tone. 'Given the warrior heritage that Cleece embraces, he was chosen to bear weapons.' He pointed towards Madrigal. 'You have your own warrior, do you not?'

McGuire wasn't happy, but he saw the reasoning behind it. 'Madrigal, Cleece; you lead. Blast anything that moves.' His only information about rock-snakes came from holovid documentaries, but he knew that they were vicious – one blast could take out a man's chest. 'I'll follow behind, if you'll be so kind as to reach into your bag of weapons and get one for me.'

Madrigal grunted, and pulled out a plasma repeater. 'You'll need this, McGuire; a thousand pulses per second. You'll hardly need to aim it.' She thrust the heavy black gun into his hands. He hefted it, trying to get the balance right.

Aklaar folded his arms across his chest in prayer. 'The Labyrinth of Lost Pride is the last obstacle before we reach the holy ground of G'chun duss Ssethiissi; may the beneficence of Oras guide the weapons of Cleece, Madrigal and McGuire as we approach our destination.'

As the Abbot continued to pray, McGuire felt a small tremor of unease. A childhood of strict Catholicism under the Order of Saint Anthony had moulded him into a proper God-fearing adult, giving him a moral framework and a knowledge of right and wrong that had directed him through adolescence, marriage and parenthood. But then the Greenies had struck, ripping his soul apart as easily as they had ripped apart the rail network. The resulting emptiness had eventually become endurable, but it was still there. A void.

And yet, as McGuire listened to the old Martian praying to his god, his cracked voice strident with belief, he found himself tentatively reaching into himself, probing for that void.

Somehow, for some reason . . . it was smaller.

* * *

Rachel wandered round the perimeter of their room, exhausted but afraid to stand still. Perhaps a moving target would prove more difficult to hit. It was obvious that the Ice Warriors were keeping them for a purpose; from what Michael had told her, military nests tended to react towards trespassers with brutal efficiency. They didn't put them up for the night in guest quarters. Until now.

One didn't have to be a genius to work out what was going on, even though she was. She and Felice were subspace engineers, and the Martians had a subspace manipulator in the basement. Logic suggested that it wasn't fully operational, otherwise they wouldn't have shown such obvious avarice towards her and Felice's talents – indeed, they would have used it against Earth or the invaders before now. Even without knowing its full capabilities, Rachel could envisage the effects of wide-scale subspace manipulation: grabbing a ship and changing its course would be easy – it was simply a matter of twisting the subspace striations into another direction; that same ship hitting Earth at lightspeed would be as devastating as the asteroid which had wiped out the dinosaurs.

So the Martians needed Rachel and Felice's assistance, and she doubted that they would have much choice in the matter. She looked at the others: Felice was helping Chris with what looked like a map of the base. What was Rachel doing to assist in their escape attempt? She was making herself extremely useful by pacing around the room. Hmmm. She began to smile at the absurdity of the situation, but a noise behind her made her turn. The door was swinging inwards.

She swallowed; somehow, she had thought that they would have had a little more time. And then she frowned; the Ice Warrior that walked into the room wasn't empty-handed, but he wasn't wielding a sonic disruptor in their direction, either. He was carrying a large tray of food.

'The Grand Marshal hopes you are comfortable,' he said, obviously not at all comfortable with being so – so pleasant to humans. 'He asks that you eat, sleep and rest.' With that, he deposited the tray on a side table and lumbered out of the door, which started to close behind him.

'Room service? It gets worse,' said Felice as the door clanged shut.

Chris got up and examined the food. There were twelve small bowls, three for each of them: four bowls contained a mushy, green, rice-like substance mixed with some grey herb; another four held some sort of braised root vegetable, gnarled orange stumps with white blotches; and the others were full of a thick yellow broth full of disturbing brown lumps.

'A healthy vegetarian diet,' muttered Felice, standing next to him. 'I suppose we're lucky that we didn't get raw meat and buckets of blood.'

'The Ice Warriors are vegetarians,' Rachel pointed out. 'Despite all the myths about their eating babies during the Thousand Day War.' Michael had told her of his amazement over the wide range of native vegetables, and the versatility of Martian cooking. Indeed, Martian chefs were highly prized in the caste structure. So it was with some regret that she looked at Chris. 'I may be starving, but I'm not convinced that this is healthy.'

'They've poisoned it?' asked Felice.

'It's probably drugged,' Chris agreed. 'Which means that they'll probably come for us – well, you and Rachel, anyway – in a few hours, when they think it's taken effect. We'll have to be ready.'

'Ready?' snapped Rachel. 'Ready in what way, Chris? We've already been here for over two hours, and you haven't been exactly forthcoming with a plan.' As Adjudicators went, Chris wasn't the most dynamic she had ever met. Then again, she hadn't met that many; the 'ravens' of the Adjudication Bureau were an aloof lot.

'That's because I was waiting. And that's what we're going to do; wait.' He sat down on his bed and began to pack lots of small, unfamiliar objects into a pouch that he had made out of the fabric of the rucksack. 'Unless I'm completely wrong about this, I'd guess that you two are going to be forced to work on the manipulator, and I'm going to be shot.'

'I'm glad to see that you're keeping your spirits up,' said Rachel.

He smiled. 'That's the worst-case scenario, Rachel. But, knowing that, we should be able to take advantage of the situation . . .'

As dinner got cold, Rachel listened to Chris's plan with mounting disbelief. It was outrageous, but understandable – and Rachel couldn't see any alternative. Michael would be turning in his grave.

'By your command, Your Excellency,' Draan announced as he entered the Grand Marshal's chambers. The summons had been an urgent one, and Draan knew better than to keep Falaxyr waiting. Not just because of the Grand Marshal's rank, although the rigid chains of command were the foundation of the Martian military. No, Draan obeyed Falaxyr through a sense of honour, duty and respect. The first two were givens. But the third . . .

Draan's father had been ruthless, ambitious, and ultimately a failure. If his mission of a century ago had been a success, he would undoubtedly have been offered a place on the Eight-Point Table. Instead, he had died in disgrace, leaving Draan an orphan in the care of his nest. Such orphans rarely prospered; although the sins of the father were not formally passed down the generations, too many Martians considered failure to be hereditary. Draan could have ended up like that, had it not been for the patronage of his father's commanding officer, Falaxyr.

When Falaxyr had welcomed Draan into his home, he had been a Supreme Lord. But success and a thorough knowledge of the machinations of Martian politics had assured his rapid ascent to the Eight-Point Table. And, as Falaxyr rose through the ranks, so did Draan; just before the War, he had been promoted to Supreme Lord – a rank higher than his father had ever attained – and assigned to Falaxyr's personal staff as his adjutant. He momentarily wondered whether he would have accepted the position had he known of the decades in isolation that they would have to face, but immediately chastised himself. He owed it all to Falaxyr, and would have followed him into the sun if ordered.

Standing to attention before the Grand Marshal's desk, he

waited while Falaxyr finished reading something from the monitor inset into the cold stone surface.

'Your analysis of the situation, Lord Draan?' asked Falaxyr without looking up.

'The taller male is an Adjudicator, and familiar with our culture, Your Excellency. It is probable that he suspects a trap.'

'Probable?' Falaxyr replied, smiling. 'I would say it was inevitable. The Adjudicator has already neutralized our surveillance devices. Remember, the Bureau is a fearsome and honoured opponent – many of the most honourable conflicts of the Thousand Day War were those between our forces and the Adjudicators.'

'I assume that the food has been drugged?' asked Draan. Falaxyr seemed to be relishing the idea of having captured an Adjudicator; in Draan's opinion, the human was of no possible value to them, and should have been executed immediately. It was almost as if Falaxyr expected him to provide some sort of welcome challenge.

'Naturally. But it is just as inevitable that they will not have eaten it.' He stood up. 'Do you remember our games of chess back in the Fortress of Ooss-Ett-Jassiir?' Draan nodded as Falaxyr walked over to a curtained alcove and pulled back the iridescent green drape, revealing the hexagonal shape of a chess board. 'That was nothing more than one of my opening gambits.' With his clamp, he picked up one of the pieces, an intricate carving of a Grand Marshal in yellow orbstone. 'This is our Adjudicator, Draan; the enemy. And I am the opposing Marshal.' He held up a similar but grey piece. 'We are both aware of the other's strategies and tactics, we are both familiar with the arts of war.' He replaced the chess pieces and turned round.

'The Adjudicator must be considered as dangerous as a *Riis-utt-Ssethiss*, Draan. He must be treated with honour, but given no quarter. That is why I did not execute him upon his arrival. It would be dishonourable.'

Falaxyr's obsession with Martian honour was legendary, but even Draan baulked at the idea that the Adjudicator should be treated as a *Riis-utt-Ssethiss*; the Bloodswords of

Ssethiss had been the Martian assassination elite, trained killers whose order had been wiped out millennia ago in one of the Primal Wars, and their prowess was now the stuff of legend. This Adjudicator was only human, wasn't he? In Draan's opinion, the Grand Marshal was over-reacting. 'What will you do, Your Excellency? Challenge him to a blood-duel?'

Falaxyr's clamped hand struck Draan across the face, knocking his helmet to the floor. 'Do not insult me, *Lord* Draan. Despite our friendship, I am still the only remaining Supreme Grand Marshal on Mars – and your superior. It was misjudgement of the enemy that led to the death of your father and one wing of our space fleet, Draan. Unlike Slaar, I do not intend to underestimate my opponent.'

Retrieving his helmet, Draan tried to hold back his anger. Some of that anger was due to the shame of being struck – his comment about the blood-duel had been insulting, since the duel could only be fought between Martians – but the major part was in response to Falaxyr's insult. Draan's father had been betrayed; if Slaar's plan had succeeded, New Mars would have been founded on Earth, not on some Ssethiis-forsaken rock on the far side of Arcturus. But Draan kept his counsel; it was the wisest course.

'We will make our move in an hour, Draan; I will instruct Cassaar to pump anaesthetic gas into their room in case they have not eaten the food. After it has taken effect, take four of your Warriors and bring the two scientists to the Brain-Rack.'

Draan nearly questioned the need for four Warriors, but thought better of it. In Falaxyr's mind, the Adjudicator had become an opponent of epic proportions; if four Warriors made the Grand Marshal happy, then so be it. 'By your command, Your Excellency.' He bowed, straightened, and walked towards the door. And then he stopped. 'What of the Adjudicator, Your Excellency?'

Falaxyr was standing by his chessboard. 'Our Amber Marshal? Attempt to apprehend him alive, Draan.'

Draan nodded and opened the door.

'And Draan? If he is to die, ensure that it is an honourable death.' Falaxyr tapped his clamps together. 'I'm sure we understand one another.'

'I can hear things,' whispered Carmen, looking around the dark city with obvious trepidation. For once, Roz could sympathize with her; Sstee-ett-Haspar was decidedly unlike the relaxing, open city of Ikk-ett-Saleth. The gloom didn't help: centuries of neglect meant that the bio-luminescent fungus was giving out barely a glimmer – even less than the faint glow that had illuminated the service corridor. The members of the human expedition had broken out even more torches, and the Doctor had started playing around with his everlasting matches again, but all that the extra light did was show exactly how uninviting the city actually was. That included the smell: a musty, cloying odour that Roz couldn't place – not that she really wanted to.

It certainly lived up to its name as the Labyrinth of False Pride – that was obvious from the moment that they entered through the circular hole and the Plague Seal was replaced. There was no way of knowing exactly how big the city was, because it wasn't possible to see for more than a couple of metres without there being a wall in the way.

The walls of the Labyrinth lacked the smooth, decorated lustre that they had come to expect from Martian architecture; they were made of rough grey stone, carved with very primitive-looking hieroglyphics. The walls were also unbelievably tall, but their precise height was immeasurable since the upper reaches were lost in the shadows of the roof.

The actual path through the city was only two metres wide, an uneven, dusty surface that constantly snapped through ninety degrees as another wall forced a change in direction. It made Roz feel like a laboratory animal.

The creepy atmosphere was made even worse by the constant background noise of hisses and clicks which endlessly echoed around the Labyrinth, bouncing back and forth and ensuring that the true source was indeterminate.

'The hissing is the mating call of the rock-snake,' ventured Sstaal to Roz. 'It is in a permanent mating frenzy.'

'And that horrid clicking sound?' asked Carmen.

'That is the feeding triumph,' Sstaal replied. 'It usually follows the mating call. They are also permanently hungry.'

Understanding Sstaal's implication, Roz decided to change the subject.

'Where's the actual city?' Roz asked. 'At the centre of this maze?'

'This *is* the city,' said Sstaal. 'The walls of the maze are the buildings.'

'So why is the city built as a maze? Some sort of defensive strategy?'

Sstaal shook his head. 'Most certainly not. It is one of eight such cities built during the J'Kassaar Dynasty, four thousand years ago. They are all patterned after a map in the Blessed Apocryphal Glyphs of Oras.' He lowered his stuttering, lisping voice. 'They are considered blasphemous by certain Orthodox sects of my religion,' he added guiltily.

Roz quickly glanced around to check what everyone else was up to; the Doctor and the Abbot were conducting a subdued yet gesticular conversation about some subject or another, while Esstar was tagging along with Carmen, Sstaal and herself. That left Cleece and Madrigal, leading the party through the maze; the Ice Warrior's concealed disruptor scanned directly ahead, while Madrigal looked from side to side, plasma rifle in hand. And then there was McGuire, trailing behind and guarding their rear.

'How much longer have we got to go, Roslyn?' asked Carmen. 'I feel sick, knowing that there are those – those things out there.'

'We're going to be all right, Carmen,' said Roz without the slightest trace of true concern; she just wanted to shut the woman up. 'Those *things* won't come anywhere near us.' Roz waved her torch around to prove that they were alone.

Santacosta screamed, pointing at the illuminated ground with a shaking finger. The desiccated body stared up at them with empty eye sockets set into yellow parchment skin. It was slumped against one of the walls, where it had presumably been since dying of sleeping fever, centuries ago.

'The ghosts of our dead will watch over us,' intoned Sstaal.

Santacosta immediately burst into tears.

Draan strode down the corridor towards the holding cell that contained Falaxyr's precious 'Amber Marshal', flanked by his own personal guard. Ssell, Gaar and Ossarl were vicious, uncompromising Martians who were fiercely loyal to him; currently, loyalty was just what Draan needed. If the Grand Marshal thought that this was a suitable task for a Supreme Lord of the Martian aristocracy, then Draan had seriously misunderstood the relationship between them. No, he corrected himself; it was Falaxyr who had misunderstood. Draan's gratitude to his patron was finite; the time was approaching when Draan would pay Falaxyr back for the humiliations which he had constantly heaped on him.

Christopher Cwej would die, the subspace scientists would serve the Martian cause . . . and Draan would be remembered as the Martian who had forged a new empire.

Draan sighed. Who was he trying to deceive? Falaxyr held his life in his clamps; one tug and Draan would be less than nothing. His hopes sublimating into anger, he continued down the corridor towards his meeting with the so-called 'Amber Marshal'.

Chris sat on the bed, trying to push away panic. Rachel and Felice were already unconscious – the colourless gas that had been pumped into their cell had been instantly effective. Chris's nose filters had succeeded in keeping him awake, but the smell of the anaesthetic was rather too much for him, and he had to keep from retching – the room smelt like somebody had just had a very bad attack of flatulence.

It was pretty likely that the Ice Warriors were on their way – why else would they have flooded the room with gas? Chris just hoped that his inventiveness – and imperfect memories of various courses on Ponten IV – would be sufficient. Returning his attention to what he had been working on, he tried to thread the filament through the small opening in the hastily rigged circuit, but he angrily realized that his hands were shaking too much. He grunted, and put the device down alongside him.

Come on, Chris – get a grip. This is the opportunity that you've been waiting for. One man against the world, the hero who gets the girl. All you've got to do is outwit a group of Ice Warriors.

He took a series of deep breaths – through the filters, of course – and was relieved to feel his heartbeat slowing. He had just one last thing to do; then he would be ready for them.

He hoped.

Roz's insistence that they had nothing to worry about was suddenly torn apart, yet more proof that the universe had a pretty lousy sense of timing. The sharp retort of a plasma burst echoed around the Labyrinth, followed by the screech of a sonic disruptor and two screams. Only one was human, but both were death rattles.

Roz ran the five metres to the nearest junction and stepped into a pool of light provided by somebody's torch. She immediately saw what had happened. Madrigal's body was still smoking from the attack and Cleece stood over her, unmoving, his disruptor still trained on what remained of a rock-snake in front of him. Its middle section was missing, but the plasma-hurling sting and the bulbous eye were still intact, twitching. Cleece tensed his clamp once more, and the rock-like remains of the snake buckled and warped under the sonic disruption, leaving nothing but charred ground.

Roz fell to her knees and examined Madrigal's wound, but even a cursory look showed it to be fatal: the bio-plasmic sting of the rock-snake had burnt through her jacket and body armour, virtually eviscerating her. Roz sighed; in her century, the rock-snake was almost extinct, but there were still reports of fatalities in the less-developed regions of Mars. The rock-snake was a vicious predator that served no purpose in the Martian foodchain, just one of those nasty quirks of evolution.

'There is no brain activity,' said Sstaal sadly. He was kneeling next to Roz, a palm-sized device made of glittering trisilicate in his clamps.

'If you don't mind moving back,' said McGuire coldly. As Sstaal and Roz complied, he scanned Madrigal's body with a micro-tablette. 'She's dead.'

'That was my diagnosis,' muttered Sstaal. 'I was not aware that human technology was any more sensitive than ours.'

'Perhaps I wanted to prove it myself,' McGuire snapped. 'Just to be certain.'

Roz could understand McGuire's attitude; indeed, she had behaved the same way on more than one occasion. Losing somebody under your command was never easy, and if there was the slightest chance of a mistake ... But the gaping, cauterized plasma burn in place of Madrigal's chest was undeniable proof that the last member of McGuire's original expedition was dead.

Roz stepped back towards the Doctor, who was staring at Madrigal's body without a flicker of emotion.

'Seems straightforward enough. Or was Madrigal killed by our mysterious assassin as well?' she asked, well aware that her anger over the marine's death was boiling over and she was having difficulty containing it.

The Doctor tapped his chin with two fingers. 'No, Roz, this is just what it appears: a pointless tragedy. Unfortunately, we don't have a lot of time to grieve.' He moved out of the way to allow Cleece to continue patrolling round the party.

'A trained colonial marine, taken out by a sodding rock-snake? Surely even you can see how unlikely that looks?'

The Doctor gazed downwards, and it was clear to Roz that the events unfolding around him were somehow irrelevant. All that mattered to the Doctor was reaching the Pole and solving the mystery of the Vortex rupture; the fate of the joint expedition was beneath him, the pointless scampering of creatures as below him on the evolutionary scale as the rock-snake was below Roz. She turned her back on him and looked over at the others.

'Find something to cover her with,' said McGuire. 'We're going to have to leave her here, but it's only right that we collect the body on the way back. I'd – I'd like there to be something left to bury back in Jacksonville.'

Aklaar beckoned Sstaal over to him. After a brief exchange

in their native language, Sstaal took off his hide backpack and reached inside.

'Please, accept this warding shroud,' he said to McGuire, handing over a folded bundle of metallic cloth. 'In our traditions, the body of a fallen warrior is consigned to the flames with respect and ceremony. However, there are circumstances under which the body must be left unaccompanied for some time; to prevent desecration, a warding shroud is used. It is impregnated with chemicals which repel scavengers.'

McGuire accepted the shroud with a grateful smile. 'I am honoured, Pilgrim Sstaal.' He began to unfurl the fabric, accepting Aklaar's assistance with good grace.

Roz found the scene touching, and she looked around to gauge the others' reactions. Then she noticed: Carmen was missing. She glanced up and down the narrow road between the high buildings, but there was no sign of the singer. Groaning with irritation, she was just about to mention the absence to the Doctor when Carmen appeared from a small alleyway. For a brief moment, her expression was hard, cold and calculating, but then she saw Roz's attentive look and smiled warmly.

'Call of nature,' she said chirpily, noticing the attention.

Really, thought Roz. In a hostile environment crawling with rock-snakes and spider-lizards, was it really likely that the timid Carmen Santacosta would wander off down a dark alleyway to relieve herself? Roz decided that the woman merited much closer attention from now on.

'I suggest we carry on,' said the Doctor to McGuire. Madrigal's body was now covered by the shroud, its edges weighted down with lumps of masonry which had presumably fallen from the surrounding buildings during their centuries of neglect. 'We still have another two days before we reach the Pole.'

McGuire nodded, but the grief was vivid in his ashen face. 'You're right, Doctor.'

Roz joined Cleece in the vanguard position; she was the best suited to be the marine's replacement, wasn't she? Without saying a word, McGuire handed over Madrigal's plasma rifle and nodded, a silent thanks for her stepping into the breach.

She gave the rifle a brief once-over to check that it hadn't been damaged by the plasma blast, and then did a double take: the safety catch was jammed. With some effort, she bent the mechanism back into shape, but it puzzled her. Had the catch jammed when the rifle dropped from Madrigal's lifeless fingers, or had it been deliberately bent? If the latter was true, the marine wouldn't have stood a chance. It would definitely explain how a crack member of the Colonial Marines could fall prey to something so humble as a rock-snake.

So, accident or deliberate sabotage? As the party continued through the maze of streets in funereal silence, leaving Madrigal's shrouded body behind them, Roz felt more uncomfortable than she had for ages. Not only were they under threat from rock-snakes and spider-lizards, but there was a possible threat from within. And, despite all of her instincts, Roz couldn't help suspecting that innocent, whimpering, timid Carmen was anything but the harmless nightclub singer that she claimed to be.

It was just a pity that she no longer felt that she could take the Doctor into her confidence. She just hoped that that pity didn't turn into an even bigger tragedy.

The room was silent, the lighting low. But pitch-blackness was no hindrance to cybernetically enhanced night vision. Four sleeping figures occupied the cots by the far wall, their belongings piled up on the floor. To the side, a small, low table held the remains of dinner, twelve empty bowls. Draan smiled; Falaxyr's assurances of the Adjudicator's superiority had obviously been misplaced. This Cwej had probably eaten the food to begin with, making the gas wholly irrelevant. The faint chemical smell of the anaesthetic gas still remained in the air; the lingering odour of a compound harmless to Martians but instantly effective on mammalian life.

In the open doorway, Draan considered the situation. Perhaps the Amber Marshal wasn't quite as legendary as Falaxyr had warned – but was that warned or hoped? Draan had long suspected that the Grand Marshal still yearned for the days of battle and conquest; and, even though the GodEngine project would give them back their racial honour and glory, century-long plans didn't cater to the immediacy that coursed through most Martians' blood.

Then again, if Falaxyr was that desperate to polish his fighting skills, why wasn't he personally overseeing the abduction of the captives? Perhaps Falaxyr was so old, so weary, that he just liked to talk about it all the time. A lot of old Martians were like that.

Gesturing to his squad of three Warriors, Draan stepped into the room, vaguely insulted and bitterly disappointed that Falaxyr's promises of a testing skirmish against a ruthless foe had become nothing more than a simple fetch-and-carry exercise. The Adjudicator had undoubtedly fallen for the drugged food – where was the challenge in that?

Draan was suddenly rocked back on his feet by an explosive concussion that erupted from the middle of the room. Losing his footing as the force of the detonation hit him in the chest, he crashed into Gaar and Ossarl and sent them sprawling onto the floor. Stumbling to his feet, he scanned the room, but the explosion had also released clouds of obscuring noxious vapour – extremely noxious to Martians, his head-up-display informed him. 'Activate breathing filters!' he ordered. At the same time, he tried to find some part of the electromagnetic spectrum that wasn't blanketed by the gas. After far too long for Draan's liking, his inbuilt sensor net informed him of the frequency at which the gas was transparent; as his visor automatically adjusted, he used his command override to electronically force his Warriors' visors to do the same.

The familiar retort of a sonic disruptor distracted him from his sensor readouts. Despite his instincts, Draan knew the displeasure that would await him if the Adjudicator was killed dishonourably, and indiscriminate shootings under these conditions was anything but honourable. 'I gave no order to fire!' Draan yelled at Ssell. 'Close the door!'

As Ssell and Gaar moved to obey him, another explosion came from the direction of the door. Draan managed to stand his ground this time, but the two Warriors staggered back from the doorway, clearly dazed.

The gas released by the second explosion was beginning to obscure the visual frequency that Draan had selected earlier, so he instructed his sensors to find another. 'Is that door shut yet?' he barked at the dark shape of the nearest Warrior.

'A few seconds, My Lord,' grunted Ssell. Another shape appeared in the grey gloom, a shape too small to be one of Draan's Warriors.

The shriek that erupted from Ssell was bloodcurdling; Draan recognized it as the Warrior's brain being scrambled by feedback from his armour's cybernetic systems. Before Draan could react, the smaller shape had vanished through the door and into the corridor.

Draan knew he had no choice. He linked into the base's communications suite and accessed the general address system. 'This is Supreme Lord Draan. There is an escaped prisoner in the base. He is currently in section Ull-teth-Kliis. Apprehend him but do not kill him.' He cut the connection and looked around the room. The two scientists were still asleep – and they were the true prize.

Besides, how much trouble could one human being cause? It wasn't as if the Adjudicator was a real threat to their project, was it? Leaving Gaar and Ossarl to bring out the scientists, he stepped into the clearer air of the corridor. He could already imagine Falaxyr's growling tones: 'I warned you of the dangers of underestimating the enemy, Draan. You are no better than your father.' With a roar of anger, Draan slammed his clamp into the rock wall.

This Chris may have had the initial advantage; but now he was up against the might of a Martian military nest.

The Adjudicator didn't stand a chance.

PART TWO

THE CAULDRON OF SUTEKH

Chapter 8

'Two days, Draan!' hissed Falaxyr, knocking over the chessboard and scattering the pieces across the floor. 'The Adjudicator has been loose in the base for two days!' The Grand Marshal strode forward and held his clamp only inches away from Draan's visor. 'Do you realize how much this has inconvenienced me?'

Draan knew exactly how much it had inconvenienced his superior, because this was the third time they had had such a dialogue since the human had escaped. He also knew that keeping quiet was his best defence when Falaxyr was as angry as he was now.

'The project is unravelling before my eyes, Draan. Unless the Daleks see some tangible proof that the GodEngine is functional, they will conquer this world as easily as they did Earth.'

Draan couldn't see his people allowing the Daleks to simply annex them without resistance. 'We are Martians, Your Excellency –'

Falaxyr growled, and turned his back on his adjutant. 'Ninety-nine per cent of our race is currently on another planet, Draan, or had you forgotten the Great Exodus? We need the GodEngine; if not as a bargaining tool, then definitely as a means of defence. I have watched these Daleks systematically annihilate the outer colonies of the Earth Alliance with weapons that we could not begin to understand, let alone counter; they are merciless and without honour. If they decide to invade Mars, we will be powerless to stop them.'

'But we have the two scientists –'

Falaxyr thumped his desk. 'But I cannot spare the technicians to put them through the Brain-rack! Thanks to your inherited incompetence, all of my personnel are currently hunting down this Adjudicator!'

Draan wanted to point out that it was Falaxyr's desire to treat the Adjudicator *honourably* that had led to his escape, but thought better of it. He remained silent, trying to let Falaxyr's anger wash over him. It was difficult.

'However, my need for the scientists is now too great to ignore, especially since they will begin to suffer permanent neurological damage if they are anaesthetized for much longer. Therefore, you will replace Technician Yeess on watch.'

Draan ran a quick diagnostic of his helmet's cyber-net, but his enhanced hearing wasn't malfunctioning; Falaxyr had just ordered Draan, a Supreme Lord of the Martian Military Elite, to go on guard duty like a common Warrior.

'Your Excellency, I must protest! I am –'

Falaxyr's voice was quiet yet threatening. 'You are a bungler, Draan. Yeess is the only Martian left to me who can operate the Brain-rack, and therefore of importance.' *Unlike you, Draan*, was the unspoken corollary. 'A perfectly logical decision, I believe.' The Grand Marshal reached down and picked up the Amber Marshal chess piece from the floor. 'Now go, Draan, before I decide to let Yeess practise on you.' An empty threat – the Brain-rack was specifically designed to influence human brains – but the insult was cutting.

Draan left the chamber without comment, but his course of action was clear. He would find the Adjudicator and deliver him personally to Falaxyr.

After torturing him, of course.

Chris Cwej's lanky frame was squeezed uncomfortably into a tiny little cubby-hole, but he wasn't that bothered – he was safe, and that was what counted. He suspected that the Ice Warriors didn't even know that the space existed; it appeared to be nothing more than a gap between three walls, and he doubted that they would even consider looking there.

He was more concerned about the others. When he had formulated the plan, he had made it quite clear to Rachel and Felice that there were risks; although it was almost certain that the Ice Warriors wanted them for their scientific knowledge, there were ways and means of extracting such information. But they had agreed that, given the circumstances, there wasn't really a lot of choice. Chris had to escape – the Ice Warriors would have undoubtedly killed him without a second thought – and the others had to play along.

The plan did have some benefits – in addition to Chris's continued living, of course. Rachel and Felice could get nice and close to the subspace manipulator, and find out what the hell the Ice Warriors were up to; and Chris could ride in like a white knight and save them all at the last moment. At least, that was the plan.

Escaping from the Ice Warriors had been easy, but Chris had the Doctor to thank for that. The kit had offered a very eclectic version of first aid: dozens of tiny chemical phials, reels of superconducting filament, and a small manila envelope full of electronic components. There had even been what had initially appeared to be a locket; closer inspection had revealed that it was a personal shroud field. Although not powerful enough to render him completely invisible – hence his cramped hidy-hole – it was more than sufficient to scramble his life signs and prevent detection by whatever sensors the Ice Warriors possessed.

When the gas attack had come, Chris had been protected by a set of nose filters from the kit; the others had reluctantly agreed to be rendered unconscious for the sake of verisimilitude. As they quickly dozed off, Chris had been putting the finishing touches to his very special welcoming present for the Ice Warriors; using the starchy vegetables from dinner as a chemical base, spiced up with a few extra ingredients from the phials, he had produced two handy gas bombs. With a touch of cunning, he had deposited the remainder of the food underneath one of the beds; if the food had been drugged, the Ice Warriors would have seen the empty bowls, and assumed that they were all definitely unconscious.

But Chris was experienced enough to realize that he might need more than clouds of slightly poisonous smoke to ensure that he escaped. So, having finished the bombs, he had set to work on something a little more direct. With a few inches of filament and a superconducting circuit from the envelope, he had produced a very serviceable bio-cybernetic feedback scrambler.

Chris had a lecture to thank for that: he clearly remembered listening to a grizzled old veteran of countless interstellar conflicts, who had pointed out that the vast majority of Man's foes had chosen to evolve artificially using cybernetic augmentation. The Daleks and the Cybermen were the pinnacle of this false evolution, having surrendered almost all of their so-called humanity to cold positronic nets of silicon and steel. But other races were catching them up: the Sontarans implanted their clone musters with countless electronic 'improvements', and the Ice Warriors' cybernetic techniques were legendary. Much of their legendary fighting skills were derived from their armour; despite their organic appearance, the carapace and the helmet were grown in nutrient tanks and augmented with cybernetics. As well as increasing an Ice Warrior's already formidable strength, it provided a direct link to the Martian battle-net and boosted reaction time by five hundred per cent. But, like all cybernetic systems, it relied on feedback between the electronic and the organic components to function.

And when that feedback was scrambled . . . Chris had to admit, he had been extremely pleased with himself when the Warrior had collapsed.

Unfortunately, the scrambler was a rather limited weapon; the chances of getting close enough to an Ice Warrior to actually slap it onto its armour were fairly slim, especially without clouds of obscuring gas. And there were rather too many Ice Warriors around to take them all out personally. No, if he was going to rescue the others, he needed to play the Martians at their own game. Which was the art of war.

He leant back in his cubby-hole and smiled. The last two days had been both terrifying and exhilarating as he had darted throughout the base, always one step in front of the Ice

Warriors; his one regret was that Roz hadn't been around to see him adjudicating his socks off. He wondered what she would have made of his 'arrangements', solid proof that he had been paying attention during those endless lectures about terrorism and clandestine warfare. Then again, he wondered what she would have done in his position; knowing Roz, she would already have freed the others and be back in the TARDIS ... Chris shuddered. He had no reason to believe that Roz or the Doctor were even alive, and no idea what to do once Felice and the others had been sprung. For the first time in over a year, there wasn't a set of blue doors and subsequent sanctuary waiting for them.

One step at a time, Chris, he told himself. In three hours' time, the Ice Warriors would discover what he had been up to over the last two days. And while they were dealing with that, Chris would grab his colleagues and make a break for it. To somewhere.

Assuming his 'arrangements' worked as planned, that was. He shrugged. If there had ever been a time for cheery, devil-may-care optimism, this was it. He closed his eyes and waited for what he hoped was the inevitable.

The gods who watched over the Labyrinth of False Pride had obviously decided that the meaningless death of Christina Madrigal was a sufficient sacrifice to permit unmolested passage through the maze. Either that, or the gestalt air of defiance that positively radiated from the party was enough to ward off the hostile denizens of the Labyrinth.

In the two days since the death, things had definitely changed in the group: McGuire noticed that Roz was invariably in the company of the singer, Santacosta – an odd pair, but at least it stopped the latter's whinging; the female Martian, Esstar, seemed to spend most of her time with nervous, timid Sstaal, while Cleece kept his own company, stoic and silent like a model Ice Warrior. McGuire himself had spent most of the tiring – yet thankfully eventless – journey talking to the Abbot, Aklaar.

There didn't seem to be a single topic that the ancient Martian didn't have some sort of an insight into, and his fresh views on subjects that McGuire would have imagined were all but exhausted gave McGuire the intellectual stimulation that he had all but forgotten about. They had discussed Madrigal's eventual burial back at Jacksonville, and he had learnt from the Abbot of the complex and reverential death ceremonies reserved for war heroes; the Abbot had even helped McGuire compose a fitting obituary for the marine.

So, all in all, the group was actually bonding, in some strange yet fascinating way. With a tinge of uneasy sadness, he just knew that Vincente would have been chuffed with the way things were going – except that he couldn't, of course. There was still Vincente's death to consider, and that was a gnawing puzzle that couldn't be solved. Yet.

Indeed, the only outsider to the group was the one person that McGuire had initially considered a threat: the Doctor. The odd little Scotsman had spent most of the journey through the Labyrinth withdrawing into himself, even giving Roz short shrift when she had tried to talk to him. She hadn't persisted. It was as if he was privy to some horror that was too much to share, yet too much to bear alone. McGuire just hoped that he didn't turn out to be a liability before they finally reached the Pole.

The Pole – now only a few kilometres away – was going to be . . . interesting, McGuire had decided. The Abbot had explained that his pilgrimage would end with a public renouncement of the Martian warrior ethic, marked by the ceremonial breaking of the Sword of Tuburr. The Sword was thousands of years old, the ultimate symbol of their warrior heritage, and breaking it would serve to direct the remaining Martians down a new path, one of peaceful co-operation with their neighbours. The fact that Mars's current neighbours were vicious tyrants didn't faze the Abbot in the slightest; he was convinced that the invasion and blockade were nothing more than a temporary set-back, and that mankind – aided and abetted by newfound allies on Mars – would soon reassert its claim on Earth. And, for some reason, McGuire believed him.

Aklaar had also assured McGuire that he would personally ensure the success of his own mission as well. Although the nest at the Pole was small, there were undoubtedly enough supplies to share with the colonists at Jacksonville, and Aklaar would make sure that negotiations were opened up to provide a lifeline for the isolated human population until the blockade was finally broken.

So Antony McGuire was a fairly happy man when they approached the borders of G'chun duss Ssethiissi – the Cauldron of Sutekh, according to the Doctor's translation, although that didn't make much more sense than the Martian version. Fairly happy until they reached those borders, that was.

'Another Plague Seal?' McGuire had seen the end of the wide and winding road that connected Sstee-ett-Haspar to the North Pole some time back, but had imagined that there would be some kind of door in the upcoming barrier. Instead, they were confronted by a wall of blue metal that stretched from left to right without any obvious break.

Aklaar stepped forward and stroked the smooth, unmarked surface. 'I – I am puzzled, Antony. The level of technology – the level of security – is not consistent with my knowledge of this place.'

'It's the hull of an Osirian WarScarab,' stated the Doctor quietly. 'An alloy of light neutronium and osmidium. Unbreakable.' He tapped it with the end of his wholly irrelevant umbrella. 'And unexpected. Your pacifist nest has been both busy and resourceful, Abbot.'

'I do not understand, Doctor,' said Aklaar curtly. 'What are you implying?'

'I'm implying nothing, Aklaar. I just find it . . . odd, shall we say, that a pacifist nest should choose to protect itself with the remains of an Osirian vessel. I would have thought that they would have found it rather blasphemous.'

'Hang on, hang on,' interrupted McGuire. 'Who the hell are the Osirians? More aliens?'

'Were, Mr McGuire, were. The Osirians were an ancient, amoral race that manipulated countless civilizations in this quadrant of the galaxy. They were cruel, aloof mental giants, but even they were horrified by one individual they bred who embodied all of those qualities in abundance: Sutekh.

He destroyed his home planet, Phaester Osiris, and fled the vengeance of his peers. The final battle was on Earth, but the remaining Osirians' bridgehead was here, on Mars. From the Martian North Pole, the Osirians finally managed to cage Sutekh on Earth. There were two other Osirians of note: Sutekh's brother, Horus, and his sister, Nepthys. All three of them have become part of both human and Martian mythology: Ssethiis, Oras and Netysss, in your language, Abbot.'

'Not only do you know our ways, Doctor, but you know our secrets as well,' hissed Aklaar.

'Oh, indeed I do,' replied the Doctor quietly. 'For example, the layout of the Labyrinth was based on a neural map of the Osirian cerebellum. But what currently concerns me is this barrier; leaving aside the religious connotations, since when have the pacifist caste possessed the skills and techniques to shape Osirian metal? I thought that was the right and privilege of the artificer caste.' And then he frowned. 'Or certain guilds of the warrior caste.'

'What about the Divine Sight of Horus?' asked Sstaal hesitantly. 'That was forged from an Osirian star-sapphire.'

'There's quite a difference between a star-sapphire and the hull of a WarScarab, Pilgrim Sstaal. And besides, the Divine Sight would have been extruded by an artificer.'

'Please, Doctor, your suspicions are unfounded,' protested the Abbot. 'I give you my word that I had no idea we would encounter such a barrier.'

The Doctor sighed. 'The universe is full of people wanting me to trust them.'

Cleece waved his clamp menacingly. 'Do not insult the Abbot, human. His word is his bond.'

As the verbal fencing continued, nobody noticed Carmen Santacosta slip away into the shadows. Nobody, that is, apart from Roz, who turned and followed at a distance.

Rachel hated hangovers. Especially a hangover that blotted out the night before. If she had to suffer, at least she ought to remember why. Then she did remember, and realized with a wave of nausea that alcohol had had nothing to do with it.

Instead of her quarters on Charon, she was strapped to a

bench in a low rock-walled room. It looked like step one of Chris's plan had been successful: they had been captured by the Martians. She turned her head with difficulty. 'Felice? Felice, are you awake yet?'

'Don't. Shout,' the other whispered through gritted teeth. 'I feel like death. How long have we been unconscious?'

'No idea,' Rachel replied. 'I wonder what happened to Chris? Do you think he escaped?'

Before Felice could answer, a grinding noise made her strain her head to look in front. A door was opening in the rock wall; seconds later, a Martian strode through. But he was unlike any Martian that Rachel had ever seen. Instead of ridged green body armour, he was wearing a plain brown hide tunic and kilt, and his head was helmetless. Despite Michael's letters, it was Rachel's first look at a 'real' Martian, and she was intrigued.

Even without his cybernetic enhancements, the Martian would have proved a formidable opponent; he was well muscled and well proportioned, over seven feet of fighting reptile, his leathery skin sparkling in the overhead lighting. Tufts of black fur grew from his elbows, knees and wrists, and around his shoulders; and without his boots and clamped gloves Rachel could see he possessed surprisingly human fingers and toes. But the biggest surprise was the head. It was quite small in proportion to the rest of his body, and smooth, with tiny flaps for ears. Two cat-like yellow eyes stared at her, nictitating membranes occasionally sweeping across the slitted pupils.

'I am Technician Yeess,' he announced, his head oscillating in a snake-like movement. 'I am here to process you.'

'What do you mean?' asked Felice.

'You are Dr Felice Delacroix,' Yeess stated. It wasn't a question. 'Both of you possess technical knowledge required by the Grand Marshal. Although you may offer your services willingly, we cannot risk any . . . mistakes.' He squeezed his fingers together, obviously forgetting that he wasn't wearing a clamped glove.

Rachel made the deductive leap rather more quickly than she would have liked. 'Brain-washing?'

'A curious term, Professor Rachel Anders, but I understand the cultural reference. The Brain-rack creates artificial neural pathways in the human mind. These pathways dominate existing thought processes and ensure obedience.'

'You don't have to do this,' said Felice. 'We will help you willingly – I give you my word.'

'Perhaps you would help us. But we are at a vital stage in our work here. It would prove more . . . convenient to ensure your allegiance.'

Rachel swallowed. This was one thing that Chris's plan had not taken into account. She wondered what *obedience* entailed.

Santacosta was standing in a small alcove back down the corridor, whispering into her watch.

'Dictating your memoirs?' Roz smiled at the look of surprise on Santacosta's face, but that look quickly faded, to be replaced by the hard and calculating expression that Roz had caught earlier. 'I take it that's a long-range communicator?'

'Observant, aren't you?' Santacosta stepped from the alcove, her body poised for a fight.

'So the nightclub singer was a façade. Not a very good one, I must say.'

'Good enough to fool McGuire and his party. And the Greenies wouldn't have noticed if I'd been wearing a sign round my neck with "impostor" written on it. All they care about is their damned pilgrimage.'

Roz was pleased that her instincts could still be relied on, but that still left a massive problem: if Santacosta wasn't a singer, what was she? The communicator looked strangely familiar, but she just couldn't place it. Playing for time, she continued. 'What about Esteban? I assume you killed him.'

Santacosta nodded. 'Esteban was a known Greenie sympathizer; although we had no proof, we suspected that he was a member of the Martian Axis – a group of human terrorists who've been committing acts of violence to further their cause. I couldn't take the chance that he'd foul up my mission. Still, the Greenies got the blame; who would expect the culprit to be a harmless nightclub singer?'

'You knew that the Gree–, the Ice Warriors were in the city?'

Santacosta laughed, a rich, fruity laugh. 'You don't get it, do you? This entire expedition has been a set-up from the very beginning. I'm on a mission to the North Pole. When my shuttle crashed, I had to switch to the backup plan and infiltrate McGuire's party.'

Roz had heard enough – she had to bring this woman down hard and fast and warn the others. Spinning, she lashed out with her foot, expecting to catch the other woman in the solar plexus and bring her down.

Unfortunately, it didn't work that way. Santacosta reacted even faster, grabbing Roz's foot before it could connect. Pulling her off balance, Santacosta sent her sprawling to the ground. But Roz was an Adjudicator, with all the martial arts skills that that office represented. Rolling to one side on the dusty floor, she leapt to her feet – and Santacosta was there again with a chop to the stomach which left Roz wheezing against the rock wall.

And then Roz recognized the technique – Hi Shu's Defence. She had learnt it twenty-odd years ago on Ponten IV. When a stray thought informed her that the basic moves had remained virtually unchanged since the formation of the Guild, she realized that Santacosta was fighting like an Adjudicator. Any further speculation was stopped by the stabbing pressure of two fingers against her neck: the Herzgang Manoeuvre, another Adjudicator favourite. Any more force and Roz would die of a brain haemorrhage within moments.

'You're an Adjudicator?' But the question was Santacosta's; she must have recognized Roz's fighting technique at the same time that Roz had recognized hers. Roz was stunned; what was a Raven doing on Mars? She thought back to the Guild History classes on Ponten IV, but she couldn't remember hearing anything about Adjudicator activity on Mars during the Dalek invasion. Their time had come later, once the blockade had been broken, when their base on Oberon had become the centre of the resistance movement.

Santacosta let Roz go, but it was clear that any sudden moves would be immediately countered; and, although Roz had started the fight full of confidence, that assured self-certainty had been considerably eroded by Santacosta's prowess. They may have both learnt the same moves and the same techniques, but Roz's skills were dulled by nine hundred years of teaching by rote, as a succession of instructors across the centuries had forgotten the true meaning that lay behind them; Santacosta's were fresh and original, and probably taught by the actual originators of the skills. Roz then realized where she had seen the wrist communicator before: in the museum on Ponten IV, part of a display of standard Adjudicator field equipment from the twenty-first century. Final proof, if she really needed any.

Santacosta shook her head. 'No, you can't be. No Adjudicator would let herself be taken down like that. You're just not good enough.' Ouch. That hurt. 'Who are you, Roz?'

Roz knew that the situation was at an impasse; somehow, she had to let the others know what was going on, and that called for a bit of lateral thinking.

This was going to hurt even more than the woman's slight; Roz knew that. But she wasn't exactly in a winning position, was she?

Roz threw herself at Santacosta, catching her a glancing blow to the chin. Not too hard, but sufficient to get a reaction.

Santacosta almost fell to the floor, but managed to regain her balance within seconds. That gave Roz enough time to step back, but she didn't want to get too far out of range. She just hoped that she had gauged the other Adjudicator correctly; there was a certain move that all Adjudicators tended to think about when cornered, and that was exactly what Roz wanted to happen.

'Bad move, Roz. I don't need you, but I was prepared to let you live. I can see now that you're too much trouble. Far too much trouble.' As Santacosta leapt forward, Roz moved herself in a subtle and hopefully unnoticed way, taking the attack face on, but with certain muscle groups tensed. Santacosta behaved exactly as Roz had hoped; the chop to the shoulder was almost a relief.

When it was first taught, the Cthalz manoeuvre was invariably fatal, immobilizing the autonomic nervous system and causing instant death. Unless, of course, one knew the defence. The defence hadn't been discovered until the twenty-eighth century, so Roz knew that Santacosta was unaware of it. So she tried it.

She wasn't convinced that her plan had been particularly successful. Lying on the floor, unable to breathe, Roz realized that her clever defence hadn't worked. Her heart wasn't beating, her head felt like it was being compressed into a neutron star, and she knew that she was going to die.

As the heavy pounding blackness poured in and swamped her thoughts, Roz found herself thinking of Chris. Was he still alive? How would he feel about her death? Would he ever know? And then she passed out, knowing that she had only pre-empted the inevitable; she would have ceased to exist anyway when the laws of time caught up with her, so dying now was only being premature.

By the time Santacosta returned to the expedition, the niggling arguments had subsided, with everyone too preoccupied with the metal barrier and looking for some means of entry to notice her presence. The Doctor was waving his metal probe around, making it buzz and screech but without any noticeable effect, while the Greenies were kneeling in a circle and praying. This worried her; wasn't the whole point of meeting up with the Greenies only to take advantage of their ability to open the barrier? What good was prayer going to do? Somebody on Oberon was going to pay for their woolly analysis of the situation; she swore it.

Santacosta had known all about the impenetrable barrier for quite a while: it was the reason that she was on Mars. She just hoped that *someone* would open the damned thing so that she could drop the pretence and get on with her job.

'Have you seen Roz, Ms Santacosta?' the Doctor called over his shoulder, taking a second's break from his sonic probe.

'She's answering a call of nature, Doctor,' she replied timidly. 'Like I was.' God, the number of times she had used that excuse over the last five days; the others must think she had bladder problems. Still, it would all be worth it – as long as her colleagues on Oberon were on the ball, and, more importantly, somebody opened the bloody barrier.

He turned. 'Really?' The suspicion was clear on his face. 'I find that –'

The sound took them all by surprise, a high-pitched whine that came from the reflective blue barrier. As everyone turned to locate the source, a strip of metal about two metres wide slid smoothly upwards, revealing a brightly lit but empty corridor within.

That was the cue that she had been waiting for. She reached into her jacket –

'Stop her! She's an Adjudicator!' It was Roz, coming towards them in a limping run. Santacosta was shocked: how could she still be alive? But it didn't matter – the game was up. She raised her gun before anyone else had a chance to move towards theirs.

'Too late, Roz. The time for playacting's finally over.' Santacosta pulled out a small sphere from her jacket and gave it the once-over. As she had been told to expect, it was no longer white as it had been when she had looked at it earlier – it was black, indicating that the gap in the barrier had created a window in the subspace interference surrounding the North Pole.

Holding the sphere in her palm, she squeezed it. As it started to vibrate in her hand, she threw it onto a clear space on the ground about two metres away and watched as it started to grow. Dozens of straight black strands shot out from the sphere and rooted themselves into the rocky soil, creating a spoked wheel about four metres across. Further strands then began to develop, crossing and recrossing to link the whole thing together like a huge black spider's web. Then the black fibres began to pulse with an eerie pearl light which ran up and down the strands in a regular pattern – just how Professor Ketch had said it would happen.

'What the hell's that?' asked McGuire, staring at the glowing arrangement of cables.

'A Transit-web,' replied the Doctor. 'A portable stunnel

terminus. I believe that Adjudicator Santacosta is bringing in reinforcements.'

Santacosta dropped the giggly pretence. Thank God. 'Very perceptive, Doctor.' She moved towards the gap in the barrier – the best position to keep an eye on everyone – and unholstered her pulse laser.

'So it's all been an act?' said McGuire. 'But how? The shuttle crash –'

'Was not part of my original plan, I'll admit that. The Adjudicator base on Oberon managed to get me to Mars in a survival pod disguised as a meteorite where I met up with my squire – he was the pilot. But we made a mistake: we assumed that the invaders would ignore low-level shuttles.'

'The invaders ignore nothing,' said the Doctor coldly. 'So your shuttle crashed, and your squire was killed. I assume that you were actually heading towards the North Pole?'

'Quite right, Doctor. Thankfully, there was a backup plan – the shuttle's flight path was worked out so that it was in the same direction as McGuire's expedition. In the case of a crash, I was to locate McGuire's expedition, pass myself off as a civilian, and infiltrate the group.'

'But why?' asked Esstar. 'You are all humans, so why are you acting so clandestinely? Why aren't you working together?'

Santacosta sighed; these pilgrim Martians were too nice for their own good. She momentarily wished that they had all been Warriors; at least you knew where you stood with a Warrior. 'Since the invasion, Adjudicator Intelligence on Oberon has been monitoring the inner planets closely, trying to analyse what the invaders were up to. Then, about three months ago, we detected subspace emissions from the Martian North Pole. We were very interested; especially when our scientists claimed that it represented a level of subspace technology far beyond anything we currently possessed.'

'Useful in the war effort, then?' said the Doctor.

'What do you think? Thanks to Professor Ketch and his subspace researches on Oberon, we're making progress in finding out how to beat the blockade, but we're still nowhere near ready to take on the invaders. But with whatever the

Greenies are hiding at the Pole –'

'So why go to all this trouble?' interrupted McGuire. 'Why not just Transit your troops into the Pole and take it by force?'

'Because there is a subspace jamming field affecting a radius of about two hundred kilometres around the Pole, McGuire; even with the Transit-web, Ketch's team couldn't resolve a Transit beam within that field, and a group of heavily armed Adjudicator shock troops making their way to the Pole would be rather . . . noticeable. Despite what everyone thinks, we knew that there were still Greenies on Mars. It might have been taken as a hostile act – and a skirmish between Martians and Adjudicators so close to whatever they're hiding at the Pole would probably have merited the invaders' attention. As the Doctor said, they ignore nothing.' She nodded at the blue barrier. 'I presume that that's responsible for the jamming field around the Pole?'

'The hull of a WarScarab is opaque to subspace fields,' explained the Doctor. 'A necessary consequence of the Osirians' version of FTL drive.' He tapped the barrier with his umbrella once more. 'The Osirians built their shielding into the molecular structure of their vessels. Typical Osirian efficiency.'

'I can see that this metal's going to be a bonus for the Bureau.' She checked the Transit-web; the glow was deepening to a throbbing blue, meaning that the stunnel would be open within a couple of minutes. 'When we found out about the Mayor of Jacksonville's plan to send an expeditionary force to the Pole, we had hoped to use it as cover. But the Mayor hand-picked the team, and decided to include both a member of the Colonial Marines and a known Martian sympathizer. We didn't know what to expect at the Pole – if we'd had to do some double-dealing to secure the subspace device, we couldn't have Marines and Greenie-lovers spoiling things.

'Then again,' she continued, looking over at the Abbot, 'we were more interested in the Abbot's pilgrimage than the Jacksonville expedition.'

Aklaar raised a clamp. 'How would the human Bureau of

Adjudicators know of our holy mission? It was conducted in sacred silence, known only to the Holy Bishop and the leaders of the Polar nest.'

Santacosta smiled. 'It isn't solely a human Bureau, Abbot,' she replied enigmatically; did the Abbot really think that the Bureau wouldn't have recruited a few Martians; they were the only other intelligent life form in the Solar System. She quickly checked the progress of the web: a sphere of iridescence was forming above it, the visual interpretation of a subspace meniscus. 'It stood to reason that you would know a way in – it was the reason for your pilgrimage. My mission was to ensure that I reached the Pole at the same time that you did, Aklaar; then all I had to do was wait for a breach in the barrier and then activate the T-web.'

She grinned. 'Now we're all here, the barrier is open, and a crack squad of Adjudicators is about to arrive.'

'You would dare to profane the holy grounds of Oras with your human belligerence?' hissed Aklaar. 'What sort of a person are you?'

'A practical one. You've got a subspace manipulator in there which can help us get Earth back, Abbot. And if getting our hands on it means a bit of desecration, well . . . this is war.'

Roz listened to Santacosta's explanation and shook her head. The woman had had it all worked out from the start – Roz could see that the ancient Bureau of Adjudicators was as clandestine as the Guild in her own time. A movement distracted her; far down the corridor, a blue shape was resolving. Knowing exactly what it was, she nudged the Doctor.

'Doctor – there's another one!' she hissed.

The Doctor looked puzzled for a moment, before following her gaze. The expression on his face when he saw what was floating towards them was almost indescribable: a mixture of disbelief, shock and pure joy. Then he frowned.

'Another one? You've seen this phenomenon before?'

She nodded. 'Twice so far.'

'And you didn't see fit to tell me?' he snapped. 'This changes everything!'

Roz knew that she should have said something earlier, but the Doctor had erected a cold, hard barrier around him since their arrival on Mars, a barrier that Roz had felt uncomfortable getting close to. 'Is it important?' Stupid question; of course it was important.

'More than you could ever imagine,' he muttered. 'But this is too soon.' He looked around the group; thanks to their position, none of the others had seen the TARDIS yet. 'We can't let it interact with the Transit-web, Roz – the result would be disastrous!'

He moved towards the coruscating sphere of susbspace energy.

Santacosta trained her gun on him. 'I really wouldn't recommend it, Doctor. This is Bureau business.'

The hissing voice from behind was unexpected. 'Drop your weapon.' Santacosta spun round to see three Martians standing in the doorway, sonic disruptors aimed in her direction. For a second, she wondered whether she could make a break for it, but then she thought about the Transit-web; the stunnel terminus was almost complete, a globe of sparking green light that hovered about ten centimetres above the web. In less than a minute, fifty Adjudicators would come pouring through, and even three Greenies wouldn't stand a chance. She just had to keep them busy for a few seconds more.

They all saw the translucent shape at the same time, a large blue box coming out of the corridor, floating about a metre above the ground. What the hell was it, wondered Santacosta. Whatever it was, it appeared to be heading straight towards the Transit-web.

Cursing herself, she remembered the Doctor. He was right next to the T-web, hurling a metallic object into the stunnel terminus. She suddenly realized that it was the Divine Sight of Horus that he had pocketed earlier.

'No!' she shouted. She didn't know what he was up to, but she did know that the Doctor could be incredibly resourceful – and was probably a Martian sympathizer into the bargain. She aimed her gun at him, but he was standing directly behind the terminus; Santacosta knew better than to fire a directed energy weapon into a subspace field. She could only watch as the surface of the terminus began to ripple and fluoresce.

She groaned as the terminus started to collapse.

Then there was no terminus, just a contracting blur of radiation and a low, teeth-rattling groan. The blue box, which had been only metres away from the T-web, disappeared at the same time, simply popping out of existence. She cast her gaze to the ground, and watched with a sinking feeling as the strands of the web contracted into the central sphere. The stunnel had been aborted, and that was that.

The Doctor stared at the T-web nucleus, dabbing his forehead with a large spotted handkerchief. 'That was very close. Too close.'

'You idiot! Do you know what you just did?' yelled Santacosta. 'The T-web was our only chance!' She began to aim her gun at his head, but realized that it would be a waste of effort. The damage had been done.

The Doctor nodded. 'Indeed I do, Adjudicator Santacosta. Thanks to the deleterious effects of Osirian technology on subspace fields, I narrowly prevented a minor subspace infarction. Minor, but enough to consign all of us to an early grave. You should be grateful; the feedback would have blown up the stunnel generator on Oberon into the bargain.' He turned and doffed his panama hat towards the unusually patient Martians waiting in the doorway. 'Anyway, we appear to have a reception committee. I presume you were expecting this, Abbot Aklaar?'

But the elderly Martian remained silent. Frightened, even. Great, thought Santacosta; the whole operation goes down the pan, and now we could all be in even more trouble.

Roz sidled up to the Doctor. 'I'd appreciate your making a window in your diary to explain what the hell is going on. Why are we being haunted by the ghost of the TARDIS?'

But the Doctor wasn't listening. He was staring at the Martians in front of them with a frown twisting his mobile features. 'Why is Abbot Aklaar's religious pilgrimage being met by a squad of Ice Warriors from a military nest, I wonder?'

With that disturbing comment fresh in her mind, Santacosta followed the others through the opening in the metal wall.

She failed to notice the Doctor reach down and shove the inactive Transit-web nucleus into his pocket.

Chapter 9

Felice freely admitted that she was terrified. She and Rachel had been unstrapped from their beds by Yeess – none too gently, come to that, although what had she expected? Hotel service and a massage? – and escorted from the 'waiting room' to yet another welcoming chamber carved from solid rock, presumably the location of the Martians' precious Brain-rack. She tried not to look at the complicated and possibly painful assembly on the far side of the room; she'd rather wait until the inevitable. Chris's proposed plan had culminated in their rescue, but how could they be rescued if their minds had been coerced into obeying the Martians? The idea that she might be forced to gun Chris or Rachel down – or betray her own race, come to that – under the influence of the Greenies wasn't reassuring.

'There are no harmful side-effects to the Brain-rack,' Yeess assured them, not particularly convincingly. 'It wears off after a week or so, as the artificial engrams decay and your natural pathways reassert themselves. And a week should be all that we need for you to complete the GodEngine.'

'And what will you do then?' asked Rachel. 'Kill us?'

Yeess shook his head. 'Despite your propaganda, we are not barbarians, Professor. We are an ancient and honourable race with tenets forged in fire and blood.'

'Don't you think I don't know that?' Rachel snapped, and Felice was surprised by the ferocity of the reply. It was as if something deep within Rachel was taking its last chance for freedom. 'My brother spent a year in one of your military nests.' Felice frowned; she had known that Rachel had had a brother – Michael – but the circumstances of his death had been a mystery. Felice had gathered earlier that Rachel was far more familiar – and comfortable – with the Martians than most humans, but this was a revelation.

'Michael was assigned to the UN peacekeeping force on Mars about ten years ago,' Rachel explained. 'At first, he was like the others, regarding the Martians as nothing more than monsters. Then he fell in with a group called the Martian Axis.'

'The Axis?' repeated Felice. 'But they're terrorists.'

'They weren't at first. In the beginning, they just wanted peaceful coexistence with the Martians. Michael joined them, and bought into their ideals. It was only later when he realized their true purpose.' She looked at Yeess. 'They were using their cover to further their own cause, which was nothing more than civil disobedience.'

'But the Axis always claimed that their actions were sanctioned by the Martians,' said Felice. How could she forget the images of carnage that the news broadcasts had shown, the dead and injured that followed each atrocity?

Rachel shook her head. 'That was exactly what everyone was supposed to think – it gave a sick sort of justification to what they did. All their well-known attacks – the bombing of Coventry, the destruction of the Montreal monorail system – were nothing more than plain and simple terrorism, and the Martians got the blame.'

Felice touched Rachel's arm. This was the big question, but she had to ask it. 'What happened to Michael?'

Rachel closed her eyes, clearly torn apart by what she was about to say. 'He left the Axis when he realized what they were really up to. He wanted to seek out the real Martians. He made his way off Earth, and tried to find the planet where the Martians had settled. He never found it.'

'He found our base on Cluut-ett-Pictar,' stated Yeess.

Felice suddenly realized that she was at a disadvantage; Yeess and Rachel both knew the circumstances far better than she did. 'Your brother found a Martian base?'

Rachel nodded. 'Their exodus fleet made a brief planetfall on a world in the Rataculan system – the Martians called it

Cluut-ett-Pictar. A few stayed behind, and Michael found them.' She sighed. 'He did more than that, Felice; he joined them. That's how I know so much about Martians; Michael wrote to me every week, passing his letters through a dumb satellite that Earth had forgotten about.'

Yeess's fingers made some very odd, almost nervous, movements. 'Your brother is a hero of the Martian people, Professor. He died defending the nest on Cluut-ett-Pictar against an Arcturan strike-force.'

Rachel suppressed a choking sob. 'I – I never knew how. The letters just stopped, but I just knew that he'd – he'd gone.' She thrust her face upwards towards Yeess. 'I got his last letter, though, telling me that it was time that Earth knew the truth about the Martians – about their honour, their loyalty.' She looked up at Yeess. 'I know your ways, Yeess – if Michael was a hero, why are you treating us like this?'

Yeess's voice was tinged with regret as he replied. 'Sadly, I have no choice, Professor – it is not my decision to make. The GodEngine must be completed, and your knowledge is invaluable. If it means anything to you, though, I am no longer happy about this; there is something ... dishonourable about subjecting the sister of a Martian hero to the Brain-rack.'

'What is the GodEngine?' interrupted Felice, mainly to take the pressure off the clearly upset Rachel. 'The subspace manipulator?'

Yeess nodded. 'In our own tongue, it is *Ssor-arr duss Ssethissi* – the Engine of Ssethis, and the means of restoring our glory. But you will learn more after you have been processed. The Brain-rack will increase your learning rate by three hundred per cent.' He gestured towards the only object in the room, the thing that Felice had been at pains to ignore: a tall construction of silver pipework interlaced with the unmistakable amber of trisilicate. There was a man-sized gap in the centre. Actually, it looked rather too Felice-sized for her liking. That was when she discovered that she had tempted fate. 'You first, Dr Delacroix.'

Felice gulped, but knew that she had no choice; even without his body armour, Yeess could easily overpower her.

Stepping into the gap, she closed her eyes tightly, waiting for the inevitable searing agony. But it wasn't like that. She felt a delicate, almost tickling feeling across her scalp, a soothing sensation that forced her to relax. Suddenly, she experienced a surge of panic as she realized that she was being anaesthetized, but it was far too late for that. Any thoughts of a last-minute rescue attempt by Chris receded rapidly as brand-new thoughts began to flower and bloom in her mind. But these thoughts were nice thoughts, thoughts free of any negative feelings.

As she opened her eyes, she saw Rachel standing in front of her. But she didn't recognize her as a friend or colleague: she was simply another resource pledged to the service of the GodEngine.

'Welcome to G'chun duss Ssethiissi, honoured guests. I am Supreme Lord Draan.' The Ice Lord, dressed in the full regalia of smooth-domed helmet, tabard armour and cloak, was standing behind an impressive stone table, with two Warriors flanking him. Roz shared the Doctor's concerns; this really did not feel like a pacifist nest. What the hell was going on? Not for the first time, she wished that Professor Bernice Summerfield, or Mrs Jason Kane, or Benny Kane-Summerfield, or whatever she was going to call herself, had been with them, rather than a few blurred memories of a few blurred conversations.

'Lord Draan – when will the ceremony take place?' It was Aklaar, his tone of voice understandably eager.

Draan bashed his clamps together and clearly agreed with Roz's analysis. 'I understand your eagerness, Abbot, but I also realize that you have all had a strenuous and tiring journey. I suggest that you take some rest before we proceed.' He looked over at Sstaal; more specifically, he looked at his backpack. 'And that is the Sword of Tuburr. Excellent. The ceremony will mark a new beginning for Mars, the start of an entire new history for our people. I share your anticipation, Abbot, but am sure that you will enjoy the ceremony far more if you have rested. We have waited a long time for this moment; a few more hours will not matter.'

With that, the Ice Lord dismissed them.

'Short and sweet,' said Roz as they filed out of the room with their escort.

'Too short, too sweet,' replied the Doctor. Roz had noticed that the Doctor's odd behaviour of the last couple of days had abated somewhat. Was it to do with the mysterious floating TARDISes, or the fact that Aklaar's pilgrimage wasn't as innocent as it had first appeared, justifying his mistrust? It did seem to her that the Doctor was looking for any opportunity to expose the Ice Warriors in what he believed were their true colours. 'Draan is an Ice Lord – which makes it quite clear that this is not the pacifist nest that the Abbot thought he was heading towards. But Draan isn't in charge here.'

'Why do you say that? He seemed pretty sure of himself.'

'Because he isn't senior enough, Roz. From the size of this base, it merits a Marshal at least. Possibly even a Grand Marshal.'

'But you said the Grand Marshals were executed after the Thousand Day War.'

'All but two,' corrected the Doctor. 'Falaxyr and Abrasaar. The two most brutal, sadistic and unpleasant of the lot. Their bodies were never found.' He growled, 'Aklaar was expecting to be met by pilgrims; instead, there's a military reception. And I'm sure that I recognize Draan . . .'

'You've never met the Ice Warriors in this time period. Unless the TARDIS databanks were lying to me.' She had occasionally surfed the TARDIS's memories, curious of the Doctor's past actions.

He pouted. 'They do occasionally, but not about this. Ice Warriors can live for nearly three hundred standard years, but Draan is too young to have been involved in the T-Mat crisis. Anyway, there was only one Ice Lord on the Moon, and that was Slaar. Brutal, sadistic and unpleasant.'

'A typical specimen, then?'

A momentary frown was replaced by a self-admonishing grin. 'I am getting a trifle involved, aren't I? Then again, there was something of a family resemblance . . . Believe it or not, I do trust Aklaar; he represents a type of Martian I could never have hoped would exist in this time zone. Unless I'm sadly mistaken, he's the victim of a set-up, and we had better be ready to lend a hand.'

Roz smiled. 'I'm an Adjudicator; I'm always ready.'

He grinned at her in return. 'So how did you let Santacosta beat you, then, O old and wise Adjudicator?'

'Too old, too wise,' she laughed.

Chris checked his watch. Still over half an hour left before he set off his indoor firework display. The two days he had spent in careful observation meant that he was well aware of the various routines and exercises that the Martians carried out in their oh-so-precise fashion; in just over half an hour, quite a lot of Ice Warriors would come very close to quite a lot of important corridors and intersections as they carried out their duties.

The little boy inside Chris – the one who had stared out of his bedroom window and dreamed about the Hith dogfights going on, far out in space – just couldn't wait.

Rachel watched as Felice stepped out of the Brain-rack. She smiled and walked over to her, a look of beatitude on her face. 'Once you're processed, Rachel, we'll be able to start work on the final stage of the GodEngine. Oh, Rachel, this is going to be magnificent. Forget the work we were doing on Charon – this is centuries beyond our technology, possibly even millennia. Professor Ketch would give his eye-teeth to see this. The Martians –' Felice broke off as Yeess came over and gently escorted Rachel over to the metal assembly. She knew that there was no point in struggling – this was it.

Yeess positioned her inside the Brain-rack matrix. 'I am sure that your brother would have understood the expediency necessary during a wartime situation.'

As the jittering tendrils of the rack reached towards her head, Rachel asked one, final question. 'Who are you at war with, Yeess?'

The Martian's head made little circling movements. 'We are at war with everyone, Professor. Everyone.'

No, Yeess, you're at war with yourselves, thought Rachel. That had been Michael's last message, his final realization that the honour that the Martians prized above everything was nothing more than an inherited illusion. And then the Brain-rack began to infiltrate her thoughts, and Michael was replaced by seductive images of a glittering pyramid of Egyptian relics.

The Martians led Aklaar and McGuire's party to a lower level that seemed less finished than the rest of the base: instead of polished amber walls and decorative murals, Roz noted that the surfaces of the tunnels through which they were currently being taken – they were too crude to be called corridors – were rough and unadorned.

After about ten minutes of silent trudging, the Ice Warriors motioned for them to stop. They had reached a long gallery that was dimly lit from above, a perpendicular space with four archways evenly spaced in front of them.

Behind the archways were plain white walls, an incongruous touch of artificial plastic set into the natural rock.

'You will rest here until you are sent for,' hissed one of their escort, before opening each of the doors in turn. There wasn't much chance of choosing your room-mate either; they were ushered in, two at a time, according to their relative positions in the group.

Roz watched with interest as the members of the expedition-stroke-pilgrimage paired off. Understandably, Esstar was quartered with her mate Cleece, and yet Roz knew that they weren't going to be playing happy families. Roz herself was quartered with Carmen, a situation which she was less than happy about, to say the least, while McGuire was sharing with timid little Sstaal. Mmmm. That would prove interesting. And as for the Doctor . . . he and Aklaar were heading into the same room. She smiled; at least the Doctor was with the one Martian whom he came close to liking.

As she entered the room, pulling off her rucksack, she looked around. The room was very different from the comfortable yet simple habitation in Ikk-ett-Saleth; it was as if a prefabricated cube of some sort of polymer had been assembled inside a medium-sized cave in the rock. There were two basic beds – large enough for the bulking frame of an Ice Warrior – and a table. There was also an object in the corner that Roz eventually recognized as a toilet.

'Comfortable for a jail cell,' muttered Santacosta, taking off her jacket. She smiled. 'Sorry about earlier, Forrester.'

'What? Trying to kill me? It happens all the time in this job – you should know that. But don't worry – I'm not one to bear a grudge,' she replied sardonically.

Santacosta shrugged. 'The joys of being an Adjudicator; sometimes you have to get down and get dirty because of the bigger picture.' Then she frowned. 'What do you mean – this job?'

Before answering, Roz pondered the woman's words. She remembered her recent career, when being an Adjudicator had been the be-all and end-all of everything – she and her partner, Fenn Martle, fighting for truth, justice and the Imperial way. She then remembered his death – as if she could ever forget it, short of having the memories surgically removed again – at her own hands, when she had discovered the first signs of the cancer that was infesting the Guild and the Empire itself. Now she and Chris were exiles from their own planet, their own time, simply because they had held onto their ideals while everyone else had sold them to the highest bidder.

But Santacosta was an Adjudicator from an earlier, simpler time; the Guild didn't even exist in the twenty-second century. She belonged to the Adjudication Bureau, an organization which still believed in the outdated ethics for which Chris and Roz had been condemned.

'What is the bigger picture, then?'

Santacosta shook her head. 'I'm sorry, Roz, but that's still confidential – explain what you meant earlier,' she insisted.

Roz thought for a second, but knew that she only had one course of action if they were to gain some sort of advantage over the Ice Warriors. Reaching into her trousers, she pulled out her Adjudicator ID – the one item that she could guarantee to keep with her at all times. Sometimes, she was even more sentimental than Chris. 'Does this give me sufficient clearance, Carmen?' She leant back and waited for the reaction.

Santacosta examined the small black wallet, her face impassive. Roz knew that the formal credentials of an Adjudicator had remained virtually unchanged since the formation of the Bureau; even though the badge was, by her time, purely symbolic – advanced forgery techniques meant that the only true identification was a sub-dermal chip – it should still have some effect on Santacosta.

She wasn't mistaken.

'Where did you get this?' Santacosta asked urgently. 'Where?'

'At my graduation ceremony on Ponten IV. I can assure you that it's genuine.'

' "Roslyn Sarah Forrester, Class of 2955" . . . what is this telling me, Roz? What are *you* telling me?'

'That I'm also an Adjudicator from over eight hundred years in your future. The Doctor and I are time travellers; that blue box that appeared just before he cancelled your Transit-web is all that remains of his space-time vehicle.'

Santacosta threw her head back and laughed. 'A time-travelling Adjudicator? And yet . . . those moves you tried on me were definitely Raven-training – if a bit on the rusty side.' She passed the badge back. 'Okay, okay, suppose I accept what you're telling me. My God, it's hardly the sort of story you'd come up with to impress me, is it?'

Roz grinned. 'Hardly – I'm not known for my over-active imagination. Nor am I known for my trusting nature, but we're going to have to trust one another, Santacosta. Because, unless you're the most inept Adjudicator in the Bureau, you must have noticed that this situation is spiralling out of control.'

'If you mean the preponderance of Warriors in a so-called religious nest, then yes. If you mean the way that your friend shut down the Transit-web –' She frowned. 'Not very clever.'

Despite the Doctor's recent aberrant behaviour, she knew that he wouldn't have done something like that unless there had been a very good reason. She hoped. 'I told you that the Doctor and I were time travellers?'

Santacosta giggled with a faint trace of her songbird persona.

'One of the less believable aspects to your story, but yes.'

'The emphasis is on the *were*. Our – our time machine blew up three days ago. But that blue box which was floating towards your T-web was some sort of after-effect, I suppose. According to the Doctor, it would have interacted with the subspace field and caused a massive explosion.'

'Really?' replied Santacosta, fixing Roz with her near-black eyes. 'I heard him say that as clearly as you did, but the important question is: do you believe him?'

Roz opened her mouth to protest, but suddenly realized that she couldn't. Not any more. Perhaps she needed to trust Carmen Santacosta a lot more than she needed Santacosta to trust her.

'Rooms designed for human habitation, Aklaar. Doesn't that strike you as odd?' The Doctor pointed at the toilet in the corner. 'Almost as if they expected your pilgrimage to have included others.'

The Abbot continued folding his shimmering cloak in the ritual manner of the winding sheet of Oras. 'Extremely odd, Doctor.' He placed the cloak on one of the two beds, laid his thick wooden staff next to it, and then lowered himself into a sitting position, ignoring the jolts of pain which resulted from the movement. Martians were long-lived – on those rare occasions that they failed to die an 'honourable' death – and could expect to continue for nearly three centuries. But Aklaar was over two hundred and eighty, and easy prey to all of the vicious ailments of old age. After six months of pilgrimage, his joints burnt as though they were on fire, and his exhaustion was almost tangible.

But he felt no desire to sleep; he knew that he had to talk to this Doctor, this infinite well of secrets that appeared to know each and every facet of Martian life and tradition, and yet could not give his trust freely.

'But Oras has taught us to relish each diversion from the expected as a fresh challenge to fortify the soul.' Aklaar gestured around the room with a clamp. 'This mystery will undoubtedly unfurl in a myriad of wondrous and awesome ways.'

'Oras? Oras?' The Doctor hurled his hat at the prefabricated wall with unwarranted anger. 'Oh, Aklaar; you quote parables and aphorisms and attribute them to an Osirian who died thousands of years ago, an Osirian who considered your race as nothing more than insects, little crawling things which occasionally proved useful when he needed a Sphinx or a pyramid building. The Osirians were all alike, Aklaar: selfish and duplicitous. And if they ever deigned to acknowledge you, it was as their servants and inferiors. Horus never uttered a single word that you attribute to him!'

Aklaar nodded sagely. 'I know. The Osirians were exactly as you described them, Doctor: callous godlings whose extinction was a blessing for the universe. But know this first, before you condemn our religion so offhandedly: a faction of our race – even then, seven thousand years ago – knew that by committing our entire race to war we were dooming ourselves to the same fate, the same extinction, that befell the Osirians. They took advantage of the race memories and legends that had sprung up around the Osirians, and created a new religion, one based on compassion, on peace. They hoped that even this thread of pacifism could restrain our baser instincts; if not, it could serve as the nucleus of a new age. This is that new age, Doctor.'

But the Doctor's look of venom didn't change. 'In four thousand years' time, a liar and a criminal called Maximillian Arrestis will create a religion called the Lazarus Intent, preaching exactly the same holy tenets. He wanted power and immortality, Abbot. What do *you* want?'

Aklaar cast his gaze to the smooth floor as he considered his answer. The Doctor's intimation that he was a time traveller came as no great surprise; there were quite a few references to time travellers in the all-encompassing history of Mars. Quite apart from the tales of the Osirians – who had discovered time travel but abandoned it as a sterile waste of their talents and a sociological dead-end – there was the mischievous alien called the Monk who had allied himself with a military nest many years ago, and those stories surrounding Grand Marshal Paxaphyr's disastrous attempt to seize control of the human's matter transmission control centre on Earth's moon. On that occasion, the time traveller had called himself ... Aklaar looked up sharply and stared the other in the face, almost unable to believe it. Surely this couldn't be the same Doctor who had thwarted Paxaphyr and Slaar's conquest? Then he remembered the question.

'What do I want, Doctor?' He opened his clamps in supplication. 'I want what all followers of Oras want. What all followers of Oras have always wanted. Forgiveness for our sins. And peace.'

McGuire threw his rucksack onto the bed and looked around the room. 'Oh, very cosy. You Gree–, you Martians really know how to treat your guests.'

Sstaal tried to view his surroundings charitably, but he knew that he could never have described it as being cosy. But that didn't explain McGuire's outburst – the room had clearly been tailored for humans, and he should have been pleased. 'I do not understand your displeasure, Antony. Steps have been taken to make this room suitable for human habitation.' He pointed a clamp towards the object to his right. 'That is a latrine, is it not?'

McGuire had taken off his thick jacket and thrown himself onto one of the beds. 'What's the difference? Or do you crap in the corner like most lizards?'

Sstaal removed his rucksack, making sure that the Sword of Tuburr lay flat on the quilted fabric of the bedding, and then sat on the other bed. *Crap* meant *defecate*, and that was something that Martians did rarely. So rarely that their dwellings didn't even need separate areas for it. 'No, Mr McGuire. Millions of years ago, our race was migratory, and we evolved so that almost all of our waste products were recycled. This armour boosts even that efficiency – nothing is wasted.'

'What a perfect life you must have, Sstaal,' McGuire sneered. 'You don't even have to go to the toilet. All the qualities of a galactic master-race.'

Sstaal understood the reference, but still didn't understand McGuire's belligerence. 'We are pilgrims –'

'Cut the crap, Sstaal.'

Sstaal was puzzled by yet another scatological reference. 'But I have already told you that we do not need to defecate.'

McGuire sat up on the bed, his eyes narrowed. 'That's not what I meant. You may be a typical Martian pilgrim – short and stunted and unable to talk without falling over yourself – but your big Warrior friends killed my wife and children. And you expect me to sit here and listen to a dwarf bastard like you stuttering away about your spiritual leanings?'

Stunned by the ferocity of the verbal attack, Sstaal coldly considered McGuire's words. As Martians went, he *was* small. From his earliest days in the seminary, he had been ridiculed about his stature, and he could only assume that the constant, cruel ridicule of his peers had led to his general nervousness and his unfortunate stammer.

Sstaal was still only a teenager in human terms, but he would happily have given up the hundreds of years of life that lay ahead of him to be built like Cleece. Despite McGuire's theories, all Martians should possess the stature and bulk that characterized their race across the solar system, whether they be pilgrims, warriors, artificers or farmers. Sstaal was a deformed runt, he knew that only too well; and that insecurity was always there, a furious sandstorm barely held at bay, always ready to overwhelm him and plunge him into depression. Growing up, he had stared at his larger brethren with all-consuming envy, never fully accepting that he might possibly have gifts – such as his intellect – which they might have coveted.

Which made his feelings for Esstar all the more puzzling. What could he offer the proud Esstar that she couldn't get from Cleece? Why had she even deigned to look at him? He looked at McGuire, a strange feeling shooting through him like a burning stomach cramp, as if he had eaten too many hot okk-tet leaves. With a sudden flash of realization, he knew that it was anger. Without thinking, he stepped forward, bearing down over the small human being.

'Neither of us has a choice in this, McGuire,' he whispered. 'We must stay here until Lord Draan is ready for the ceremony. So we can either sit here in silence, or attempt to have a civil conversation. If you cannot conduct the latter, I would prefer the former, since I find your constant xenophobia offensive. Your race has no reason to be proud of its barbaric behaviour either.' There, he had said it. As the green haze that had flickered around his field of vision faded, he wondered whether Esstar would have been proud of him, before remembering with another sickening feeling that she was quartered with her mate. The anger continued. 'Thanks to your people, Mars is a lifeless, soulless world –'

'I'm sorry, Sstaal.' McGuire's voice was quiet, lost. Soulless.

The Martian was momentarily lost for words. His outburst had simply been a means of shutting up the human. Sstaal had never expected that it would invite an apology. He gathered his thoughts before replying.

'Silence or civility?'

McGuire forced a smile. 'I just don't feel comfortable here. After talking to Aklaar over the last few days, I thought that I was beginning to come to terms with your race, but this . . .' He patted the bald spot on the top of his head. 'And I shouldn't have been rude about your size; I'm not exactly the tallest man on Earth, am I?'

Sstaal reached out and gingerly laid his clamp on McGuire's shoulder, and was pleased that the human didn't flinch. 'Not all Greenies are the same, Antony.' And then he remembered some of what he had overheard between McGuire and the Abbot. 'Please, tell me about your family.'

McGuire looked at him, his eyes like glittering trisilicate. Sstaal realized that the human was crying. 'All right. But afterwards, I'd like you to tell me about you and Esstar.'

Sstaal was taken aback – was it that obvious? But he was also reassured: talking of such personal matters was a first step to true understanding between their peoples. Whether Esstar was proud of him or not, he was proud of himself, and that was unprecedented. So it was a very big first step.

'Alone at last, Esstar.' Cleece dropped his rucksack on the floor, and urgently started feeling for the hidden catches which would release his carapace. Even through the red tint of his visor, Esstar could see the avarice in Cleece's eyes. It repelled her. 'I have waited a long time for this. Despite the tenets of Abbot Aklaar, I am only Martian.' Hurling the carapace onto the bed, he pulled off his clamped gloves and reached for her.

Esstar drew away in disgust. 'What sort of an animal are you, Cleece? I am with child, but all you can think of is sexual congress?' His reaction wasn't unexpected, but it was definitely unwelcome – and not just because of her condition.

Bereft of carapace, helmet and gloves, Cleece stood before her and smiled cruelly. She could see that his genitalia were descending from their protective internal sac, and she felt sick at the prospect of him taking her as if she were some mindless creature whose sole reason for existence was to please him.

'Why, what are you thinking of?' he asked. And then his eyes narrowed. 'Sex with Sstaal, perhaps?'

Esstar had been prepared for this insult; it was one of Cleece's favourites, always hurled as a last resort when reasoned argument failed; with Cleece, that was always rather quickly. During the year-long pilgrimage, she had held her tongue and put up with his foul attacks; Abbot Aklaar wouldn't have stood for such behaviour. But here, now . . .

Her own insult had been honed and polished over the last year, and she loaded, aimed and fired it with relish. 'At least he is true to his caste, Cleece, and not a changeling like you.'

Totally prepared for his reaction, she moved to one side as Cleece lunged at her, but she had the advantage; although he was male, and naturally stronger, she was still dressed in her armour. With her cybernetically amplified musculature, she grabbed his arm and flung him to the floor. As he lay there, dazed and prone, she grasped his neck with her clamp; for a second, she wondered whether the slight effort needed to snap his neck would be worth it, but decided that there were other, less final ways of teaching her mate a lesson.

Cleece looked up at her, his expression one of disbelief mixed with confusion. But he was powerless, and Esstar liked that.

She smiled down at him. 'It is time we talked of the future, Cleece.'

Chris checked his watch. Only seconds remained before his preparations came to fruition, and he knew that he had to be ready. He had planned the route from his cubby-hole to the manipulator chamber with calculated precision over and over again in his mind; he could get there in a matter of minutes. He just hoped that that was where Felice and Rachel had been stationed by the Ice Warriors. He had already decided that searching for them was fruitless; they could be anywhere in the base. If they weren't where he expected them to be, his only option was to make a break for it and get back to the survivors.

Assuming that they hadn't been slaughtered by the Ice Warriors, of course. Falaxyr had been expecting them to arrive; was it too much to hope that he wouldn't have sent a search party to the parliament building? Chris's watch suddenly bleeped at him. And sent a blanket pulse across the complex.

His little hidy-hole shuddered as fifty separate explosions rocked the Martian base, each of them carefully placed to cause the maximum amount of confusion. And that was only the start.

Chris smiled.

It was time to begin.

Chapter 10

Falaxyr looked up from Hoorg's latest report on the status of the GodEngine, aware that he had been disturbed, but not quite sure by what. But the next disturbance was clearly recognizable: it was an explosion, just outside the doors of Falaxyr's chambers. Through the circuitry built into his helmet, he patched into the base communications suite.

'Report!' he demanded.

The reply was distorted by static and barely decipherable. '... multip ... explos ... througho ... complex ... casualties ...' Falaxyr closed the useless connection and stood up. He attempted to summon Draan, but there was even more interference across that channel. He had no choice: he would have to find out what was going on for himself. Hissing with anger at the situation, he strode over to the main doors of his room and pulled the handle.

Nothing happened. He examined the doors and immediately saw the reason why: the door frame was buckled at the top, jamming the doors and making them totally immovable, despite Falaxyr's enhanced strength. Without hesitation, he raised his arm, aimed his clamp at the line where the doors met, and then sent the necessary signals to his inbuilt weapon.

The sonic disruptor mounted on his wrist gave a sustained, shrill warble, and the surface of the metal began to ripple as if seen through a heat haze. Unfortunately for Falaxyr, the doors were heavily reinforced, a legacy of an earlier time where even a base commander had to protect himself from ambitious underlings and internecine struggles. It would take at least ten minutes at full force for the doors to give way under the sonic barrage.

Trying to feel the patience that had kept him sane over his long years of isolation, Falaxyr started waiting for the rippling metal to melt.

Chris hauled his backside out of the cubby-hole and dropped to the ground two metres below. The string of explosions was still continuing, and should carry on for another two minutes if he'd wired everything up properly. Some of the bombs had been nothing more than smoke and noise, akin to the ones he had used to elude the Ice Warriors earlier. But the others had been far more destructive.

The Doctor had thoughtfully included a handwritten inventory in the kit, including instructions on the usage of the various phials and bottles that it contained – like the late, lamented TARDIS, the kit seemed to be bigger on the inside than out. Two of the phials contained chemicals called nitro-twelve and nitro-thirteen, which the Doctor's spidery handwriting described as 'rich, full-bodied and fruity vintages a thousand times as powerful as nitro-glycerine'; sadly, Chris hadn't ever heard of nitro-glycerine, but he had used the chemicals sparingly. From the sound of the continued explosions, even those single drops had been overkill.

Ripping handfuls of insulation from his atmosphere jacket, he had dripped various chemicals into the hanks of white fibres and attached short lengths of filament to the impregnated areas. And then he had wired the filaments into tiny, pinhead-sized detonators which were apparently controlled by the watch that was coiled up in the kit.

He had made other preparations: small collections of circuitry which would act as milder versions of his cyber-scrambler, placed at strategic points and effectively blocking the Ice Warriors' communication net; ultrasonic squealers which would completely disorientate any Ice Warriors in the vicinity, and one, last, special surprise for his hosts. He checked his watch once more; according to the timing sequence, that should be going off about –

He had to steady himself against the smooth stone wall as

the ground bucked beneath him, while an echoing roar came from deep in the complex. One last bomb, soaked with the remainder of nitros twelve and thirteen, had been placed right next to what Chris believed to be some sort of auxiliary generator.

And from the way the lights were flickering up and down the service corridor he was in, he had guessed correctly. Now should be the time of maximum disruption – Chris's opportunity to mount his white charger and rescue the fair damsels from their distress. Smiling at the thought of Rachel as a damsel, he set off down the corridor, following the route that he had etched into his mind.

As the series of explosions continued, Aklaar instinctively tried to tap into the base communication net, before realizing that his helmet lacked the necessary security protocols. He looked up at the Doctor. 'The base is under attack.'

Aklaar prided himself on his ability to read human expressions and emotions, but the smile on the Doctor's face was inexplicable. 'Doctor?'

'That isn't an attack, Abbot. It's a distraction, and – if the culprit is who I think he is – a very, very welcome one. I suggest we sit tight and await developments.'

Aklaar was puzzled, but he could see that this Doctor was like the plasma vampires of the great southern plains; for centuries, they would wait just beneath the surface, on the borders of life and death. But as soon as their unfortunate prey stepped onto it, they would rise from the sand and engulf its victim. The Doctor would act; but only when it suited him to do so. Aklaar just hoped that the Doctor wasn't quite as lethal as the plasma vampires.

'Why did you stay on Mars?' asked the Doctor suddenly. 'Why didn't you join the majority of your race and leave?'

'As you say, Doctor: the majority. There are still hundreds of thousands of my people on Mars: pilgrims, warriors, artificers . . . This is our home.'

'I meant on a personal level, Aklaar. Why did you stay? Or was the Blessed Order of Oras barred from New Mars?'

'I stayed because there is still much work to do among my

people. The Thousand Day War, and the skirmishes that preceded it, were the last throes of a weak and desperate military. The Eight-Point Table longed for one last triumph, one last war that would re-establish their authority over this planet and show your Alliance that we were still a force to be feared.'

'So you invaded T-Mat Central on the Moon, and followed up that little débâcle by dropping an asteroid on Paris. Did you really think that Earth wouldn't retaliate?'

Aklaar held up his clamp. 'The Eight-Point Table was desperate, Doctor. There was a serious possibility of a coup –'

'You seem to be very familiar with the workings of the military mind for a wise old Abbot. Is military history a hobby of yours?'

Aklaar smiled, but he didn't mean it, and wondered whether the Doctor could tell. Probably, he decided. 'Know thine enemy, Doctor. The retaliation from Earth was swift and unexpected, and tore the heart out of the military. The aftermath was far less bloody, but even more devastating; the collective soul of the Martian people was tainted, stained by the actions of their rulers. Most of my people chose to make a new start on Nova Martia, where they could learn from the painful lessons of their ancestors and leaders –'

'Is that the destiny of the Ice Warriors, Aklaar?' the Doctor interrupted. 'To run from planet to planet, afraid to face their true nature?' He smiled sadly. 'The galaxy is very large, Abbot, but even you'll run out of homes eventually. You don't exactly make the best neighbours, do you?'

The Abbot stood up and faced him. 'You asked me why I had stayed on Mars, Doctor. *That* is the reason why: because I am prepared to face that true nature – to face it and to conquer it. Both here and on Nova Martia, there are Martians whose very beliefs have been violated, whose spirits scream for absolution from their crimes. The Order of Oras will counsel and guide them, and point them in the new direction of peaceful coexistence.'

The Doctor cocked an eyebrow. 'So, you're galactic social workers now? I'm sorry, Aklaar, but I can't believe that the Ice Warriors have changed so much, so quickly.'

'Then you are no better than the people you mistrust, Doctor. How pure is your soul?'

The Doctor frowned. 'That's the problem, Aklaar. I'm not sure I know any more.'

Aklaar placed his clamp on the Doctor's hand. 'Then perhaps, through the wisdom of Oras, we could find out together.'

'What the hell was that?' yelled Roz. The explosion sounded like it had come from just outside, and she moved sharply to one side to avoid a lump of ceiling that dropped to the floor with a dull thud.

'Come on, Roz!' snapped Santacosta. 'Even in your time, they must have taught you to recognize a terrorist attack?'

Terrorist? Roz realized that Santacosta was right; it bore all the hallmarks of a standard Adjudicator raid. 'Your backup?'

'I doubt it, unless Ketch has found a way of breaking through the barrier. And if he could do that, the Bureau would have come in force, not like this. This is the McClane Approach, by the textbook – a one-person raid.'

Roz was puzzled; if Santacosta's colleagues weren't responsible, who was? It had to be an Adjudicator. One particular Adjudicator came to mind, one who had once spoken wistfully of his lectures on subversive warfare on Ponten IV, and of a heartfelt wish to put his education into action.

Chris.

'I've got an idea of the guilty party, Carmen, and that's our cue to get out of here.' She looked around the plain white walls, hoping that the ceiling wasn't the only part of the room to sustain damage. It wasn't. Just next to the toilet, a jagged vertical crack had appeared. She went over to it and shoved the wall between the crack and the toilet, and was gratified to feel it give slightly. 'Over here,' she called, requisitioning Santacosta's aid.

After less than a minute of sustained shoving, the whole section of wall fell inwards, revealing a gap of about a metre between the prefabricated polymer walls and the rock face of the cave: the Ice Warriors had simply erected the room in a convenient cavern. Roz stepped through the hole first, with

Santacosta right behind.

'Since I seem to be squiring you, what's the plan?' asked Santacosta.

Roz shrugged. 'We get out of here, find my partner, and release the others.'

'Your partner?'

Roz was suddenly aware of a warm feeling of completeness inside her. Although she would never admit it, she was extremely fond of Chris; the idea that he had died when the TARDIS had been destroyed had been like a cold black hole in her stomach, a twisted knot that she had ignored with fierce determination. For a moment, she thought about Fenn Martle; had he ever felt like that about her, or had it all been an act for his paymasters? When she finally returned to Earth – as she knew she had to, one day – she would start digging, and carry on until the corruption at the core of the Empire was revealed as the rotting canker that it was.

She realized that Santacosta was talking to her. 'Are you telling me that your partner decided to take on an entire military nest single-handed?'

Roz grinned. 'That's the type of guy he is. Irresponsible and sometimes downright stupid. All part of his charm.' At that point, they reached the front of the cave, where the prefabricated wall was partially welded to the cave mouth. But there was a thin crevice between the polymer slab and the rock; it was less than half a metre wide, but it opened directly onto the corridor beyond. Not that they could see much of the corridor: a drifting cloud of some foul-smelling gas obscured almost everything, and what they could see was gloomy due to the lack of illumination. Smoke, power cuts; Chris has been busy, thought Roz.

Squeezing through the crevice with some difficulty, she looked up and down the corridor – although she would only have seen an Ice Warrior if one was right on top of her – before helping Santacosta through.

'Do we find your partner first, or release the others?'

Roz shook her head. 'Releasing them wouldn't be a good move; they'd only slow us down. I wouldn't mind seeing the Doctor, though –'

That plan was strangled at birth by the sound of at least two Ice Warriors coming towards them, their heavy steps too close for comfort. Roz knew that the reduced visibility wouldn't prove much of a problem to the imaging systems of an Ice Warrior helmet, so she set off down the corridor in the opposite direction, as quickly but as quietly as possible. As expected, Santacosta followed without needing to be told.

They reached a junction after a few minutes. The air was clearer, but Roz still had no idea where to go. In order to accomplish such a bombing campaign, Chris must have had a fairly good idea of the layout of the base; something that Roz and Santacosta lacked. But Roz felt sure that the chaos that resulted from the explosions must have been for a reason; a cover for something else. Chris was using it as camouflage, and it was up to her and Santacosta to find out exactly what was going on.

This time, she saw it at the far end of the left-hand corridor. Translucent, blue and floating, another phantom TARDIS, bobbing away from them. Roz's instincts kicked in, and she gestured to the manifestation, saying words which she never thought she would utter.

'Follow that TARDIS!'

Well, it seemed like a good idea. And Roz needed all the good ideas she could get at the moment.

As the TARDIS sailed across a junction, Roz ran after it, Santacosta close behind. Reading between the lines, the phantom vessel was homing in on something, waiting for something to happen; what were the chances that that was where everything was going on? If so, it stood to reason that Chris would be heading in the same direction.

Roz hurtled round the junction, trying to keep the TARDIS in view – and ran head first into a tall broad figure. Before she could retreat, it reached out and grabbed her in an unbreakable hold.

Falaxyr had soon realized that the reinforced metal of the doors was disintegrating far faster than he had expected, indicating that others were trying to get in – at least somebody in the base had bothered to think about him. After only a few minutes, the metal crumpled like wet paper, revealing the corridor beyond – and Draan, flanked by two guards.

Falaxyr stepped through the hole, making sure as he did so that his purple cloak didn't catch the red-hot edges. 'What is happening, Draan? Why is the base in uproar?'

His subordinate looked distinctly uncomfortable, and so he might. From the scene of carnage behind him, the situation was even more critical than Falaxyr had expected. There had been a rock fall in the corridor, and the Grand Marshal could see at least two casualties partially buried under the rubble. To his left, the corridor was all but blocked where the ceiling had caved in.

'There has been a sustained series of explosions across the base, Your Excellency. Preliminary reports estimate over two hundred dead and injured, and a considerable amount of collateral damage.'

Falaxyr's immediate reaction was one of boiling anger at himself. He was in no doubt whatsoever as to the identity of the perpetrator: it could only be that damned Adjudicator, and Falaxyr was to blame for his continued freedom. But Falaxyr hadn't risen to the Eight-Point Table by indulging in self-recrimination. Anger was power, and he knew exactly how to channel it.

'When this is over, Draan, I will have you fall on the Sword of Tuburr for your stupidity. Fortunately for you, I still require your meagre services. Continue your report.'

Draan was clearly shaken by the threat, especially since it had been delivered in front of his own subordinates. But he continued anyway. 'Communications are disrupted across the base, we are using emergency power, and . . .' He hesitated. This meant very bad news, and Falaxyr hoped it wasn't as bad as he suspected.

'. . . and the auxiliary power feeds to the GodEngine have been severely damaged. Thankfully, the device itself is unharmed.'

Just what Falaxyr needed. Had he spent seventy years preparing for this moment, only to see it fall around him because of one, single human being? 'What is Hoorg's estimation of the damage?'

'Chief Technician Hoorg is among the casualties, Grand Marshal.'

Falaxyr hit the wall so hard that he started another rock fall. His little game with the Adjudicator had now turned into an unmitigated disaster, and Falaxyr knew he had only one course of action.

'Bring me the head of Christopher Cwej, Draan-Utt-Slaar.'

Draan nodded and hurried off in the unblocked direction of the corridor. Falaxyr nodded at the two Warriors. 'Inform Technician Sleeth that he is now in charge of the GodEngine project. Then bring all the prisoners here at once.' The promise of one last game of combat with the Adjudicator had blinded him to his duty, and that had almost ruined everything. 'It is time to end this charade.'

Cleece was silent. He had been silent since Esstar had released him from her grip. Even the series of explosions that had rocked the room had failed to elicit a reaction from him.

He had nothing to say.

Despite their constant arguments, despite the animosity that burnt between them, Cleece had never doubted their relationship. Martians bonded for life: that was their tradition. Not just Warriors, but pilgrims, artificers, cooks ... all of them pair-bonded early in life, and that bond was the nucleus of the family. From the family came the caste, and from the castes came the nests. The pair-bond was the foundation of Martian life.

And then his mate, the mother of his unborn children, had told him that she wanted to dissolve their bond, that she wanted to perform the ceremony of *Fass-jul-Aqq* – the Sundering.

'I have no feelings for you, Cleece, save ones of disgust and pity. For the sake of the seminary, I agreed to the bonding, hoping perhaps that you would moderate your intolerable ways, that you would embrace the teachings and beliefs of your adopted family. But your hankerings for the glories of war and bloodshed are too deeply ingrained, too fundamental, for you to change.

'You are not fit to be the father of children, Cleece. You belong to an age which caused the rape of Mars, and I belong to a better future. As is my right and privilege under ancient law, I will humbly request that the Abbot perform the *Fassjul-Aqq*, and dissolve this parody of a bond.'

'So you can be with Sstaal?' he had muttered numbly.

'So I can provide a new life for my children, Cleece. What I choose to do, who I choose to bond with, cease to be your concern after the Sundering.'

'To end this bond, you need a valid reason. The Abbot will not agree simply on your whim,' he stated. Bonding was always for life, unless there was some reason which was acceptable to an Abbot. As far as he knew, Esstar had none.

She had smiled, but it was the cruellest smile he had ever seen. There was no trace of love, of passion, only a cold emptiness tinged with pity. Pity for him. But that was only the precursor to a cruelty that he knew he could never forgive, never forget.

'The Sundering will take place so that I can be with the father of my children, Cleece.

'I want to be with Sstaal.'

Now dressed in his armour once more, he sat and waited. But the armour afforded him no protection from the unimaginable agony that clawed within him, a pain that he prayed to Claatris would end. But it didn't end, it just grew and grew and Cleece had no way of stopping it.

He just wanted the universe to end.

'My people were not responsible for your unbearable loss, Antony; terrorism has never been the way of my race. The Warriors of Mars would never stoop to such despicable behaviour.'

'They found Martian ideograms carved into the wreckage,' he growled. 'It must have been you.'

Sstaal shook his head. 'Even hidden on Mars, we observed events on your planet. We learnt of many atrocities that were committed in our name by your own people, yet we could do nothing to prove our innocence for fear of revealing our presence.'

McGuire peered at Sstaal through bloodshot eyes, and realized that he wasn't looking at the hated face of an enemy who had haunted him for the last five years. Instead, he was looking at a young Martian monk, no more than a teenager in human terms, who understood more about humanity than McGuire ever would. Aklaar's wisdom came through centuries of experience, but Sstaal's came through innocence and faith, a faith that McGuire had lost amidst the twisted wreckage and smouldering carnage of the Montreal monorail system. If Sstaal was right – and something in the pilgrim's manner demanded that he be believed – McGuire had spent five years of his life hating the wrong enemy. He felt the final, hard, unyielding shackles that had chained his mind to single-minded hatred begin to fall away – the result of a process begun by Aklaar, but completed by his follower, Sstaal.

Sstaal asked, 'But if you hate my race so much, why did you come to Mars? Surely that can have only served as a constant reminder of your loss?'

How could McGuire explain what had happened? How he had lost his job as a psychometric assessor at IMC because he had become hooked on Vraxoin just so that he could cope with the agonizing struggle of going from one day to the next? How his gradual decline into apathy and certain death had only been halted by an uncle who had realized what was happening and had stepped in just in time?

But he tried; he owed Sstaal that much. 'After my family were killed, life was pointless, just a constant battle to stay alive. What did I have to stay alive for? I lost my job, my self-respect ... I just didn't care about anything any more. But one of my relatives whose finances had survived the Great Crash – that was when the Earth's economy collapsed – was looking for me – some sort of family business. What he found wasn't much – a hopeless, worthless drug addict who had completely given up – but he pulled me back.' McGuire shrugged. 'God knows how. I can't even remember that period of my life. Thanks to him, I managed to claw back my dignity. He suggested that I start a new life, away from Earth and all the memories, so he found me a position in

Jacksonville in one of his companies.' He sighed. 'I know it sounds absurd – moving to Mars when I thought you were responsible for what had happened to me – but it was a chance of a new life. Besides, Jacksonville was a self-contained human colony; I could have been anywhere in the solar system.'

Sstaal frowned – he had removed his helmet and armour some time ago – and raised an ungloved finger. 'But that doesn't explain why you would lead an expedition to the North Pole. Surely you realized that you would have to deal with my people if you wanted to share any supplies that you might have found?'

McGuire nodded. 'Of course I did. That's why I approached the Mayor and suggested the expedition after Vince had detected the energy readings. After three years here, three years of pent-up anger and hate, I wanted to face up to the people that I blamed for the mess that was my life. I had to. I needed to know what would happen to me. I needed to know whether I could forgive.'

'And now that you have faced up to us, Antony – how do you feel? Has the pain subsided, or will you allow it to consume you for the rest of your life as well? Or perhaps you have become comfortable with it?'

The answer was simple, a tenet over two hundred years old.

'I can forgive, Sstaal. But I can never forget. If you're right, though, I haven't anything to forgive you for.' He reached out and grabbed Sstaal's hand. 'But can you forgive me for my hatred?'

Sstaal squeezed McGuire's hand. 'I can only do that once you have forgiven yourself. And that, Antony, is going to be the hardest thing of all.'

The door opened, and a Martian entered. He gestured to them. 'You have five minutes to ready yourselves,' he hissed. 'You have an audience with the Grand Marshal.'

McGuire looked over at Sstaal. 'Grand Marshal? What the hell's going on?'

Sstaal appeared as disturbed as McGuire felt. 'I don't know, Antony. But I am not reassured. If we needed further proof that this is not the religious nest that the Abbot expected, that is it. Grand Marshals are only to be found in military nests.'

As Sstaal hurriedly dressed himself in his armour, McGuire glanced at the Ice Warrior in the doorway, and realized that he didn't hate him. He was one Martian amongst many, and McGuire didn't have the right to condemn an entire race for the crimes of a select few – whatever he thought.

He knew that he was learning. He just hadn't expected that the education would come from a Greenie.

In a way, he was glad it had. It was the sort of poetic justice that convinced him that there was a God after all.

'You idiot, Chris!' shouted Roz, punching him gently in the stomach. He grinned, almost unable to believe who he was seeing. Without thinking, he grabbed her in a bear hug and spun her around.

'Roz – you don't know –'

'I do,' she replied curtly. 'And before you ask, the Doctor's here as well, although he's safely under lock and key.'

'What are the Ice Warriors running here – some kind of penitentiary for refugees?' And then he remembered his primary mission. 'I'm after two people who arrived here with me.'

'From where?' asked the woman with long dark hair who was standing behind Roz.

Chris frowned at the unfamiliar voice. 'Who's this?'

'Christopher Cwej; meet Adjudicator Carmen Santacosta.'

'Adjudicator?' How had Roz managed to team up with another Adjudicator? Then again, what the hell had she been up to since the destruction of the TARDIS?

Roz grinned. 'A long story. Did the TARDIS dump you on Mars as well, then?'

He shook his head, but he was unwilling to go into too much detail. They were too visible, too vulnerable. 'No, on Charon.' And then, relishing the odd looks he received: 'Another long story. We're about three hundred metres from the subspace manipulator chamber where I think the other two are being held. I suggest we grab them, and then attempt to free the Doctor.'

'And the others,' added Roz. 'An expedition from Jacksonville and a party of Ice Warrior pilgrims.'

Chris snorted. 'It's never simple, is it? Okay, okay, explanations can wait. Time for the Guild to come to the rescue.'

'The Bureau,' corrected Santacosta.

'The Guild,' corrected Roz emphatically.

Chris didn't care. His life was coming together again. And he couldn't remember the last time he had felt so exhilarated.

The Doctor, Aklaar and the others were standing before Draan's desk once more. But Draan himself was absent. Four Warriors stood at each corner of the large room, disruptors trained on the travellers.

'Any idea what this is about, Abbot?' whispered McGuire.

'None, Antony. I am sorry to confess that nothing has been as expected since we arrived at the Cauldron of Sutekh.' Not as expected, he thought. But as *suspected* was a different matter.

A grinding noise alerted them to a door opening at the back of the room. Aklaar knew that the others were probably expecting Draan to make his entrance, but Aklaar *suspected* otherwise. Just as he *suspected* that the entire pilgrimage was nothing more than an elaborate trap sprung by a very old enemy. A trap which he had blindly fallen into.

And, as the figure entered the room, Aklaar saw that he wasn't mistaken. With a twisting, nauseating feeling of hateful, vile memories being stirred from their enforced sleep, he recognized the gold and purple armour of a Supreme Grand Marshal, the ceremonial uniform only worn by the privileged: the eight rulers of the planet Mars.

Falaxyr, one of only two survivors of that same Eight-Point Table that had led Mars into bloody, futile war against mankind, the Eight-Point Table that had accepted ritual suicide as atonement for the consequences of that war – all except two. One was Falaxyr the coward; the same Falaxyr who cast his gaze across the group. When his attention reached Aklaar he paused. And smiled.

'As you probably realize, I am in absolute command of this

base. Any deviation, any questioning of my orders, will be met with immediate execution. None of you is indispensable. Am I understood?'

'Perfectly,' muttered the Doctor. 'Typical black-or-white thinking.'

Falaxyr gave a thin smile. 'But that is the way of the Martian military. Isn't it, *Abbot Aklaar*?' The words were sharp and pointed, designed to cut away at him.

No, Falaxyr. Not this time. Aklaar made a decisive step forward. For nearly seventy years, he had been the wise old Abbot of an ancient and respected seminary, the spiritual leader of his followers in Oras. Now all that was lost, gone for ever, because Aklaar hadn't recognized that he was leading his pilgrims into a calculated trap. That fact only served to fuel his current anger.

'Make your point, Falaxyr. Dramatic performances were never your style.'

'Or yours, *old friend*.' Aklaar could hear the whispers behind him, and feel the curious glances burning into his back. But there was nothing he could do. This was the moment that had only come to him in nightmares before now, excruciating, agonizing nightmares that had been his constant companion for seventy years. But no more.

Falaxyr continued. 'In another life, you too preferred the direct approach.'

'What other life?' asked Esstar. 'Abbot Aklaar, I do not understand. Do you know this barbarian?' There was a nervousness in her voice, indications of the gentle dawning of a hideous truth. His pilgrims were clever, but were they clever enough to understand *why*?

Falaxyr placed a too-friendly clamp on Aklaar's shoulder. 'The Abbot and I are old and dear friends, although I knew him by another name.'

Before Falaxyr could say it, before Falaxyr could delight in the death of Aklaar's dreams and the realization of his darkest nightmares, the Abbot knew what he had to do. He still had his pride, and he owed his pilgrims the truth from his own lips, not through the twisted lies of a coward like Falaxyr. He straightened his aching body with a vigour unknown for centuries, and faced the Grand Marshal squarely and without intimidation.

'Falaxyr and I have a history forged in blood, my friends,' he announced. 'But he indeed knew me by another name: he called me Abrasaar, also known as the Butcher of Viis Claar . . .

'The last survivor of the Eight-Point Table.'

Chapter 11

The atmosphere in Falaxyr's chambers was colder than the hoarfrost of the North Pole that lay five hundred metres above them. Everyone, humans and Martians alike, was staring at Aklaar. Or Abrasaar. Or whoever he was.

McGuire's stomach was clenched tight in unbelieving shock as he pondered the Grand Marshal's inferences and Aklaar's own confession. Over the last five days, McGuire's admiration for the ancient old Martian had grown; in a way, he saw him as a wise mentor, one who transcended hatred and those baser emotions that McGuire had embraced, and fervently believed that one man – or Martian – could make a difference. Aklaar had spoken of a new destiny for Mars, a new role for his people that would bury the crimes and injustices of the past and bring new glories of peace and understanding. McGuire had bought into those dreams.

Except that Aklaar was Abrasaar, the notorious and reviled Butcher of Viis Claar, the war criminal hated by humanity and disowned by the Martians. McGuire could tell from the others' expressions that the magnitude of that title wasn't lost of any of them.

Viis Claar was the Martian name for the Valles Marineris, a deep, wide valley near the Martian equator. It was also the name of the only significant defeat for the human forces in the Thousand Day War. Earth Intelligence had discovered that there was a heavily guarded Martian weapons dump at the eastern end of the valley, and UN Central Command knew that the dump had to be captured before the Martians could relocate their weaponry. One of the elite teams –

General Burkitt's King's Fusiliers – had been put on standby waiting for an assault window.

Finally, after weeks of patient monitoring, a transmission had been intercepted and easily decoded; the Grand Marshal responsible for the dump – Abrasaar – informed the Eight-Point Table that his forces were being redirected to a nearby city that was currently under siege. Burkitt had taken that as the signal to move in, and fifteen thousand troops had Transitted in and advanced on the weapons dump, expecting only minimal resistance.

They hadn't expected ten thousand Martian Warriors.

The engagement lasted three days before culminating in the annihilation of the dump in an explosion that was visible unaided from the southern hemisphere of Earth. Although the contents of the dump would no longer be able to further the Martian war effort, the confrontation at Viis Claar had cost fifteen thousand human lives – over a third of the final death count – and severely dented Earth's sense of invulnerability.

But the dump had not been destroyed by Burkitt's men: the Martians had sabotaged it themselves. Abrasaar had done the unthinkable: he had lured the humans into a trap by transmitting a false message using an old, broken code that he knew would be intercepted. Such behaviour was irreconcilable with the Martian war ethic, a codex which embodied honesty and honour above all else. Indeed, after the war had ended, many historians concluded that the battle of Viis Claar had so shocked the Martian military that their own edge was subsequently dulled. It would explain why the War ended soon afterwards.

Abrasaar was presumed to have been one of the legions of the dead, one of the twenty-five thousand humans and Martians who had been vaporized when the anti-matter cannons and sonic piledrivers held in the dump had exploded in an all-consuming fireball of plasma and gamma radiation that had washed up and down Viis Claar.

Obviously, that presumption was wrong.

'So, Abrasaar, you do value the truth,' said Falaxyr, his reptilian face twisted in a cruel, satisfied smile. 'After your conduct at Viis Claar, I had begun to doubt it.'

Aklaar looked over at his pilgrims, but neither Esstar nor Sstaal would meet his gaze, preferring to stare at the floor rather than accept their spiritual leader's true identity. Only Cleece could look the Abbot in the face, but he was wearing an expression of awe and wonder that disgusted McGuire. *Disgusted?* McGuire realized that his feelings for Aklaar were unchanged; seventy years ago, he may have been a member of the Martian high command, he may have lured fifteen thousand human soldiers to their deaths ... but he was now an Abbot of the Holy Order of Oras. Aklaar had embraced his new life, turning his back on a past of blood, and he and his followers had taught McGuire to accept his own pain and move forward.

McGuire knew that Aklaar was a different person from Abrasaar, even if the Abbot's pilgrims – two of his pilgrims – were having difficulty accepting the fact. He walked over to Aklaar and put his hand on his shoulder.

'Abbot? Are you all right?'

Before the Abbot could reply, the Grand Marshal stepped forward. 'Well, well, well, Abrasaar; I see that your pathetic attempt to hide yourself in the spineless Order of Oras has even attracted vermin to your cause.' Falaxyr sneered. 'Still, it is of no consequence.'

'What do you really want, Falaxyr?' said Aklaar. 'My pilgrims and I were invited to G'chun duss Ssethiissi to participate in a ceremony of peace. Obviously, that is not to be the case; you and peace should not be mentioned in the same breath.'

'You mouth the words, but is the belief there, I wonder?' Falaxyr retreated behind his desk. 'But fear not; there *will* be a ceremony.' He gestured towards one of his guards, who walked over to Sstaal. 'There is one thing that I need, Abrasaar; one thing that I have searched this planet for. After the war, its location was unknown, but my agents eventually tracked it down; I found it an irony of the highest order that it should be in your possession.'

'The Sword of Tuburr.' The Doctor watched as the Ice Warrior took the serrated blade from Sstaal. 'You engineered the pilgrimage to bring the Sword here.'

Falaxyr gave the Doctor a look of disdain, if the curve of his mouth was any indication. 'Who is this mammal?'

McGuire had asked himself a similar question on a number of occasions over the last few days, but he wasn't surprised when the Doctor took up the challenge. At last the Doctor had been proved right about the Martians.

'I'm the Doctor, Grand Marshal Falaxyr. Is your adjutant around?'

'Draan?' His mouth suddenly indicated that a frown was going on under his helmet. 'What part does he play in this?'

'I just wondered whether he was as incompetent as his father.'

Falaxyr stepped forward. Even though he was shorter than most Martians, he still towered over the Doctor. 'You know of Slaar?'

The Doctor grinned. 'I should do. Thanks to me, his attempt to invade Earth was a complete and utter disaster. Thanks to me, the Third Wing of your mighty space fleet flew straight into the sun.'

Falaxyr laughed. It was a brittle, empty laugh. 'Mad as well as impudent.' He turned back to Aklaar, ignoring the Doctor. McGuire suspected that the Marshal had just made a serious mistake. 'As we were saying, Abrasaar, I brought you here because of the Sword.' He reached out and took it from his guard, twisting it so the light sparked off the sharp teeth and ornate hilt. 'I need it.'

'To further your petty ambitions, no doubt,' countered Aklaar. 'In the seventy years since the end of the war, have you brooded and festered in this nest of evil, Falaxyr? If so, it would not surprise me to learn that it has addled your mind.'

'My mind is as keen as this Sword, Abrasaar. And my plans are far from petty. Once I have succeeded, Mars will once more be our sovereign territory. We will be masters of Mars.'

'And this plan has something to do with establishing a monopolar magnetic field around the North Pole?' asked the Doctor quietly.

'Your mammal is inquisitive, Abrasaar.' But Falaxyr sounded irritated rather than impressed. 'Yet perhaps it is time to show you our great work. Indeed, it would only be right and fitting, since you were one of the architects.'

Despite the obscured face, McGuire knew the expression under Aklaar's helmet. Pure, unrefined horror.

The journey to the manipulator chamber was quiet, and Chris could only assume that most of the Ice Warriors who had survived his delightfully noisy firework display were busy trying to sort out the mess.

'Here.' He indicated the ten-metre-wide metal door.

Roz turned to Santacosta. 'This is it, Carmen. The reason why you came to the North Pole.'

'A fat lot of good it's going to be without backup,' she complained. 'Still, I can't deny being curious. From what Professor Ketch was saying, it's far beyond anything he could come up with.' She frowned. 'Not that it'll mean a lot to me – I'm hardly a subspace engineer.'

Chris pushed the centre of the door, and waited as it swung open. As soon as the gap was wide enough, he gingerly poked his head into the chamber, alert for Ice Warriors. But, to his relief, the only people in the room were Rachel and Felice. He beckoned Roz and Santacosta to follow him in.

'Felice! Rachel!' he called out, trotting over to them.

They didn't turn round. One side of the glass pyramid had been removed, and some of the artefacts had been taken out and placed on the cold stone floor, glittering cables still attaching them to barely visible power sources, buried deep in the heart of the pyramid. The two women were working on the artefacts: Felice was examining the base of a canopic jar, while Rachel was sitting on the floor, holding the head of a statue of Anubis, but they were totally oblivious to Chris's cries.

Chris tapped Felice on the shoulder. She turned and looked up. 'Hello, Christopher,' she said cheerfully, before returning her attention to her stone head and carrying on working away with a probe as if nothing had happened.

'I don't like this,' said Chris to the others. 'It's as if they've been hypnotized or drugged.'

'Brain-rack,' stated Santacosta. 'Nasty technique – introduces alien thought patterns into the human mind. It wears off, but while they're under the influence, they're completely susceptible.'

'Can we break the conditioning?' asked Roz. Chris knew she was thinking about the mind control used in their own time, which could only be broken using psychotropic drugs. The fact that the end result was a person free of mind control but clinically insane was another matter.

Santacosta chewed her bottom lip. 'There's not been much research, although I do remember something about ECT . . .'

'ECT?' asked Chris.

'Electro-convulsive therapy – applying controlled electric shocks to the brain. Although the Martian neural pathways are dominant, they're not stable. ECT causes them to break down prematurely.'

Chris was horrified. This ECT sounded barbaric, but if it was the only way to free Felice and Rachel from Martian control . . . He looked around the chamber for some source of electricity, but realized that he knew so little about Martian technology that a power-point could be staring him in the face and he wouldn't have spotted it.

But Roz must have been reading his mind. 'Try this.' She held out a pencil torch, and Chris recognized it as the twin of the one he had found in his first-aid kit. The one that had provided some added kick to the jamming device which was still interfering with the Ice Warriors' communications.

'Perfect!' He pulled it apart, revealing the small yet incredibly powerful battery within. He then reached into his pocket and pulled out his last reserves of filament.

'Where did you get that from?' asked Roz.

He grinned. 'Leaving present from the Doctor.' Pulling off two twenty-centimetre strands, he attached one to each terminal of the battery, and then stripped the insulation from the last centimetre of the wire. 'What sort of voltage do we need, Santacosta?' Not that he knew any way of regulating the output from the battery with the equipment available, but at least it made him sound as if he knew what he was talking about.

'As high as possible, and as brief as possible. The pathways are extremely delicate; a short burst at high voltage should be enough to shake them loose. She'll have a headache, but she'll be free of the Greenies' mind control.'

Chris chewed his bottom lip. 'I don't like this. I don't like it at all. But if there's a chance, well, we've got to take it.' Of course, the chance was that he would burn out Rachel's mind, and the woman hadn't exactly given her consent. He made a quick adjustment to the circuitry around the battery with a small probe that had been lying next to Rachel, making sure that the current was discharged through the wires rather than the bulb. He nodded at the scientist. 'You'd better grab her.'

As Santacosta and Roz laid gentle but ready hands on Rachel's shoulders, Chris switched on the torch. The two filaments were now live. He hesitated, but it was the only option. He brought his hands together, touching the bare ends of the filaments to Rachel's temples as briefly as he could.

The result was immediate: she went rigid, her back arching before she collapsed. Santacosta supported her, and laid her on the floor. 'She should come round in a few moments and be in full possession of her faculties.'

On cue, Rachel started groaning. Chris knelt down beside her. 'Easy, Rachel.'

Rachel's eyes managed to focus on him. 'Oh, Chris,' she whispered. 'I tried to fight it, but I couldn't. Their thoughts were in my head, telling me what to do . . .' Her eyes were misty as she fought back tears and tried to regain her normal self-assured composure.

'It's all right, Rachel,' he said, trying to comfort her. She was suffering from the typical reaction to mind control: feelings of impotence and degradation. He looked over at Felice, and found himself dreading her release from mental slavery; the thought of her elfin features twisted in guilt and self-disgust was not one he was looking forward to.

'No, it's not all right. You don't know what they're doing here. It's monstrous.' She glanced at the partly dismantled gold and glass pyramid. 'We've got to destroy that thing before it comes on-line. If they get that working . . .' She shuddered. 'You don't know the consequences.'

'Then you'd better tell us,' said Santacosta curtly. 'I've

come a long way to find out what this is, and I'm rather impatient.'

'It's called the GodEngine,' Rachel replied quietly. 'And it's a weapon. An enormous weapon.' She nodded towards Felice. 'Please; free Felice.'

'That's not an option, I'm afraid,' said Roz. She was examining the interior of the torch. 'You've fused the battery, Chris.'

'Damn!' Chris snapped. 'All right, we'll take her with us. We're sure to find another electrical source.'

Rachel shook her head emphatically. 'She won't go. The GodEngine is her life now. Take her with us, and she'll turn hysterical; the Martians will find us straight away.'

'We should go,' said Santacosta. 'The longer we stay here, the more chance of being discovered. At least we've got Rachel. If we survive this, she might know enough to explain this GodEngine to Ketch.' Chris frowned, but said nothing; this woman was hard.

Roz put a hand on Chris's arm. 'She's right, Chris. We have to retrench. Once Rachel tells *us* about this GodEngine, we might have a better chance of saving the Doctor and the others.'

Throwing a regretful backwards glance at Felice, Chris shrugged. 'We'll go back to the service tunnels below the complex. We'll be safe there.' And then he looked at Rachel. The horror that lurked behind her eyes indicated that the GodEngine was her biggest nightmare. Would any of them be safe if it was as bad as she seemed to believe?

Leaving Felice with her canopic jars, Chris and the others left the GodEngine chamber. But as he walked through the doorway a terrifying thought occurred to him.

If the GodEngine had to be destroyed, would he have to kill Felice in the process? More importantly, *could* he kill Felice?

Aklaar had known that Falaxyr was obsessed. Obsessed with power, obsessed with glory, and obsessed with the Martians reclaiming Mars. He just hadn't expected his fellow Grand Marshal to dedicate himself to a plan that was both insane and unworkable.

'The *Ssor-arr duss Ssethissi*?' he said. 'You are telling me that you have built the *Ssor-arr duss Ssethissi*?' It had been a longshot even then, a last, desperate idea from an Eight-Point Table bereft of choices.

'The Engine of Ssethiss,' muttered the Doctor. 'What an intriguing name. Of course, a less mythical translation would be *GodEngine*. Been playing around with Osirian technology, have we?' And then he tapped himself on the forehead with his hat. 'Of course; the WarScarab. From warriors to scrap dealers in one easy move. How are the mighty fallen.'

Falaxyr squeezed his clamps together. 'It was left here, Doctor. It is our legacy.'

'You don't know what you're doing, Falaxyr; Osirian technology is far beyond your comprehension. You're like clutchlings playing with sonic disruptors,' he said desperately.

Falaxyr laughed unpleasantly. '*You* don't know what *we're* doing, Doctor. The GodEngine is our greatest triumph. With the GodEngine, we can reaffirm our supremacy and take our rightful place in the galaxy.'

'What is the GodEngine?' asked Esstar.

Falaxyr stared at the ceiling in supplication. 'Nothing short of our apotheosis.'

'It's a weapon,' explained Rachel. 'The Osirians – they're some ancient race of aliens who influenced both Egyptian and Martian civilization – left a lot of technology on Mars. For thousands of years, the Martians ignored it, partly because it belonged to their gods, and partly because they didn't understand it. But when Earth retaliated against the attack on Paris, the Martians knew that they had to match our own technology to stand any chance of winning. They knew that the Osirians' technology was based on subspace manipulation, and they knew that the Martian Sphinx was something to do with that. For the last seventy years, they've been trying to turn the contents of the Sphinx – and the crashed wreckage of an Osirian starship – into a weapon.' Her eyes narrowed. 'They've almost succeeded.'

Roz was both fascinated and worried. 'But what is it?'

'When it's finished, the GodEngine will be able to manipulate the electromagnetic, gravitational and subspace fields of stars. It causes stars to emit coherent, superluminal beams of plasma. It's an FTL plasma cannon!'

Santacosta shook her head, snorting. 'A giant death ray? Oh, come on.'

Chris raised his hand. 'Hear her out, Santacosta. She's the scientist around here.'

Rachel smiled, but it didn't touch the fear in her eyes. 'The technology they're using is so far beyond anything we've even dreamed of. The whole assembly is powered by a nano-accretion disk and a magnetic monopole, and we can't even solve the equations for that yet.'

'But does it work?' asked Roz.

'It will do, once Felice has finished. She's the genius around here.' Chris was amazed; Rachel's feelings towards her assistant had definitely changed, and he briefly wondered whether it was a side-effect of the Brain-rack. But she dismissed his apparent look of disbelief. 'No, I mean it. The reason that the Martians have been working on the God-Engine for seventy years without success is that they didn't know what they were doing. They had a rough idea of the equipment they were using – the Martians are far more intelligent than a lot of people believe – but not the information that would allow them to bring the GodEngine completely on-line. But Felice knew – God knows how, but she knew. After they – they took us over, she was able to understand the inscriptions round the base of the GodEngine. The Martians thought they were nothing but prayers to the cult of Oras – they were written in an archaic and virtually unknown Martian dialect – but they weren't. They were the instruction manual. Don't ask me how, but Felice was able to decipher the language and see where the problem was. They were so very close, but without Felice's knowledge . . .' She obviously remembered Santacosta and Roz's questions.

'If Felice finishes what she's doing, the GodEngine will be ready to come on-line. They still need something which appears to be an ignition key, but once they've got that, the GodEngine will be able to fold the subspace manifold around stellar cores. It can create polarized funnels of subspace and accelerate coherent plasma down them. Imagine it: a plasma gun powerful enough to incinerate planets, to ignite super-Jovians, to turn stars nova.'

'Well, that settles it,' stated Roz. 'We've got to put a stop to it.'

'And that's the *Ssor-arr duss Ssethissi*?' asked Sstaal quietly after Falaxyr's explanation. 'A bringer of death?'

Esstar was equally horrified. The fact of this abomination's existence was appalling enough; the intimation that their beloved Abbot was something to do with it was blasphemy itself.

Falaxyr pursed his lips. 'You pacifists are a cancer in our race. If you were a true Martian, you would glory in the power that we wield, you would revel in the chance of conquest. Instead, you reject our birthright and burrow into the soil like plasma-vampires. Then again, your attempts at peace have delivered the Sword of Tuburr to me, so you still have your uses.'

'But you have not got it right yet, have you? A few of the details elude you, eh?' It was the Doctor.

Falaxyr looked round. 'Ah, the mad mammal. Yes, there have been delays, Doctor, but no more. Two human subspace scientists, late of the Charon Subspace Research Facility, are aiding us. The GodEngine, to use your crude terminology, will be ready within the hour.'

'Charon,' muttered the Doctor. 'That explains Cwej.'

Falaxyr turned on the little man. 'What do you know about Adjudicator Cwej, vermin?' he shouted.

The Doctor smiled in defiance of Falaxyr's anger. 'I know enough, Grand Marshal, but that's unimportant at the moment. I would like to know what you plan to do with this GodEngine – if you ever get it finished, that is. Destroy Earth?'

'Nothing so futile, Doctor,' said the Grand Marshal, easily brought back to his favoured topic. 'Earth is already conquered – our vengeance by proxy. It is now in the hands of our allies.'

The Doctor's odd features folded into a frown. 'Allies?' he

yelled. 'Allies? Do you realize who – *what* you are dealing with?' He sounded furious.

'Indeed I do,' Falaxyr nodded. 'Like minds, Doctor. Like minds.'

'What?' yelled Forrester. She couldn't believe what Santacosta was saying. Getting down and get dirty was one thing, but this?

'Don't you see, we could use the GodEngine, Forrester. With Professor Ketch on the case, he could soon work out how to use it. How long would the invaders remain in the solar system if we're holding a loaded gun to their slimy heads?'

'No, no, no,' protested Rachel. 'You don't understand the magnitude of this. The GodEngine can't be fine-tuned. Even at its tightest focus, it can still take out entire moons. Any attempt to focus any further puts too much strain on the subspace lens.'

'Ketch will find a way.' She pulled out a pencil-sized grey rod. Roz recognized it as a rather nasty five-shot disposable projectile weapon colloquially called a scalper. Another design classic. 'If you don't help me, I count that as treason against the Earth Alliance. And – as you should know, fellow Adjudicators Cwej and Forrester – treason is the crime that we swear on our graduation to avenge with death.'

Falaxyr had not let go of the Sword of Tuburr since they had left his office, Sstaal noticed. He also noticed the anger that still raged within himself, hot, tearing feelings which were alien to his upbringing. But his anger was no longer aimed towards Antony McGuire; the human was an object of sympathy and brotherhood. It was firmly targeted on the Grand Marshal, treasuring the Sword as if it were his bloodright.

Sstaal was jealous, and he had no idea why.

Felice replaced the canopic jar in its appointed place on the lowest level of the *Ssor-arr duss Ssethissi* – the level of the primary subspace attractor – and checked that the trisilicate cabling was still attached correctly. If the connections were in error, the initial meniscus penetration would fail, and that would bring dishonour upon Felice. She turned to face her superior with a smile of beatitude across her face, as glory and honour flooded her mind – the glory and honour of the Martian race.

She bowed to the tall figure before her. 'That is the final component of the *Ssor-arr duss Ssethissi*, Technician Sleeth.' Felice was aware that her first superior, Hoorg, had died, but her allegiance had immediately been transferred to Sleeth.

The Martian shook his head. 'Not the final component, Dr Delacroix; that awaits, and is entrusted to others. But there are further duties ahead of you.' Sleeth indicated the bank of control panels inset into the amber walls. 'Once the *Ssor-arr duss Ssethissi* has woken, it will require attendants. You will be one of the attendants.'

Felice was more honoured than she could ever remember.

'What do you suggest, then? A head-on assault?' asked Rachel coldly. Her old mentor Professor Gregory Ketch was a genius, her only peer in the esoteric realms of subspace engineering, but she doubted that even he possessed the knowledge necessary to turn the GodEngine from a weapon whose lowest setting was nothing less than planetary destruction to the device that Santacosta thought he could create. Would the invaders really take the Adjudicators' threat seriously if their main bargaining tool would destroy Earth in the process?

Santacosta held the scalper steady. 'Of course not. We need to revert to my original plan and breach the subspace barrier around the base. After Cwej's recent bit of terrorism, the place is in uproar; fifty Adjudicator Special Operatives could secure it without breaking into a sweat.'

'Won't the Transit-web work in here?' asked Roz.

Chris looked puzzled. 'Transit-web?'

Rachel nodded in understanding. 'Gregory's magnum opus. A portable stunnel terminus.' An image of Ketch's face, glowing with triumph over his latest discovery, appeared in her mind. 'So he finally built one?'

'Yes, but it won't work inside the barrier,' said Santacosta.

'The Martians have surrounded the base with the hull of an alien vessel called an Osirian WarScarab,' explained Rachel. 'The metal is made from molecules which extend into subspace, creating a natural shield against subspace penetration. At least, that's what the Martians told me.'

'So we get outside the base and use this Transit-web?' offered Chris.

Roz shook her head. 'It's not as simple as that. Is it, Carmen?'

'I don't have the web any more. I left it outside the base.'

'So we get outside the base and grab the web.'

'It's not outside the base,' said Roz.

Santacosta looked at her sharply. 'What do you mean?'

'The Doctor pocketed it. If you want the Transit-web, you've got to find the Doctor,' she replied. 'He picked it up as we were being brought in here.'

'Great.' Santacosta shoved the scalper back into her jacket. 'There's no point in threatening you when our only option is to do what you want, is there?'

Rachel sighed. There was still time to dissuade the Adjudicator from her stupidity. If she couldn't do it, she hoped that the Doctor could.

'So this is the GodEngine?' stated the Doctor. 'Looks like the Mitterrand extension to the Louvre.' McGuire had to agree; rather than a doomsday weapon, it looked like a museum exhibit of ancient Egyptian relics. He also noticed the petite blonde woman standing next to it, and presumed that she was one of the kidnapped scientists from Charon.

'This is our greatest achievement – our birthright,' stated Falaxyr. 'The GodEngine will give us back that which is rightfully ours.'

The Doctor was indignant. 'Rightfully yours? Rightfully yours? You squandered Mars, Falaxyr. You led your people into bloodshed and lost any claim to it.'

The Grand Marshal shrugged. 'Just as you have lost any claim to Earth, Doctor.'

'Earth never was mine, but that's beside the point. However impressive this GodEngine is, you can't enter into an alliance with the invaders. I can assure you, Grand Marshal, they will not honour the agreement.' And McGuire could have sworn that there was a hint of desperation in the Doctor's voice, as if he knew who the invaders were – and was frightened of them.

Falaxyr shook his head. 'They have no choice. Unless they give us the sovereignty of Mars, we will target Earth. The GodEngine will incinerate the planet.'

The Doctor shook his head sadly and muttered something beneath his breath. It sounded like 'the web of time'.

Falaxyr turned to a Martian standing to his left. 'Technician Sleeth: is the *Ssor-arr duss Ssethissi* ready to be brought on-line?'

'Yes, Your Excellency. Junior Technician Delacroix completed the final adjustments to the manifold polarizers just before you arrived. According to the final diagnostic, the *Ssor-arr duss Ssethissi* is fully operational. I commend her work.'

Falaxyr nodded. 'I will see that her name is entered in the List of Heroes.'

'Falaxyr – reconsider this!' shouted the Doctor. 'The creatures that have invaded Earth are without pity, without compassion. If you give them the GodEngine, you will change the course of history. Armed with the GodEngine, they will be unstoppable.'

'The GodEngine is ours. They will request its use, but we shall be the ones in control of it.'

'And what's to stop them from taking it from you by force?' asked McGuire. 'If they can overcome Earth's defences, they can easily overcome the few of you that are left on Mars.'

'The GodEngine would be useless to them,' stated Sleeth. 'The *Ssor-arr duss Ssethissi* depends on a number of factors to operate. It needs a planetary mass to tether it against the subspace fields it generates, and it will only function in the absence of a bipolar magnetic field. Mars is the only planet in the solar system that is both large enough, and lacks a magnetic field.'

'So that's why they did it,' mumbled the Doctor. And then his tone became one of unrestrained anger. 'You idiot!

In three years' time, the invaders will start hollowing out Earth's magnetic core. They fully intend to steal the GodEngine, and they fully intend to install it on Earth!'

Falaxyr smiled, calm against the Doctor's storm. 'Any invasion attempt will be met by the full might of the GodEngine. If the Daleks make a single move to take what is ours, we will obliterate them – and Earth.'

He stepped over to the glittering pyramid, clamping the Sword tightly. 'After I have demonstrated the power of the GodEngine, Doctor, the Daleks will think very carefully about their future plans. Very carefully indeed.'

'What's he doing?' whispered McGuire to the Doctor. 'What does he need the Sword for? And who the hell are the Daleks?'

Before the Doctor could answer, Aklaar tapped McGuire on the shoulder. 'Towards the end of the War, the EightPoint Table was torn apart by internal squabbling. With a breakdown of trust between the Supreme Grand Marshals, measures had to be taken to ensure that the proposed GodEngine would not be used to further the ambitions of any single Marshal. It was designed so that it could only be operated if a single component was present . . . The Sword of Tuburr.'

'Well put, Abrasaar,' said Falaxyr, inserting the serrated blade into a thin slot set into one of the golden struts that defined the pyramid. He rammed it home with an audible click, as if internal mechanisms were locking it into place. 'And, thanks to your pilgrimage, you have delivered it to me. As you were supposed to.'

Aklaar hung his head, and McGuire could see the strength draining from him. A lifetime of penance for a previous existence, wiped out in an instant; he couldn't begin to understand the depths of the Abbot's despair.

'Now we begin. The first act of the GodEngine will be the cleansing of Mars, the extermination of vermin. The destruction of Jacksonville.'

Falaxyr gestured to Sleeth. The Martian technician stepped forward to the control panels set in the rock walls, and indicated for Felice to do the same.

'No!' McGuire lunged forward, but one of Falaxyr's guards grabbed him and threw him to the floor. Winded, and with the business end of a sonic disruptor in his face, he could only watch as the banks of controls lit up, heralding the end of Jacksonville.

Chapter 12

Nothing happened. Absolutely nothing. The hushed and expectant atmosphere in the GodEngine chamber rapidly evaporated into one of desperate activity, as Martian technicians scurried around the equipment attempting to trace the malfunction. The enslaved human woman was assisting Sleeth at the base of the GodEngine pyramid, but none of them seemed to be able to identify the reason why it wasn't working.

Esstar was relieved. If the blasphemous device didn't work, then perhaps there was a chance for them all.

'Problems, Grand Marshal?' said the Doctor smugly. 'If this is the best you can do, I doubt that your allies will be particularly impressed.'

'Be silent!' hissed Falaxyr. He turned as Sleeth approached him. 'Have you located the malfunction?'

Sleeth stepped forward and nodded. 'The problem lies with the initiation circuitry, Your Excellency.'

'The Sword?' asked Falaxyr, puzzled.

Sleeth shook his head. 'It is not the Sword of Tuburr, Your Excellency. It is a copy. An excellent copy, but it lacks the trace elements of the original. The *Ssor-arr duss Ssethissi* must validate the presence of those elements before it can initiate subspace manipulation.'

Falaxyr turned on his prisoners. 'Where is it?' he bellowed. 'Where is the true Sword of Tuburr?'

Aklaar smiled, but said nothing. Falaxyr raised his arm and aimed the built-in disruptor at the Abbot. 'Tell me or die, Abrasaar. I have waited too long for this moment; I will not allow your pathetic mask of pacifism to spoil it now.'

The voice came from behind her. 'The Sword is here, Your Excellency.' With disbelief and horror rising within her, Esstar realized that the voice belonged to Cleece. The huge Martian walked over to Aklaar and snatched his thick wooden staff from his clamp. 'Here.' Cleece held out the staff to the Grand Marshal.

Falaxyr grasped the wood and twisted it sharply with both clamps. Under the tremendous shearing force, the staff splintered in two, revealing polished metal within. The Grand Marshal unsheathed the true Sword of Tuburr from the broken wood and held it up proudly.

Esstar spun round. 'How could you, Cleece? How could you betray all that the Abbot stands for? All that the Order stands for?'

Cleece moved over to Falaxyr's side. 'I renounce the Order,' he stated. 'The time has come for me to be true to my bloodline, Taal-Iis Esstar,' he said bitterly, clearly remembering her own insult. 'I was born a Warrior, and henceforth I shall live as a Warrior.'

Falaxyr looked up from his examination of the Sword and smiled. 'You see, Abrasaar: blood is stronger than your false faith. I welcome you to your true heritage, Cleece Ett'Shturr.' He laid a clamp on the Abbot's shoulder. 'Join me, old friend. Together, we can re-form the Eight-Point Table. With the GodEngine at our disposal, we can carve out a new Martian Empire that will dominate the stars.'

Aklaar's response was immediate. He spat in the Grand Marshal's face. Even a pilgrim like Esstar knew the significance of the action: Abbot Aklaar, Spiritual Leader of the Order of Oras, was challenging Grand Marshal Falaxyr to a blood-duel.

Falaxyr nodded slowly. 'So, the spirit is still strong, Abrasaar. It pleases me that the pacifism of Oras has not completely extinguished the fire that once burnt so fiercely within you.' He raised a clamp. 'Bring me the false sword, Sleeth. It will still serve a purpose.'

The technician withdrew the sword from the GodEngine's ignition system and brought it over to the Grand Marshal.

Falaxyr held it out to Aklaar, the blade resting on his forearm. 'So be it, Abrasaar. A duel to the death.'

Aklaar smiled. 'If descending to your barbarism is the only answer to this madness, Falaxyr, then so be it.' He grabbed the sword by the blade and swung the hilt into his other clamp.

'Descending? I think not. This is the only true honour, Abrasaar.' Falaxyr nodded to Cleece. 'In the absence of my adjutant, Cleece Ett'Shturr will be my second.'

'I choose Sstaal G'Hur-Tiis,' replied Aklaar, using the Martian's formal name. Sstaal looked surprised, but said nothing, simply stepping forward to stand by the Abbot.

The two Martians stepped away from one another, seconds in tow, neither taking his gaze from the other, visors locked. Each placed their sword across their chests and bowed deeply in the time-honoured tradition of the Warrior caste.

'Falaxyr Urr'n'Jaas – I offer the challenge in blood and fire.'

'Abrasaar Urr'n'Jaas – the challenge is accepted and embraced.' Esstar was taken aback; from the giving of formal names, the two were closely related. Truly a blood-duel.

Watching the ceremony, watching Aklaar raise his sword vertically in the ancient gesture of prayer to Ssethiis and Claatris, Esstar suddenly accepted something that both terrified her and gave her hope. Wise old Abbot Aklaar, the kindly Martian who had sat her on his knee and read her fables from the Book of Oras when she was but a clutchling, was also a fierce and bloodthirsty Grand Marshal of the Warrior caste.

In their current situation, Esstar knew that, despite her pilgrim heritage, she preferred to have Abrasaar, the Butcher of Viis Claar, at her side than Abbot Aklaar of Oras.

The warning shot hit the wall, sending rippling waves of sonic disruption through the amber rock. 'Stop!' ordered the Martian. 'You will surrender now.'

'What do we do?' hissed Rachel. 'That scalper of yours won't work against a Martian.'

'I know it won't!' snapped Santacosta, furious with herself

for leading them into the situation in the first place. They were currently standing in the middle of a corridor, with no means of defence, no means of attack. Hopeless. Projectile weapons were all well and good, but the armoured carapace of an Ice Warrior wouldn't even be scratched. 'Any good ideas?' Because she certainly didn't have any. When she had trained to be an Adjudicator on Ponten IV, the Greenies weren't considered to be a threat – if there weren't any around, how could they be a threat? It was only later, after she had graduated, that the Bureau had learnt that there were still some Martians on Mars. So Santacosta hadn't got a clue about how to kill or even disable one of them.

The service corridor in which Chris had hidden while waiting for his bombs to go off was actually a level above the area in which they had been imprisoned, and, thanks to Chris's detailed knowledge of the base, they had dropped out of a vertical duct about a hundred metres from the holding cells, in a dark tunnel with uneven walls. The place stank of rotten vegetables – Chris had ruefully explained that it was an unfortunate by-product of his smoke bombs.

Carefully, quietly, they had crept along the deserted tunnel, coming within metres of the brightly lit junction that led directly to the cells before the long shadow had fallen in front of them. Before they could react, the Martian was standing right in front of them. That was what made it so infuriating; they had got so close without seeing a single crukking Greenie.

Chris tapped her on the arm. 'Try this.' He held out a small lump of circuitry. 'It's not got a lot of charge left, but it might work.'

'What is it?' asked Santacosta.

'A scrambler: it reacts with their cybernetics. But you have to get up nice and close.'

She smiled. A one-shot chance, that was all she had wanted. 'Watch me.' Santacosta stepped forward, her hands raised in surrender. The scrambler was clutched in the palm of her right hand.

'All right, all right; we'll come quietly.' She kept moving towards the Ice Warrior, slow, steady, unthreatening steps.

Behind her, she heard Cwej and Forrester also start walking. More importantly, they provided two more targets.

As soon as she was within half a metre of the Ice Warrior, Santacosta leapt; as she did so she held out her hand and slapped the scrambler against his armour. The reaction was immediate; the Martian starting to convulse, and Santacosta stepped back to avoid being crushed as the giant green form toppled to the floor. The warbling whine of his disruptor squealed, but Santacosta was pleased to see that the shot went wide of her, although it only missed Chris by centimetres.

'Not too shabby,' said Roz, looking down at the fallen Warrior. He was still twitching feebly.

'Thanks,' replied Santacosta. 'Good piece of work, Cwej.'

'Yes. An excellent piece of work. The fabled resourcefulness of our Amber Marshal.' Whatever that meant. But the voice wasn't human. They looked round in unison to see the cloaked figure come forward from the shadows, flanked by two Warriors. It was Draan. 'It has been a good fight, Adjudicator, but it is over. As much as I enjoy the games of combat, this one has run its course.'

Santacosta looked back at the others. 'We haven't got a lot of choice, have we?'

Draan smiled. 'No, you haven't.' He walked over to Cwej and stroked the Adjudicator's chin with his clamp. Santacosta was impressed by the way that Cwej stood his ground unflinchingly; it was nice to know that the best traditions of the Adjudicators' Bureau would survive into the future. 'You are a worthy opponent, Adjudicator Christopher Rodamonte Cwej, but even you must bow to the glory of the Martian military.'

McGuire watched as the two Marshals took their positions, only now noticing the similarities between them. He knew that the Abbot had claimed that he only wore the armour of a Martian Lord because of the protection it had afforded against the harsh terrain and vicious fauna of Mars, but did Aklaar feel more comfortable in the cybernetic carapace and helmet of the Warrior caste, or the tunic and long robes of an Abbot in the service of Oras that he had described to him earlier? McGuire tried to imagine Aklaar in the same purple and gold armour as Falaxyr; as Aklaar prepared himself for battle, McGuire found that it wasn't difficult.

Aklaar lunged first, a swift, arcing sweep that Falaxyr nimbly side-stepped. In return, the Grand Marshal brought his own Sword up and caught Aklaar's sword, knocking it upwards. But the Abbot's grip didn't waver; he spun to his left in a display of agility which belied his great age, bringing his sword back and parrying Falaxyr's next blow with practised ease. McGuire was impressed; at the onset of the duel, he wouldn't have given the Abbot a chance of winning against Falaxyr. But now? As Aklaar danced around the Grand Marshal, never allowing the other a moment's advantage, McGuire wasn't so sure.

Realization coldly tempered his hopes: who was he kidding? Even if Aklaar ran Falaxyr through and left the Marshal bleeding green blood on the smooth amber floor, they would still all be prisoners in the Martian nest, and the Martians would still have a weapon capable of incinerating the Earth.

The Doctor sidled up to him. 'The quintessence of the Martian race, eh, Mr McGuire?'

The Doctor's untrusting attitude irritated McGuire, even though it was one that he had shared until the truth had been revealed. 'The Abbot's fighting for our lives, Doctor.'

The Doctor cocked an eyebrow. 'Is he? Somehow, I suspect that the feud between our two Grand Marshals is a lot older and a lot more personal than that.'

Looking back at the duellists, McGuire understood what the Doctor meant.

'You are a coward, Falaxyr,' grunted Aklaar in the High Tongue, as his face came within inches of the Grand Marshal. 'The rest of the Eight-Point Table accepted their fate and died honourably. You scuttled away like a spider-lizard, hiding in this nest of evil.'

'A coward?' Falaxyr hissed. 'I never turned my back on my heritage, my bloodline – it shames me that we grew from the same clutch.' He tried to parry, but it was easily defended.

'What place has a Supreme Grand Marshal amongst the terrified and spineless Order of Oras? The Order is an abomination to all that is Martian.'

Aklaar stepped back to compose himself. 'All that is Martian? Look at what we have left, Falaxyr: on Mars, a handful of populated nests, hidden from the sun. Then there is the frightened colony beyond far Arcturus, too ashamed to announce its presence.'

'We also have the GodEngine.'

'Which you have traded with the callous beings who have enslaved Earth. With the GodEngine and the help of the humans, you could free Earth and gain the everlasting gratitude of those we once called enemies. But no; all you seek is to further this vendetta until all of our people are dead. If you use the GodEngine to destroy the humans, they will hunt us out and exterminate us. They will find the secret colony and wipe us out to the last clutchling.'

'How?' gasped Falaxyr. 'They will all be dead.' He leapt at the Abbot, taking him off guard. Aklaar tried to parry, but the blow that caught him was driven with all of the Grand Marshal's enhanced strength – and the purple armour of a Grand Marshal was superior to the green of a Lord. The serrated blade of the Sword of Tuburr tore into Aklaar's armoured tabard and ripped deep into the scaly flesh beneath. With an involuntary cry, Aklaar sank to the floor, the faux sword clattering away.

Falaxyr straightened himself and sighed. 'And so falls the Butcher of Viis Claar.'

'Finish the duel,' Aklaar urged. 'Kill me, my brother!'

Falaxyr shook his head. 'A duel of honour with a traitor? I shall let your life ebb away as befits one such as you.' He turned his back on the fallen Abbot, wiping the green blood from the Sword with his cloak before handing it to Sleeth.

'The distractions are over,' he announced to the others. 'Now we will begin.'

He looked up as the doors to the GodEngine chamber were thrown open. It was that idiot of a subordinate, Draan, but Falaxyr was gratified to note that the Adjudicator and the other escaped prisoners were in his custody.

But Draan did not appear happy with his prize. His gaze was fixed on Cleece, standing in what should have been his position behind the Grand Marshal.

'What is this?' he roared, leaving his charges with the others. 'What is this pilgrim doing in my place?'

Falaxyr raised his clamp. 'Cleece is no longer a pilgrim, Draan, just as you are no longer my adjutant. The blood of Warriors flows through him, just as the thin, incompetent blood of Slaar flows through you. He has earned his place at my side by delivering the Sword of Tuburr to me, while you were hopelessly searching the complex for our Amber Marshal.'

He turned his back on Draan; his once adjutant was nothing more than a waste of flesh. 'Sleeth: ensure that Jacksonville is still targeted.'

'No!' It was Anders, the human scientist that Draan had caught. Falaxyr neither knew nor cared how she had escaped her conditioning, but his suspicions fell on the Adjudicator: one more reason to dismiss Draan as the fool he was.

'No, you mustn't,' Anders insisted. 'The GodEngine isn't designed to focus on that small a target. If the subspace lenses hold, you'll probably take out half of Mars; if they don't – which is more likely – the GodEngine will explode. With the energies that it's barely harnessing, that'll send Mars spinning into the sun – or worse.'

'The GodEngine is our creation, Professor Anders, the pinnacle of Martian technology. Do not presume to lecture me as to its operation.' But he was still concerned enough to beckon Sleeth over.

'Does she speak the truth?' he whispered.

Sleeth shook his head. 'She underestimates Martian engineering. All will be as you have ordered, Your Excellency.'

Falaxyr never noticed the smile of dawning realization on the Doctor's face.

'Of course,' muttered the Doctor. He beckoned Rachel over. 'Professor Anders? The head of the ill-fated Charon research project?'

She nodded. Who was this odd-looking little man? 'And you?'

223

'I'm the Doctor. Chris's friend.' He gave Chris a sharp look. 'When all of this is over, Chris, you and I need to have a stern talk about the web of time.'

Chris looked slightly bashful. 'I know.'

'Apart from that, I am very glad to see you again. That was a very nice bit of terrorism.' The Doctor turned his attention to Rachel. 'Are you sure that the subspace polarizers aren't up to the task?' he asked. 'This is very important.'

She frowned, trying to remember the specifications that she had been forced to read. 'Felice did most of the work, but I'm pretty sure. The minimum resolution of the beam is at least ten times the focal width that Falaxyr's trying for.'

'Excellent,' said the Doctor. 'Let us hope that there's a big bang, then.'

'What?' She couldn't believe what she was hearing.

'Doctor – I don't want this device damaged.' It was Santacosta, still clinging onto her pipe dreams of using the GodEngine to free Earth.

He smiled. 'If everything goes according to plan, there won't be so much as a trisilicate diode left after this is played out.'

Santacosta pulled out the scalper. 'I mean it.'

He gave the weapon a look of disgust. 'Oh dear. The last refuge of the incompetent. Listen to me, whoever you are –'

'Adjudicator Carmen Santacosta – Oberon Special Operative.'

The Doctor looked from Chris to Roz and then back to Santacosta. 'Another one? What is this, a Ravens' convention?' He sighed. 'The GodEngine is the product of Martian belligerence and Osirian technology. It has no place in this time. Neither you nor the Martians – nor the invaders, come to that – has any right to it. This must end, now. And if you cannot see that, then you will have to shoot me.'

She didn't get the chance. One of the Warriors guarding them must have seen Santacosta's scalper; he reached out and snatched it from her hand with his clamp, before crushing it into a broken ruin of polymer fragments.

'Finished?' said the Doctor rhetorically. 'Good. Then

stand back and watch the fireworks. This should be quite spectacular.'

McGuire overheard the Doctor's pronouncement and joined the group, accompanied by Esstar. Sstaal was kneeling beside the dying Abbot, presumably administering the Martian equivalent of the Last Rites. McGuire wanted to pay his respects, but knew that none were needed; the Abbot would die, knowing that McGuire had finally understood.

He addressed the Doctor. 'You're just going to stand here and let that bastard destroy my home?' he growled.

'Please, Antony.' The Doctor laid a restraining hand on his arm. 'It might not come to that.'

'Might not? Might not?'

Esstar laid a clamp on McGuire's other arm. 'In his own way, the Doctor is as wise as the Abbot, Antony. Have faith in the strength and word of Oras.'

He smiled weakly, but his stomach was threatening to burst. And when he looked at the prone figure of the Abbot, he wondered how much faith Aklaar had put in Oras.

On the far side of the chamber, Sleeth had completed his second set of preparations. He nodded to the Grand Marshal, who once again inserted the Sword of Tuburr – this time, the true Sword of Tuburr – into the GodEngine assembly.

The reaction was immediate. As well as the increase in noise from the banks of controls, a tingling, grating screech erupted from the GodEngine.

'That's the sound of subspace being torn apart,' muttered Rachel. It wasn't something McGuire wanted to hear.

The Doctor leant over to Roz and whispered conspiratorially. 'In about thirty seconds, you will see something which you recognize very well. When that happens, I am going to need a diversion. Anything, as long as it gives me a chance to reach the GodEngine.'

Roz shrugged. 'Anything you say, Doctor.'

McGuire shook his head. From what he had heard, he had a ringside seat for oblivion, and there was nothing to do but wait for the inevitable.

* * *

Vastitas Borealis. The Cauldron of Sutekh. The Martian North Pole. Three names for the same cold high pinnacle of Mars. With the Martian trait of building their cities underground – the main reason why their race had remained undiscovered by humanity until they chose to be found – the thin layer of ice and frozen carbon dioxide had been undisturbed for millennia, a freezing white expanse of rolling dunes, silent save for the tinkling sound of wind through ice crystals and hoarfrost.

Undisturbed until now, that was. The crystal chimes of the ice were suddenly drowned out by a deep growl that seemed to come from the ground itself, heavy reverberations that began to shake the virgin ice fields. Huge cracks started opening, splitting the ice-sheets with black chasms that rapidly widened into a network that criss-crossed an area over two kilometres wide.

The cracks weren't empty. From the depths of the Martian crust, titanic objects thrust their way to the surface, gigantic gold and silver pyramids that were hundreds of metres tall, their polished faces adorned with ancient hieroglyphs that would have been familiar to any human Egyptologist.

It took less than a minute for the group of pyramids – over thirty of them in total – to finally complete their journey above ground; yet once they stopped moving, they did nothing. They simply stood there, relics of an age that was shared by Man and Martian alike. The age of the Osirians.

Together, the pyramids formed the external emitter array of the GodEngine: Falaxyr's seventy-year project was finally complete.

'External assembly now fully extended,' Sleeth informed Falaxyr. 'Subspace meniscus penetration at sixty per cent.'

'I hope your gods revile you for an eternity, Falaxyr,' came a thin, raspy voice. It was Aklaar, still clinging onto life with remarkable tenacity. Or was it his faith in Oras, McGuire wondered.

'Revile me?' said Falaxyr dismissively. 'Our descendants will consider me a god in my own right. Now die, Abrasaar, and leave the future to the victors.'

Sleeth turned from the control bank. 'Penetration at one hundred per cent, Your Excellency. Primary subspace manifold created.'

Five hundred million kilometres away from Mars, within the unimaginable incandescence of the solar core, the fabric of the space-time continuum began to ripple and dissolve, as a funnel of subspace materialized from beyond its weakened meniscus. After tentatively emerging into reality, the funnel stiffened; it immediately grabbed trillions of tonnes of core matter – superheated plasma – in its poly-dimensional folds and pleats, before twisting in countless directions, none of them even slightly Euclidean.

But all of them resolved in the vicinity of Olympus Mons – Jacksonville. In scant moments, the subspace manifold would convulse, accelerating the captured plasma to superluminal velocities before unleashing it on the unsuspecting human colony.

'This is it; this is definitely it,' muttered the Doctor. 'Remember, Roz – keep your eyes peeled for an old friend.' She could barely hear him above the whine of the GodEngine; it was now a throbbing, pulsing roar that was physically uncomfortable, as ancient Osirian technology and Martian know-how joined together in their deadly pursuit.

Roz had her suspicions over the identity of the old friend, and – seconds later – she wasn't disappointed; indeed, she was rather impressed. As Sleeth indicated to Falaxyr that the GodEngine was now ready to unleash its stolen plasma on Jacksonville, movement came from all around the chamber, unexpected movement that burst through the walls. The phantom blue shapes that appeared automatically brought a broad grin to the Doctor's face, and Roz couldn't really blame him.

Roz counted at least twenty of the translucent police boxes, majestically floating through the amber walls towards the pyramid of the GodEngine.

'Now, Roz!' shouted the Doctor.

As if the arrival of twenty TARDIS ghosts wasn't distraction enough, she thought.

After the Doctor's instructions, she had co-opted Santa-costa and Chris into the scheme. In addition to Draan – apparently sulking in the corner, his visored gaze fixed firmly on his usurper, Cleece – there were five other armed Martians in the GodEngine chamber. But by co-ordinating their movements, the three Adjudicators could, with luck, evade being shot, and provide the Doctor with the distraction he needed into the bargain.

Not that the Martians weren't currently preoccupied themselves; the phantom TARDISes were doing a good enough job of that anyway. Roz noticed that another wave of them was now emerging through the walls. But a plan was a plan. On cue, the three Adjudicators ran in three zigzagging directions.

The Doctor reacted as immediately as the Adjudicators. Running at breakneck speed, he reached the GodEngine pyramid in a matter of seconds. Searching in his pocket, he extracted the small black sphere which Roz, momentarily glancing back, recognized as the Transit-web nucleus that the Doctor had picked up earlier.

'Grab Felice!' he yelled at Chris as he squeezed the sphere. As it began to extrude its black filaments, he threw it into the air like a bolus. It helicoptered upwards as it expanded, hovering momentarily above the apex of the GodEngine before dropping onto the golden summit.

The reaction was immediate. The roar of the GodEngine began to warble plaintively. In the place where Felice had been standing, one of the banks of panels exploded into thrusting flames that jetted outwards before subsiding, licking at the cold amber rock. Felice, struggling in Chris's grip, had been lucky; Sleeth caught the full brunt of the detonation and fell lifeless to the floor, oily smoke curling up from his body armour.

'No!' screamed Falaxyr, suddenly realizing what was going on. 'Kill them, Cleece! Kill them all!' The Grand Marshal raised his own clamp, aiming his disruptor squarely at the Doctor, but he never got the chance to fire – his disruptor, clamp and upper arm exploded with the sickening plop of sonic disruption and ruptured flesh.

'An imbecile, am I? A fool, am I?' Draan strode over to his former lord and master as a string of explosions took out an entire wall of controls. The GodEngine itself was flickering with a brilliant pearly light; within, the statues and relics started to wobble precariously. Something was clearly going catastrophically wrong, and Roz wondered why they were all still waiting around in the chamber rather than making a run for it. She shot a questioning look at the Doctor, but he simply smiled enigmatically and held up his hand for her to stay her ground.

Draan was now standing only a metre away from the Grand Marshal. 'Your project has been a disaster, Falaxyr, and yet you call me an imbecile. You choose another as your adjutant over me, as though my lifetime of service was but nothing.' He stood facing Falaxyr, his disruptor aimed at the Grand Marshal's chest. His intention was obvious.

The sword that speared him from behind was equally obvious. Draan twisted his head round to see his murderer, only to realize that, in Martian terms, he had not been murdered; he had been executed. Cleece withdrew the dripping blade and smiled.

'You speak the truth, Draan. It was but nothing.' Cleece watched as Draan, son of Slaar, slumped to the floor and died.

Falaxyr beckoned him over. 'Come, Cleece. We must leave here. I have a vessel capable of interstellar flight in a hangar above us. Come with me to Nova Martia – we will be heroes.'

'You, maybe, coward Falaxyr,' came a voice that was no longer timid; rather, it reverberated with a new strength, a new purpose. 'But not Cleece.' Sstaal ripped the false sword from Cleece's relaxed grip and impaled him on the serrated blade.

The look of puzzlement was clear on Cleece's face. 'Sstaal the pilgrim?' he gasped, suspended from the blade.

'Yes and no, Cleece. Our lives have both been led according to falsehoods and deceptions; that was the sin that Abbot Aklaar confessed to me as he died. You were not the orphan of a Warrior caste; your parents were pilgrims, from an endless lineage of pilgrims. There was a mistake, a confusion that arose during the chaos which followed the War. When the Abbot discovered the truth, he deemed that revealing the knowledge of your true birthright would be too traumatic for you.

'I am the true Warrior, Cleece. But I choose to renounce that bloodline and embrace the heritage that I love. I am the new Abbot of Jull-ett-eskul Seminary.' Sstaal withdrew the sword; unsupported, his rival fell heavily to the floor. 'You are the dead.'

The first wave of spectral TARDISes had almost completed their slow, steady journey to the GodEngine; the device itself was now almost impossible to look at, a nexus of blinding white light. The TARDISes suddenly stopped, forming a steady, floating arc around the incandescent pyramid. Roz had stayed her ground because of the Doctor's orders, but she really didn't feel happy about it. A shout from behind grabbed her attention.

'Doctor!' yelled McGuire. 'Falaxyr's getting away!'

Bereft of his adjutants, bereft of his guards – those that hadn't been caught in one of the explosions had decided to live to fight another day and exited the chamber as fast as they could – Falaxyr was running through a door in the rock wall that hadn't been there moments earlier.

'Leave him,' said the Doctor calmly. 'He's somebody else's problem now. This' – he gestured towards the burning pyramid of the GodEngine – 'is going to be far more interesting.'

The deep thrumming noise from the GodEngine finally fell below human hearing, vibrating Roz's body like a tuning fork. She swallowed – surely this was it? This was the moment when Earth would be destroyed, the moment when the Doctor's precious web of time would be shattered and she and Chris would simply never have been?

The noise from the GodEngine unexpectedly changed tone and frequency, rising up the scale in a fiendish crescendo. As if on cue, the floating TARDISes – now too many to count, their insubstantial bulks overlapping to form an almost solid blue arc – simultaneously converged on the GodEngine, hurling themselves into its cold, brilliant fire. Roz couldn't help thinking of the myth of the phoenix as the TARDISes consigned themselves to the flames.

Then she realized that she recognized the warbling, ululating sound that now echoed off the smooth walls of the chamber, the noise that had replaced the growl of the GodEngine. It was a TARDIS – no, a chorus of TARDISes – rematerializing, their bellowings and groanings just slightly out of phase with each other. But with the passing of each long second, the chorus harmonized, eventually climaxing into one stentorian TARDIS sound.

Everyone was now gathered round the Doctor, all hoping for some explanation. But he said nothing, simply beaming as the GodEngine's burning white shape darkened and shrank, and shrank further. As the final trumpeting strains of the TARDIS were heard, the pyramid was dark once more.

But it was no longer a pyramid. No trace of the beautiful, golden doomsday machine remained. A single object stood in its place.

Solid, resolute and blue, it was the TARDIS.

Roslyn Forrester realized that her eyes were filling up with tears. 'Would you care to explain what all that was about?' she mumbled, hoping that the Doctor wouldn't see.

She needn't have worried; his own voice was thick with emotion at the reunion. 'Just a second, Roz – there's something I would like to check.' He unlocked the blue panelled doors and stepped inside the vessel that Roz had never expected to see again – at least not in its current, solid form. She followed him in, indicating for the others to do the same.

As the humans and Martians unfamiliar with the marvels of dimensional engineering tried to suppress their surprise at the huge, white console room with its hexagonal console and roundelled walls – everything in its place, just as Roz remembered it – the Doctor flicked a couple of switches on one of the panels of the console, and pointed to the scanner as it came to life.

The image showed the Martian North Pole, where a collection of melted, twisted pyramids in gold and silver covered the dark and dirty snow. 'That is what's left of the external emitter array,' the Doctor commented. 'Now, to be terribly clichéd, watch the skies.'

Moments later, a small dark shape rose from behind the wrecked array; presumably Falaxyr's starship. It was a long thin needle, clearly designed for speed. Roz wondered how long it would take the Grand Marshal to reach the Ice Warriors' new home, just over forty-five light-years away from Earth.

'He will spread his poison to Nova Martia,' breathed Esstar. 'The cycle of death and revenge will begin anew.'

'I wouldn't be so sure,' said the Doctor. 'Remember, there are others currently in residence who do not take kindly to unauthorized space travel.'

As he spoke, a spotlight of fire rained down on the ship from beyond the atmosphere, purple fire which Roz knew to be a Dalek plasma cannon, undoubtedly from one of the orbital battlesaucers which patrolled the inhabited planets of the solar system. Falaxyr's ship was caught in the beam for less than a second before exploding soundlessly in the thin air of Mars like a moth cremated in a candle flame.

The Doctor closed the scanner. 'I did warn the Grand Marshal not to trust his allies,' he said with sadness. 'You can never trust them.' Roz wondered who he meant: the Daleks or the Ice Warriors.

'Doctor.' It was Rachel. 'Although I would love to fully understand this machine of yours, I'm more interested in what happened out there at the moment. It was obvious that the subspace lenses weren't holding at the tight focus that Falaxyr had ordered. So the GodEngine should have been destroyed. In fact, the explosion that should have resulted would have taken out Earth, Mars, and a number of the major asteroids.' She thrust her chin forward. 'So why the hell didn't it?'

'Quite,' agreed the Doctor mysteriously. 'It should have been quite nasty, shouldn't it?' He moved over to Chris, who was still holding a struggling Felice. 'Brain-rack?' Chris nodded. The Doctor reached out with a forefinger and touched it to her forehead and closed his eyes tightly. A second later, Felice relaxed into a deep sleep. 'There,' he said, turning back to the others.

'That was my T-web you used, wasn't it?' asked Santacosta.

'Indeed.'

'But the subspace field wasn't anywhere near strong enough to influence the GodEngine,' commented Rachel. 'That was orders of magnitude greater. It was like expecting a candle flame to make a difference to a star.'

The Doctor started ushering them out of the TARDIS. 'Subspace had nothing to do with it, Professor Anders. From what I can remember of your work on Charon, you tried to break through the invaders' subspace barrier by brute force. Professor Ketch took advantage of the complex interrelationship between subspace, gravity and electromagnetism to achieve his results. Besides the subspace field, the T-web also generated an enormous magnetic one – a *bipolar* magnetic field, to be precise.'

Rachel smiled in understanding. 'Of course.'

Roz tapped the Doctor on the shoulder. 'Subtitles for the hard of thinking?'

He sighed. 'The GodEngine was the result of the Martians' attempts to utilize Osirian technology,' he explained. 'But the home planet of the Osirians – Phaester Osiris – is one of those rare planets without a magnetic field. The Osirians developed their technology based on the principles of the monopolar magnetic field, something which can only exist when there isn't a natural – that is, bipolar – magnetic field.' He turned to McGuire. 'That was what prompted Mr McGuire's expedition in the first place: Professor Esteban's discovery of an intense magnetic field at the North Pole, which was actually the first activation of the monopole at the core of the GodEngine. When the Osirians finally captured the renegade Sutekh on Earth, they needed to install a powerful stellar power relay to keep him imprisoned. Mars was ideal for their purpose; they were able to place the relay here and know that it would work, because Mars also lacked a magnetic field. The centrepiece of their power grid was the Martian Sphinx, which I imagine the Martians cannibalized to create the GodEngine.'

Chris nodded. 'It's about a kilometre from here –' And then realization crossed his face. 'The others!'

'Others?' said the Doctor coldly. 'You saved the entire Charon colony?' Then he sighed. 'Oh, well, who am I to talk? We'll go after them in a minute. Anyway, the interaction between the T-web's intense bipolar magnetic field and the GodEngine's intense monopolar magnetic field started a feedback cascade in the power source.'

'But that was exactly what I was worried about!' snapped Rachel. 'You're saying that you deliberately wanted the GodEngine to blow up?'

The Doctor nodded. 'But as with many things, Professor, on my own terms.' He locked the doors of the TARDIS behind him and sauntered over to the far wall, where the controls were still sparking and smouldering. 'If I had left well alone, the subspace lenses would have collapsed, the subspace funnel would have ruptured, and the superluminal plasma stream would have sprayed out into the solar system in some random direction . . . *then* the power source would have detonated. I couldn't take the chance that that would happen: I had to ensure that the magnetic monopole fell into the accretion disk and released all the energy at once, without any harmful side-effects such as random death rays sweeping across the solar system.'

'But you still haven't told us why or where that police box came from,' Rachel laughed. 'Police box, indeed.'

'No, I haven't. And I have no intention of doing so. What sort of a magician would I be if I gave away all of my secrets, eh?' He turned to Sstaal and held out his hand, but his eyes were fixed on the lifeless form of Aklaar. 'So, you are the new Abbot. Congratulations.' Roz couldn't tell whether he was being sincere or not, but decided to give him the benefit of the doubt. It had been a long day.

'It was the Abbot – the late Abbot's last request, Doctor.' He smiled. 'Of course, only I heard that request, so this could all be some fabrication.'

'No, it's no fabrication. You deserve it, Sstaal.' McGuire waited for Sstaal to release the Doctor's grip before grabbing the Martian's clamp and shaking it warmly. 'I hope that you and Esstar are very happy.'

'And so we shall be.' Esstar brushed her clamp against her new partner's arm. 'Once we return to Jull-ett-eskul Seminary, Abbot Kyren will bless us in the ceremony of partnership. Our clutchlings will be the first of a new generation; the first Martians to be born on a Mars devoted to peace and the ways of Oras.'

'There is more, friend Antony.' Sstaal bowed deeply to the human. 'I request a favour.'

McGuire frowned, but it was more in puzzlement than trepidation. 'Such as?'

'The ceremony of partnership requires that both participants choose their closest friends to witness the blessing in the eyes of Oras. I would be honoured if you would witness our blessing.'

McGuire grinned. 'You want me to be your best man? Of course I bloody well will!'

'Another wedding?' muttered Roz. 'I don't know if I can handle this.'

'How long before your clutch is born, Sidi-Ekk-Taleth Taal-Iis Esstar?' asked the Doctor.

Esstar smiled. 'You honour me with your knowledge of the High Tongue, Doctor. But I am not the Abbot's consort yet.' She laid a clamp on her lower stomach. 'My clutchlings long to be born, Doctor. It pains me to admit that they must be laid and hatched before we return to the seminary.'

'Not necessarily,' replied the Doctor. 'I can get you there rather more quickly.'

Esstar looked at Roz. 'What is he saying?'

Roz was used to this reaction. 'Trust him – he's a Doctor.' She realized what she had said, and knew why; since the rebirth of the TARDIS, something warm and deserving of respect once more burnt within him. It was good to have it back.

'If you say so, I shall believe it,' said Esstar. 'And now it is my turn to ask a favour; will you be my witness before the eyes of Oras, friend Roslyn?'

The Doctor raised his eyes to the ceiling. 'Here we go again.'

* * *

There had been two ceremonies in the ornamental gardens at Jull-ett-eskul. One was the sombre and respectful funeral of the Abbot, who was buried beside one of the bright yellow Fees-ett-Bakk bushes, as befitted an honoured child of Oras. During the lengthy and solemn prayers, the Doctor had quietly pointed out that a Warrior's funeral was far more complicated, with burnings and burials in space and all sorts of complicated traditions.

The second ceremony was a more joyous occasion. Sstaal and Esstar, now without armour and dressed in floor-length white robes, were blessed before the eyes of Oras in the delightful stone abbey that stood at the heart of the underground seminary. Roz, wearing her formal Adjudicator's robes, stood behind Esstar, while Antony McGuire – who was dressed in a plain grey suit, courtesy of the TARDIS wardrobe room – was behind Sstaal.

During the ceremony, Sstaal pledged his life to protect Esstar; in return, she also swore to protect him till death. They both then swore to raise their clutchlings according to the wisdom of Oras. As they held hands and bowed to one another, the other members of the seminary showered them with the sweet-smelling, pink and orange leaves of the Fees-ett-Bakk bush, which was apparently a reminder that life, death, partnership and birth were all stages of being.

'Santacosta's going to try to contact Oberon,' said Felice as Sstaal and Esstar accepted the congratulations of the guests. She was now fully recovered from her ordeal. 'With the knowledge that Rachel and I gained by working on the GodEngine, we think we can duplicate Professor Ketch's work and find a way to break the invaders' subspace blockade. If we can do that, the outer colonies might be able to help us free Earth.'

'The subspace interference should not be a problem for much longer,' said the Doctor. 'When the GodEngine malfunctioned, it flooded subspace with all manner of exotic particles, which will eventually play merry hell with their strange icaron generator. It shouldn't be long before the subspace blockade is over.'

Chris nudged the Doctor. 'What about the web of time?' he whispered sarcastically.

The Doctor shot him an acid look. 'This is a wedding and I am feeling magnanimous. Anyway, it is time that we went. I want to find Wolsey – he must have been terrified when the TARDIS was destroyed.' Roz smiled, and decided not to ask how the cat could have survived the destruction of the time machine. However he had managed it, it had probably taken a large chunk out of his nine lives.

She looked round the reception, and saw that the newly-weds were coming over to them.

'You wish to take your leave of the celebrations so soon, honoured friends?' asked Esstar.

'Things to see, people to do,' said the Doctor. 'But it was a lovely wedding.'

'We have a gift for you,' Esstar added. She held out a hide-covered book which Roz recognized as a copy of the Book of Oras. 'You have spoken often of your Benny, and of her study of our people. We hope that this will answer some of her questions.'

The Doctor took it from Esstar's clamp and beamed at her. 'She will be delighted, Esstar.'

McGuire rushed over. 'You're leaving?'

'I'm afraid so.'

'The colonists are coming back to Jacksonville with us. And Sstaal has promised us supplies – the seminary has an extensive hydroponic garden. We might be able to sit this war out after all.' His smile was infectious.

'Ah . . . yes,' the Doctor replied uneasily. Roz could sense that he was holding something back, but decided that now wasn't the time to ask. The Doctor indicated the TARDIS. 'We really must go, Mr McGuire.'

'Of course.' He grabbed the Doctor's hand. 'Thank you, Doctor. Thank you for everything.'

It seemed to Roz that the Doctor couldn't wait to get away. Within seconds, they were inside the TARDIS, the Doctor fussing over the console with almost unseemly haste. As the time rotor began its rise and fall, Roz slammed her fist on one of the panels.

'Okay, Doctor – what was all that about? Why the rush to leave? And are you ever going to tell us what really happened to the TARDIS?'

The Doctor stood up and shrugged. 'Very well.' He looked at both Roz and Chris. 'As you know, the TARDIS was destroyed because it stalled when a subspace infarction – Rachel and Felice's attempt to break the blockade – hit it; the Vortex rupture – the result of the disruption of future history which would have happened if Falaxyr's plan to destroy Jacksonville had happened without my interference – exploded beneath it.'

'So what were those ghost TARDISes all about?' asked Roz.

'Even though the TARDIS was destroyed, there was still a minute possibility that the destruction of Earth – and therefore the Vortex rupture – could be prevented. This created a minor time paradox, which in turn permitted the formation of future reflections of the TARDIS – the "ghosts", each one representing a possible future. They were hanging – floating – around because there was a chance that the TARDIS might not have been destroyed. By detonating the power source of the GodEngine, I provided that chance; as well as preventing the destruction of Earth, I also provided the energy that they needed to come back into existence.' He waved a hand around the ship. 'Everything happened as it was meant to.'

'But what about Charon?' asked Chris. 'They were all supposed to die when the Daleks attacked, weren't they?'

'Everything happened as it was meant to,' the Doctor repeated, his hands flitting over the controls.

Chris wasn't that easily dissuaded. 'Come on, Doctor; I shattered the web of time – you told me as much.'

'Very well. You're both old enough and ugly enough to face up to the truth.' The Doctor reached over to a keyboard on one of the console panels and tapped a few keys before pointing at the monitor screen above it. 'Look and learn,' he muttered.

Roz and Chris leant forward and read the information that was presented on the monitor; from the title, Roz could see that they were looking at a list of those who had perished during the ten-year occupation of the solar system; specifically, those inhabitants of Mars who had died.

Certain names had been highlighted, presumably by the Doctor; Roz could see the reason why, but it still seemed a sick thing to do. The highlighted entries consisted of familiar names like Rachel Anders, Felice Delacroix, Antony McGuire ... She had no reason to doubt what she was reading – even the Doctor wouldn't do something that cruel. She looked up at him, her anger at the unfairness of the universe colouring her voice.

'Why?'

The Doctor walked over to the door which led into the TARDIS interior, his face impassive. 'It's the web of time, Roz. Cosmic book-keeping.'

As he left them to their thoughts, Roz remembered the wedding of Esstar and Sstaal; how hopeful everyone had been about their plans for the future.

Except that they didn't have one.

She turned to Chris, tears in her eyes. 'Why, Chris? Why?'

He shrugged, and she could see the pain behind his own eyes. 'I wish I knew,' he mumbled.

Roz's eyes were drawn to the interior door. 'Yeah, but I bet he bloody well does.'

Epilogue

Finished Business

As the last strains of the dematerializing TARDIS echoed around the ruined waterfront, the young woman turned away from her past and buried her tear-stained face in his chest. For long moments he held her, comforted her; he was her future now. Arm in arm, they set off to build that future.

Susan Foreman and David Campbell were well out of earshot when the TARDIS reappeared in exactly the same spot as it had vacated only minutes before. But it was a very different Doctor who stepped through the open doors into the clean air of twenty-second-century London.

'This is it? I was expecting something a bit more, well, modern,' complained Chris. The Doctor had waited for a decent length of time before returning to the console room, allowing them to begin to come to terms with what they had learnt. Chris knew that the deaths of Rachel and Felice would haunt him – but he also knew that life went on. In fact, that was why they were where they currently were; the Doctor had insisted on what he called 'closure'.

'Be fair,' admonished Roz. 'The planet's been occupied by Daleks for the last ten years. They aren't exactly renowned for their urban renovation programmes.'

'Ah!' sighed the Doctor, taking deep breaths. 'It has been so long since I was last here . . . or it might have been only minutes.' He smiled. 'That's the problem with time. It is all a matter of perspective.' Chris couldn't help shivering as the

Doctor talked about time.

The three of them walked over to the banks of the sluggish grey Thames. 'Look!' The Doctor pointed towards the twilight sky with his umbrella. A burnt yet noble starship was descending from orbit, its antigrav landers glowing bright blue. 'If I am not mistaken, that's the Colonial Warship *Dauntless*. Its commander, Jarvis, broke the physical blockade of the Solar System – after that, it was a fairly simple mopping-up exercise.'

'A hero's welcome, eh?' complained Chris. 'What about us? We saved Earth as well.'

The Doctor reached up and patted him on the shoulder. 'We will get our reward in heaven, I am sure. The important thing is we are all still here. Literally.' He glanced back at the TARDIS, and Roz caught the warm smile.

'Do you still distrust the Ice Warriors?' asked Roz gently.

The Doctor gave a slight shrug. 'I don't know, Roz. But if Abrasaar was able to renounce his heritage, there is always hope.' He waved a hand to encompass London. 'It was hope that kept humanity going during the occupation, and hope which will sustain it through the coming millennia,' he said grandly, before laughing. 'Oh dear; that was a bit pretentious, wasn't it?'

A loud cheer erupted from the vicinity of the heliport where the *Dauntless* had landed. 'Our cue to leave, I think.' He started walking back to the TARDIS with a bounce in his step that had been missing for too long.

Chris caught up with him. 'There's one thing I'm not clear about, Doctor; ten years ago, the Daleks thought that they were getting a super-weapon from the Ice Warriors and started digging out Earth's core. Didn't they realize that it was a waste of time?' he asked.

'That was why they invaded Mars, Chris; they never stopped searching until the *Dauntless* broke the physical blockade, and I ruined their chances here on Earth – I and some very special people.' For a moment, the Doctor's thoughts were elsewhere – or elsewhen. 'And that was a very long time ago.'

He ushered the Adjudicators into the TARDIS before

looking back at the newly liberated London. He searched the ground in front of the TARDIS for over a minute with his umbrella, trailing it through the rubble until he saw what he was looking for, a shining piece of metal lying in the dust.

Susan's TARDIS key.

The Doctor went over and grabbed it, his face a melancholy smile. As he entered the TARDIS, he paused. London would survive. Earth would survive. But life was more than grand gestures; the little things were often just as important.

For a brief second, he wondered whether he should run around the corner and see the young woman who was so very much a part of him. Then he looked down at the discarded key, and shook his head with infinite sadness.

'Finished business,' he muttered, before stepping into his ship.

And then, for the second time in less than ten minutes, the TARDIS left an Earth that was looking to the future.

Now that it had one.

Craig's bit – more of the same . . .

That makes three books on the trot in which I've done something nasty to the TARDIS. Can we spell the word 'obsessive', people?

No long preamble this time, just a list of people. No reasons, no explanations, except to say that you wouldn't be reading this book if it wasn't for them. So, in absolutely no particular order . . .

Eddie Thornley, Mike Ramsay, my muckers at EMAP, the TransCo lot – especially Robert Wilkinson-Latham – Justin Richards, Peter Anghelides, my mum, Kevin Gibbs, Andrew Hair, Alex Musson, Berkeley, Peter Elson, Mike Tucker, Andy Lane, Rebecca Levene, Lance Parkin, David Richardson, Ben Aaronovitch and Gary Russell.

If I've forgotten anybody, I apologize. Despite what the back cover says, I am only human.

Unlike the Ice Warriors. A special thanks to Brian Hayles, for inventing the most wonderful race of aliens ever seen in Doctor Who. I just hope I did them justice.